Out of my Depth

by

GWENYTH CLARE LYNES

Grosvenor House
Publishing Limited

This book is published by
Grosvenor House Publishing Ltd
28-30 High Street, Guildford, Surrey, GU1 3EL.
www.grosvenorhousepublishing.co.uk

A CIP record for this book
is available from the British Library

ISBN 978-1-78148-976-5

The characters, events and places in this book are wholly fictitious and any resemblance to actual persons, events and places is purely coincidental.

Any mistakes are the author's entirely.

Acknowledgements

So many people have been great encouragers to me on my writing journey, my grateful thanks to you all.

Cheryl and Chris for reading the embryonic manuscript,

Phill for advice and correction of some of the prose,

Andi and Oliver for technical input and guidance,

Jon for meticulous proof reading, ensuring accuracy of the text,

Trevor for your constant, loving support,

The Staff at Grosvenor House,

What a blessing you are.

Dedication

For my parents
Hilda Irene and Aylmer Douglas Butler
Saints of God, who taught me the way of Salvation

GLOSSARY

Inspired by the bustling anchorage of Newtown, mentioned in Gillingwater's Mediaeval History of East Anglia, Newton Westerby has been placed somewhere south of the Norfolk/Suffolk border. This fishing port has long disappeared so today only exists in the imagination of the author and reader. The local inhabitants speak with a Suffolk dialect but only a few families and some of the older residents have been depicted as using such in the text.

Suffolk people have a tendency to use double negatives i.e. won't be no more/not no more.

They also pronounce 'ing' endings as en' i.e. keepen', growen', headen', thieven', somethen', builden' etc.

Frequently an 'a' is added to these words i.e. a-sayen', a-sorten' etc.

Ow/ou pronounced ew i.e. do – dew, to – tew, you – yew.
O pronounced oo i.e. so – soo, go – goo, no – noo, close – cloose.
Afore – before.
Agin – against.
Aloan – alone.
Allus – always.
An' Oi int gorn-a dew e' – And I'm not going to do it.

Arffice – office.
A-tween – between.
Bin – been.
Bor – boy.
Doan't – don't.
E' – it.
Fule/fewell – fool.
Funny – odd/strange.
Fust – first.
Git/gits - get/gets.
Gor – got.
Gorn/goen – going.
Hen't – haven't/have not; hasn't/has not.
Hev – have.
Hum - home.
Int – not/isn't.
Lorst – lost.
Mardle/mardling – to chat/chatting.
Niver – never.
Oi/oi'l/oi'm – I/I'll/I'm.
Ole/owd – old.
Putter – complain.
Roite – right.
Rud – road.
Sin – seen.
Squit – nonsense.
Thass –that's/that is.
Thowt – thought.
Ul – I'll/ I will.
Uvver – over.
Wholly – really.
Yewsel' – yourself.
Yow'n/yourn –your/yours.
Yup – yes.

CHAPTER ONE

The piercing ring of a clock alarm shattered the early morning stillness of Easter Day. Sleepily, Jansy Cooper reached out an arm from under the warm, cosy duvet to switch it off. The unremitting noise was interrupting her dreams and disturbing her beauty sleep. Once she had silenced the din she made to turn over and snuggle down again. Seconds later she forced herself up onto her elbows to squint at the illuminated digital numbers on the clock face.

Mmm! 5.40am, not time to get up yet, too dark. Drowsily she wriggled her honey-blond head into a more comfy position on the pillow and nestled back into bed.

5.40am! Gradually, the time registered. Startled, she rubbed her eyes and shook her head. *Oh, no! It can't be twenty to six already! I'll be late!* Without further thought, Jansy jumped up from her bed, fumbled to switch on the light and grabbed some clothes. In record time she was dressed, down the stairs, outside the house, and running to her rendezvous.

It's a good job Sister Calvert can't see me. 'Decorum at all times, Nurse Cooper. No running, except in emergencies,' Jansy mimicked, and then chuckled, as she pictured the reaction her behaviour would trigger off in her superior.

In the cream painted cottage, at the far end of Main Street, Dave Ransome had also woken early. He sat contentedly, drinking a mug of tea; his Bible perched on his knee open at John chapter 20. Thoughtfully he perused the verses before him. *Early on the first day of the week, while it was still dark...* Being a fisherman he was no stranger to the early morning hours or working in the dark but, today, his feet would remain firmly on terra ferma and in a short while be taking him to meet his dearest girl. In his remaining ninety-six hours ashore there was much that had to be resolved. In the meanwhile, thoughts of the approaching hour caused him to tingle with anticipation as, along with so many others, he prepared to join in the day's celebrations.

Across the Village Green and part-way down Fishers Lane another household was also stirring. Seven and a half year old Daniel Catton was a natural early riser but he struggled daily to occupy himself with early morning pursuits that would not awaken the rest of his family. However, on this particular morning he had very specific instructions to tiptoe into his parent's room and wake up his dad, Adam.

On rising Adam encouraged Daniel in his stealth so that Laura and the girls could sleep on. *Laura seems so tired these days, an extra hours rest will do her good.* His eyes lingered with concern for a moment on his sleeping wife before turning his attention to his excited son.

"Keep your PJs on under your clothes, my boy, they will give you extra warmth," Adam whispered conspiratorially. "Don't forget your hat, scarf and gloves," he continued, as he slipped his arms into his own warm anorak. "All set?" When Daniel nodded in reply Adam picked up his piano accordion and as quietly as possible unbolted the front door. Together, father and son stepped out into the dark, crisp morning their warm breath spiralling before them into the air like puffs of steam from a boiling kettle.

As they walked along the lane they could see that right around the fishing village of Newton Westerby many house lights pierced the early morning gloom as occupants busied themselves in readiness for the day. At the butcher's premises the shop remained in darkness but the living quarters of the Cooper family blazoned with light. Frenetic activity was taking place behind the closed doors as the three sisters prepared for the day. When they were finally ready they set out with their parents, who had patiently waited till the girls were suitably dressed, to walk the short distance to the quay.

Across the road at the Village Stores Emma Kemp, ably assisted by Nicky Andaman, was loading the Stores van with sealed boxes and containers filled with food.

"Here's another contribution to add to your load, Emma," Billy Cooper called out as he, with Pauline and their daughters, crossed the road. He held out two large trays of eggs and a package containing bacon.

"Thanks, Uncle Billy. We'll just drop this off at the church hall for Jilly and her helpers and then meet you on the quay," explained Emma, as she gratefully accepted Billy's generous gift towards the communal breakfast.

"Are you sure you'll have enough?" laughed Hilary, the youngest of Billy and Pauline's daughters. Peering further into the back of the laden van she remarked wryly, "Looks as though you're going to feed an army."

"You can mock, Hilary, but it's surprising how much food cold, early morning risers consume. Dad left a detailed list on record so I'm working from his experience," retorted Emma. "I don't think this year will be any different to those in the past."

"Well done, my dear, I'm sure your assessment of the situation is quite right," Billy patted her encouragingly on the shoulder knowing full well the stoical manner with which Emma had managed the village shop for the past four months following the tragic death of her parents. "We'll see you shortly."

Little by little, as the Cooper family walked along the road, the number of people joining them began to swell. Dawn had scarcely broken when between seventy and a hundred people, from the Newton villages and surrounding area, congregated on the seaward side of the quay, to celebrate the arrival of Easter morning with a sunrise service. Most walked, but those who lived in the outlying hamlets and the villages scattered along the river side made the journey by car. Others travelled from further afield, to join with them, out of curiosity or because it was tradition. All were warmly wrapped against the freshness of the early morning air.

As they met, friend greeted friend, relative embraced relative, acquaintance warmly welcomed acquaintance, youth, middle-aged and seniors came together, one in aim and purpose, to celebrate the risen Lord. Joyfully, the news "He is risen" reverberated along the shoreline with the onset of sunrise.

Breathlessly, Jansy ran to meet Dave so that they could share together the wonder of the resurrection morning as daybreak emerged over the sea. A marvellous experience; somehow more special and significant on this day than any other, as it symbolized the rising of God's Son from the tomb.

As she reached his side Dave turned towards her, his eyes shining with love. The fresh morning air coupled with her enforced exertions had heightened the colour in Jansy's cheeks. Tenderly, Dave stretched out his hand and with his finger softly caressed the rosy dimpled skin.

"Good morning, my dearest girl," a smile broadened his lips. "The Lord is risen!" The joy in his heart reverberated in his deep base voice.

"He is risen, indeed!" Jansy replied quietly, knowing it was the expected response.

"Shall we step up on to the quay? We'll get a better view of the rising sun."

Jansy nodded and slipped her small hand into the huge, work-roughened one that Dave extended to her. As it engulfed hers she felt safe and secure. She smiled up at him as they moved forwards with a spring in their steps to participate in the Easter celebration.

"'Morning, Em," Dave called out as they walked passed their friend. Emma, having completed her delivery chores, had positioned herself on the harbour wall alongside her cousin, Ben Durrant. She twisted briefly to wave a quick acknowledgement to her friends. Anxious not to miss the scene coming into view she turned back to focus the lens of her camera on the far horizon. The emerging sun seemed to come straight out of the water. Both Ben and Emma were keen amateur photographers and wanted to capture the scene on camera; Emma, as a reference point for future artwork she might be inspired to attempt, and Ben, as a record for the parish news and archives. Eagerly they clicked as a dazzling vista unfolded before them. Many people around them gasped at the stunning spectacle they were witnessing; day and night pushed apart by a waking sun on a distant line where shimmering sea and brightening sky meet.

Hugh Darnell, the vicar, allowed time for the crowd to enjoy the beautiful sight then, cleared his throat and prepared to open the service when a motorbike, ridden by a leather-clad motorcyclist, roared along the quayside drowning his words of welcome with its noise. Heads swivelled round and tongues began to wag.

"I say, mate, cut it out," Barry Piper shouted.

"Tut, tut, tut," muttered Jennifer Pedwardine, the recently retired headmistress.

"Oh dear," murmured Bernice Durrant.

"What a racket!" grumbled Billy Cooper.

"Hardly the time and place," agreed his brother, Doctor John.

"Hey, Dan, he didn't ought tew make that noise," some of the older bystanders complained.

"Can't yew dew somethen' about e'?" someone else called out.

"You ought tew 'ave a word, constable," hinted Peek, the verger.

"Shouldn't be allowed," others in unison expressed their disquiet.

"So disrespectful," muttered Mrs Jenner.

"Thoughtless, more like," countered Billy Cooper.

"Oblivious to what is about to take place," suggested Doctor John.

The motorcyclist, RK Dickinson-Bond, complete with Harley-Davidson, unaware of the furore the noisy arrival had caused, parked up the motorbike. Keen to see what was causing such interest alongside the quay the biker joined the crowd and grinned a greeting at the nearest bystanders.

In response, Dave Ransome and Jansy, still standing hand in hand, briefly acknowledged the biker's presence with a smile. On the other side of them stood Justin Durrant who nodded a cordial "Good morning," whilst the church choir leader, Adam Catton, flambuoyantly reached out his free hand in welcome. His son, Daniel, stood with eyes and mouth wide open gazing at the crimson and black machine and yelled, "Wow!"

The tall, lean, broad shouldered visitor, acknowledged their greetings in a soft, husky voice, "Hi, I'm RK Dickinson-Bond," playfully ruffled Daniel's hair then took off the safety helmet to reveal very short dark curly hair before enquiring, "What's going on?"

"Easter Morning sunrise service," came back the reply from several quarters.

"Oh, I'd better move on then. I thought you were all admiring the fantastic seascape." The visitor turned to restart the noisy engine.

P.C. Dan Prettyman though officially on duty, but not anticipating crowd trouble, was hovering on the edge of the crowd of worshippers. He casually strolled over to the group of friends with whom the biker stood hoping to placate those who were voicing their discontent at the buzzing machine.

"Best delay leaving for a little while," he quietly advised the visitor. In response the biker viewed him quizzically but did turn off the ignition key as requested.

However, as an avid motorbike enthusiast Dan quietly appraised the vehicle parked alongside the quay, then joined heartily in the singing of the Easter hymns as Adam skilfully accompanied the congregants on the accordion. "Christ the Lord is risen today," they sang with heart and voice.

At the conclusion of the hymn, Dan remained standing next to the newcomer as Rev Hugh read the account of the resurrection from St. Luke's Gospel. Dan listened again to the miracle of the Easter message whilst casting a practised eye across the assembled gathering. When the service was over Dan stayed beside the visitor. He discussed the Harley-Davidson's merits with its owner and showed a knowledgeable appreciation of the machine, then kindly explained the concerns some of the residents had about the noise.

"Perhaps they're unused to motorbikes in this quiet little backwater, because really, this machine is no noisier than most motorbikes," suggested RK, mischievously nodding towards the police bike parked further along the road.

"That may well be so, but just do your best to keep the noise to a minimum when you're riding around the village," he requested. When RK raised an eyebrow Dan explained, "No unnecessary revs," and chortled as he moved off to circulate amongst the crowd.

When P.C. Dan had gone, Adam turned to chat with RK just as Ben came up to join them.

"Have you come far?" Adam enquired.

"Lincolnshire."

"Interesting county," commented Ben.

"Mmm. Fields and fields and then, more fields," grinned RK impishly.

"Sounds as though you have experience?"

"Considerable! My father's a farmer."

"What sort?"

"Mainly root crops and flower bulbs."

"Aah! That explains it."

"What do you do?"

"I work in the nursery."

"I see..."

"Dad, are you coming?" Daniel called out to Adam impatiently.

"We usually have breakfast together on Easter Sunday morning in the church hall. You're welcome to join us."

"Thanks, I'd like to do that. I had a very early start this morning; hoped to miss all the holiday traffic."

"You'll be in need of sustenance then. Come on and meet some more of the villagers. They're a great crowd," enthused Adam. "It's not far and your bike will be fine there where it's parked."

"Yew mean 'cos Josh int 'ere, doan't yew?" spat out Ryan Saunders who caught the end of Adam's remark as he walked passed him in the company of a group of teenagers on their way to the church hall.

"I didn't say that, Ryan," said Adam defensively but Ryan scowled at him till Ben drew alongside the angry young man and spoke calmly to him in order to diffuse the hostile tension.

"No, but that's what yew meant," Ryan retorted, unwilling to let the matter rest.

Adam rolled his eyes, "Shall we move on, RK?"

"Just as you wish."

"Regrettably, Ryan's friend got involved with the wrong side of the law mainly for helping himself to other people's property and is currently residing in a Young Offenders Institute," explained Adam quietly as they joined a group heading towards the church hall.

"How unfortunate."

"Yes, this quiet little backwater, as you described us to P.C. Prettyman, has in recent times been shaken out of its lethargy by some disturbing events. Sadly, most have been attributed to Ryan's friend, Josh and his father, Joe Cook."

"Really."

"Ryan is convinced Josh has been harshly treated, thinks the law has got it wrong, and so always jumps to Josh's defence. But, let's not spoil the euphoria of this day with sombre events from the past."

Within ten minutes they reached the open door of the church hall where the inviting aroma of brewing coffee and sizzling bacon tempted their taste buds and the buzz of animated chatter created a welcoming ambience.

Adam introduced RK to his wife Laura who was helping to prepare the breakfast. She had woken up when the front door clicked as Adam and Daniel left the house despite their tiptoeing carefulness. Their daughters, too, had stirred soon afterwards so Laura dressed them warmly and bundled them outside but instead of walking down to the quay for the sunrise service she had pushed the buggy briskly up to the church hall with Kirsty running alongside to keep up with her pace. Laura was sorry to miss the Easter morning celebration but felt an extra pair of hands in the kitchen might be more useful. *"It will also be warmer for the girls."*

She was right on both counts. The warmth that greeted their entrance as Laura pushed open the church hall door confirmed that Peek, who held the combined roles of verger and sexton at St Andrews, had set the heating timer to come on early and the enthusiastic welcome Jilly gave on their arrival assured Laura she was most definitely needed. Now, she was ensuring that everyone who had come into the hall expecting breakfast had sufficient to eat. She paused in her busyness to flash a smile of welcome in response to Adam's introduction to RK before he moved the visitor on.

"And this is Penny Darnell, our Vicar's wife."

"Welcome to our Church. What brings you to Newton Westerby?"

"I needed a break from the demands of work. In a brochure I picked up in our local library the description of this place seemed to be just what I'm looking for."

"Well, I hope you're not disappointed."

"I'm sure I won't be. I can hardly wait to absorb the sleepiness and tranquillity of this place."

"Don't let this morning's peacefulness deceive you. Believe me, it's not always this calm."

"Don't disillusion me! This morning has been a fantastic start with that incredible sunrise, so unexpected. I'm really looking forward to rambling on the nearby ancient heaths and sauntering through tree-lined lanes where branches overhang with emerging buds. Most of all I'm hoping to feel the bracing sea breeze on my face and the crunch of sand and shingle beneath my feet."

"I'm glad you caught the sunrise. It is really special and spring is certainly the best time of the year. Everything is just coming to life. We do still have the occasional cold winds and high tides but that is to be expected on the east coast."

"It's the thrill of this that truly makes me feel alive, will hopefully blow away a few cobwebs and send me home refreshed and thankful for the experience."

"I hope you find all you're looking for."

"Excuse me." Penny moved back to make space for Jilly Briggs who was carrying a tray laden with full breakfast plates.

"Here we are. I hope you enjoy your meal."

As RK sat down and ate the delicious breakfast Jilly set upon the table conversation buzzed all around.

"I think it would be impossible to be lonely or isolated here."

"Oh?" Adam looked at the visitor with his head askance.

"Well, everyone seems to be included." RK indicated, with a nod of the head, the lively discussions taking place further down the table.

"Mmm, when villagers get together they chat and plan and catch up on news. You'll overhear many interesting conversations."

Adam's words were proved correct, before long RK learned that Dave and Jansy, the first of the villagers the biker met on arrival in the village, were soon to be married. Additional information, concerning the forth-coming nuptials, filtered across the tables between mouthfuls of breakfast.

"Have you found somewhere to live?" Jansy was asked.

"Not yet, we've been looking but so far unsuccessful in finding anything suitable."

"You're cutting it a bit fine, aren't you?"

"Yes, I suppose so, but none of the properties we've looked at, so far, seems right," Jansy shook her head forlornly.

"We're going to have to reach a decision this week before I go back to sea," Dave remarked decidedly.

"Or they'll be moving into your spare room at Green Pastures, Justin," Emma, Jansy's friend, joked. Laughter reverberated around the room.

"I'm sure Mum won't mind."

"No, nothing so cushy for you Jans, if you don't soon make up your mind you'll have to bunk down in Dave's boat, in between the fish boxes," further hilarity broke out as Stephen teased his sister.

"Watch it, Bro, or you'll be carrying the ring cushion down the aisle as page boy."

"Just don't go to Matty for a new build you'll end up with a shack around your ankles," called a voice spitefully from across the room.

Even RK, whose face had been wreathed in smiles at the thought of a six-foot young man dressed as a knickerbocker-clad attendant at a wedding, was startled by such a sombre warning. This Matty chap was obviously an unscrupulous 'cowboy' builder and someone to stay clear of.

Further down the table arrangements for an Easter egg hunt for the children on Easter Monday were being discussed. An Easter bonnet parade and other activities scheduled for the Bank holiday were also being finalized.

After breakfast Adam and Ben extended a warm invitation to the visitor to attend the Easter morning service to be held later that morning in the Newton Westerby Church.

"I appreciate your kindness but I'm afraid I can't accept." If the villagers were disappointed by this refusal to attend what for them was the most significant service in the Church calendar they graciously did not show it.

"I do need to find somewhere to stay for the night, though. Can you point me in the direction of a good B&B?"

"The village is not over endowed with guest houses, hotels or B&B's. We just have the Ship Inn on the quay or there's Jenner's Mill B&B at Marsh Newton. The only other available accommodation is to be found at the Station Hotel in Newton Lockesby."

"Thanks. I think as it's close by I'll opt for the Ship Inn," said RK. However, as it was Easter all their rooms were taken. Undeterred RK rang the Station Hotel at Newton Lokesby but found they were similarly packed to capacity.

As a last resort RK called Jenner's Mill B&B. After much muffled discussion they hesitatingly offered to squeeze RK in somewhere, although they too, were fully booked.

"But don't come before 4 o'clock," instructed a youthful voice at the other end of the phone. "It won't be ready till then."

With relief RK accepted the accommodation unaware of the frenzied commotion the call had created.

CHAPTER TWO

Some while later RK sat in the crowded restaurant of the Ship Inn enjoying the recommended Sunday 'roast of the day' and, at the same time, unintentionally eavesdropping on local gossip.

After leaving the church hall at breakfast time a brisk walk around the harbour and along the cliff top had generated a healthy appetite. The bright sun of the crisp, early morning now radiated springtime warmth so that RK felt a certain lift in spirits. Truth to tell, the feeling was a vast improvement. The lingering deflation caused by the constant bickering at home seemed to hang like a black cloud over RK. The gloomy doldrums had prevailed for so long they had become the accepted norm. This holiday was an attempt to break the mould and re-establish an even balance to life.

The crowd at breakfast seemed a good sort, too; welcoming and accepting, even though their hospitality had been grabbed with gratitude but the invitation to worship declined. *Can't get involved with that, however sincere they might be*, RK grimaced, *that would give Dad cause to read me the riot act and I don't want to fuel further trouble.*

However, the Ship Inn was packed. The unexpected warm weather had brought out the world and his wife intent on making the most of the Bank holiday. The tables outside along the quayside were filled and the overspill had taken their drinks and bar meals on to the harbour wall and were sitting there enjoying them in the spring sunshine.

Seats in the dining room proved scarce. RK's height proffered a good view over the heads of the other diners but the dark hazel eyes scanned for an empty place setting without much success. A group of locals noticed RK's dilemma and quickly moved chairs around to make a place available at their table which they offered to RK. Thus, squashed in to a space by the wall, RK was both captive audience and reluctant participant.

"Hent sin yew around these parts afore."

"No, I'm just visiting."

"Yew the chap wi' the noisy bike?"

"Guilty as charged."

"Nice machine but it sure dew roar."

"Oh, do you think so?"

"Doan't like noise in these 'ere parts that int nat'ral."

"Oh?"

"We lives peaceful like."

"Yup! The wind, the gulls, an' the sea be noise enough for the likes of us," agreed Peek, the verger.

"I see."

"Some 'as 'ad other notions; like them Cooks."

"Joe revved that engine of 'is up and raced around like a mad man at times. We put up wi' that but 'is thieven' and violence be somethen' a body can't tol'rate."

"An' Oi int gorn-a dew e'."

"Hope they locks 'em away for a pretty long time."

"Aah! They sure dew deserve it after what they did tew Nicky, an' Vicar's wife, an' the Kemps."

"Careful, careful now, Joe an' Josh hent bin charged with killen' the Kemps, only the break-ins an' the attacks on Mrs Darnell an' Nicky."

"Aw, come on, if it wasn't them who else could've done it?" Heads shook around the table.

"Dunnoo!"

"It's Michelle, his wife, I feel sorry for. She be the one who 'as to bear the brunt of folk's anger."

"The sooner they gets convicted for what 'appened to Mick and Val, Oi'll be well pleased, better for all concerned."

"Hardly likely, though, be e'?"

"What dew yew mean?"

"Well, Josh 'as got two years in Hollesley an' Joe be given four years for 'is part in the burglary and assaults, but yew see he'll be out in two…"

"So, what yew're a-sayen' be, if he's convicted of the Kemps' murder, he won't be in prison for very long."

"Seems that way."

"They's taken a mighty long time a-sorten' e' out."

"Well, they do 'ave to gather together all the evidence agin them."

"An' make e' stick!"

The questioning of RK ended as conversation concerning the Cook duo's presumed misdemeanours, pending trial and possible verdict, became heated and opinions flew rapidly up and down the table. It appeared that for a village where time usually stood still, and nothing much ever happened, a great deal had occurred during the last few months to upset the equilibrium of these villagers; burglary, theft, kidnapping, assault and possibly even murder. Although the diners differed in their views about how the culprits should be punished they were unanimous in their condemnation of the perpetrators whom they all believed to be father and son, Joe and Josh Cook, as Adam had intimated earlier in the morning.

"Put up wi' 'is behaviour long enough. Not no more."

"Yup, felt right sorry for 'im when 'e first lorst 'is job up the nucl'ar at Sizewell but 'is antics 'as gor out o' hand."

"I 'ear young Matty Durrant be headen' in the same direction if the gossips can be believed."

"Is that roite?"

"Stands to reason shady dealen's be bound to come to light eventually 'specially in the builden' trade."

"Well, 'e's met 'is match in Tessa Jenner. Chip off the old block, she be, and she won't put up wi' any ole squit."

"Matty's brickies has put down tools, till it be sorted, an' they be in a funny ole mess at the Mill."

"I understand Adam Catton's boss be on the case an' he's a stickler for getten' things right. If Mr Capps-Walker finds that Matty's in the wrong he'll throw the book at 'im, yew can be sure."

"No more than he deserves."

"Pity they can't do the same over his moral behaviour. The way he spreads it around be roite sick'nen'."

"How Miranda can bear it Oi'll niver know."

"It's no wonder the poor girl's gorn hum to her parents."

"But if Matty and Miranda be liven' in different places and not see'en' one another it's hardly likely to be sorted, is it?"

"S'pose yew be roite."

"Thass a tricky one, somethen' like the problem a-tween Dave an' Jansy Cooper."

"Hardly the same them's be'en' soo lovey dovey."

"Oh? From what I 'ear they don't seem able to agree on where to live after they get wed."

"They don't know when they be well off. Wish we'd had as many options open to us as they 'ave. We 'ad to settle for Sid's Mum's or mine till a place came up for rent. Not ideal but it was all we could afford and we were roite glad of it."

"Well, they've turned down Alex and Graeme Castleton's lovely old cottage in the centre of the village."

"Oooh! What I'd give to 'ave the chance to live there instead of the damp ole dump we 'ave down the common!"

"Even Lord Edmund's spankingly renovated cottages on the far side of the estate 'as been refused."

"What dew she want? A palace?"

"I'd 'eard it be a question of where it be."

"Where?"

"Yup, town or coast, city or country?"

"Well, of all things!"

As discreetly as possible RK withdrew from the after dinner chatter and offered profuse thanks for their kindness.

Just as RK was leaving the Ship Inn, thinking that it was an intriguing pattern people made of the tangled web of other people's lives, another diner blocked the doorway. He deliberately jostled RK's arm, spilling his own drink. "'Ere mate, watch it," he said aggressively. "Unless you want E's or crack," he muttered between his teeth. Taken aback, RK murmured, "Sorry," stepped warily round the unpleasant young man and quickly headed to the exit and fresh air without further incident.

Once outside RK breathed a sigh of relief. *Whoo! I really didn't appreciate that encounter.* Satiated with the delicious meal RK's footsteps were inclined to dawdle as they closely followed the harbour path, the eye drawn by the movement on the water. With time to kill before being allowed into the B&B, it seemed the ideal moment to lean idly over the harbour wall and absorb the intense boating activity that was taking place.

So much was going on yet, at the same time, it was peaceful. The yachts with billowing sails that appeared to dance to the rhythm of the breeze were fascinating and the motor boats and fishing trawlers seemed to glide effortlessly through the water. It presented a scene vastly different to the landscape of home. Even the noisy gulls added, rather than detracted, to the ambience. All very natural, as Peek, the church verger had said.

The afternoon sun grew even more intense as it travelled across the sky. It became too warm for motorcycling gear so RK removed the cumbersome leather jacket, slung it carelessly across the shoulders, and meandered towards the harbour master's office. It was a quaint construction built on top of the harbour walls with lookout windows placed strategically over the water giving clear visibility across the harbour mouth towards the sea, as well as, boating activity up and down the river. Mixed tubs of daffodils, tulips and iris brightened the way in. The open door invited entry and a chance to chat with Titus Wills. So, ducking beneath the low beamed door lintel RK gained entrance and began to ask questions of the genial harbour master about customs, searches and the like, then enquired about smuggling opportunity and the incidence of illegal immigrants along this particular stretch of the coast.

"Is the coast guard station manned 24/7?"

"Somewhat," replied Wills noncommittally looking askance at his questioner.

"What causes the greatest problem, drink or drugs, or trafficking?"

"Yew seems a might in'erested," Titus stroked his beard thoughtfully and viewed the tall newcomer quizzically. He and Sergeant Catchpole had earlier in the day discussed their concern at the appearance of this stranger in the village. Most visitors came to enjoy the sandy beaches or the nature reserve and bird sanctuary. This visitor appeared to spend a lot of time watching boats and in view of the directives from their respective department heads regarding the increase of drug and people smuggling along the east coast they stepped up their vigilance if the actions of a stranger aroused any misgivings. Wills felt the tenor of the questions now being asked seemed to support their initial suspicions. He watched his visitor closely as the conversation developed.

"Well, you hear so much on the news about these things but I don't really know how it is actually dealt with so, being here, I thought I would ask," explained RK.

"New to these parts, be yew?"

"Yes, I come from Lincolnshire."

"Aah! Bulb country."

This time it was RK's turn to look surprised.

"You know about bulbs, then?"

"I should say soo. Gits me bulbs for th' display ev'ry year from Dickinson-Bond. Best around."

"My father would be delighted to hear you say so."

"He in to bulb growen', then?"

"Yes, you could say that."

A little later, RK left the harbour master's office, curiosity satisfied, and sauntered casually back to where the Harley-Davidson had been parked all day. Eyebrows shot up to find so many people gathered round the machine but RK was even more surprised to see Ryan Saunders, the lad who had been so scathing earlier in the day, ostensibly on guard. He also displayed incredible knowledge on the subject of motorbikes and was quite unfazed by the questions that were being fired at him from the crowd about the engine. The bike was obviously in good hands with its self appointed protector.

Meanwhile, Titus Wills sat at his desk mulling over the conversation he had just had with the stranger. His size hadn't perturbed him but his questions gave the harbour master pause for thought. Therefore, after only a short while Titus picked up the phone to call Constable Prettyman.

"Dan? Wills here. Inquisitive stranger bin in. Spoke to Tom earlier about him. Needs an eye keepen' on him."

Although surprised by this request P.C. Prettyman noted the harbour master's concerns and scheduled restricted surveillance of the stranger subject to Sergeant Tom Catchpole's approval.

Totally unaware of the conversation taking place, between the harbour master and the constable and the close scrutiny they planned to give any future movements, RK thanked Ryan for his guardianship of the Harley-Davidson and prepared to ride off on the motorbike. It was almost time to book into the B&B.

"Any problems with the bike just give a shout."

"Thanks. See you around," RK called out, as the machine roared away from the admiring crowd. Following Adam Catton's explicit instructions to Jenner's Mill B&B, RK found the route led away from the harbour, along Main Street and through the village till it passed the stately entrance gates to Newton Manor House, the ancestral home of Lord Edmund de Vessey. It then took a right turn into a twisting narrow lane that was bordered by a hedge on one side and what was obviously the riverbank on the right. After two and a half miles the lane rose, turned abruptly to the right, and then crossed the river. A left-hand bend brought an imposing view across the river valley and suddenly, there ahead, was a magnificent windmill, complete with full sails.

R.K. was quite at home with country life but this was something else! There were striking mills in Lincolnshire but nothing quite like the one in view. The window slits suggested four, possibly five stories and, at some time in the past, a number of the jumbled crop of outbuildings had been tastefully incorporated to create a unified building. But at present, the approach to the Mill implied disorder and confusion. Opening a dilapidated four bar gate RK wheeled the Harley-Davidson carefully along a hole-pocked dirt track avoiding the mounds of builder's rubble.

To the right there appeared to be a market garden of sorts but there was no order to the placement of the plants. They were growing in a mindless higgledy piggledy fashion. On the left animals ran amok, chickens with pigs, geese mingled amongst the goats, cats and dogs ran side by side. Coming from a rural community in the heart of Lincolnshire, RK was used to the straight lines and vast orderly, open spaces of the fens, bordered in a regimented fashion by hundreds of dykes and droves.

Dad would have a heart attack if he saw this disorder on his farm, RK thought grimly. Mr Dickinson-Bond was a first class flower bulb and plant grower, distributor and exporter and as precise in his dealings with land as with people.

Before RK took another step, seemingly hoards of children running wild suddenly appeared, whooping and yelling, coming close to knocking over RK and the motorbike with their exuberance.

"Hi! Welcome to the Mill."

With a broad smile that encompassed them all RK said "Hello."

One of their number reached out a hand towards RK. "I'm Tessa Jenner, and these are my brood," she pointed with her free hand towards the cluster of boys and girls. She was dressed in unusual flowing apparel and looked little more than a child herself, although a gold band on her ring finger indicated otherwise, and her blue-grey twinkling eyes suggested humour and friendliness.

The group all surrounded RK and acted as escort up to the door of the Mill, the boys eyeing the Harley-Davidson with awe, one surreptitiously reaching out to touch the bike.

"We have other guests and are very full but we've managed to fix up a room for you."

"It's mi…"

"Sshh…sh."

"Thankyou, it's very kind of you."

One of the girls sidled up to RK and said, "My name's Lily, what's yours?"

"Well, my Dad calls me RK."

The children screeched with laughter.

"That's a funny name."

"My Mum named me Robyn Keit…"

"Aah, so that's where it comes from, your initials, RK?"

"As a matter of fact, Dad's pronunciation sounds like Our Kay so some people call me Kay but most just say RK."

"You're very big," said Pansy tentatively, the smallest of the children, who had been gaping continuously since she had skipped alongside her siblings to greet RK's arrival.

"Oh, that's all the Lincolnshire sausages and cabbage my Mum made me eat when I was only your size. I just grew and grew," RK grinned mischievously at the little girl.

Keir crept nearer and peered very closely.

"Are you a boy or a girl?"

"Keir!" admonished Rosie, his eldest sister, as RK's rich laughter filled the air.

"What do you think?"

The little boy shook his head, "I'm not sure, but you've got a deep voice so…uhm…" RK winked to relieve his uncertainty and flashed him a wicked, conspiratorial grin.

As the tour to the room continued it became obvious that RK had been allocated one of the Jenner children's rooms in the main Mill complex rather than a room in the guest wing, the chattering children intimating that over there the roof was leaking. RK's heart sank when there appeared to be more builders' rubble and evidence of incomplete building work. In a snake-like procession they stepped carefully around the debris and implements, Keir and Lily hinting at problems between the contractor and their parents.

What have I let myself in for? RK recalled the conversation at lunch time in the Ship Inn and realised the diners were well informed. It seemed that village communities universally displayed an inherent nosiness in other people's affairs, whether in rural Lincolnshire or coastal Suffolk.

"The bathroom is the second door on the left. As you're in the main house I'm afraid it's shared facilities," apologised Tessa as the stragglers caught up with her.

"No problem," RK assured her hostess.

"Supper's at half-past six. We all eat together in the dining room. I hope you realise this is a vegetarian establishment. When you've unpacked your things Gil will escort you down to the sitting room where you'll find tea and scones."

Vegetarian! RK's heart plummeted even lower.

Tessa flounced out before RK could voice a reply. The children trooped out en mass after her. Rosie, the eldest girl, who had caught RK's expression of dismay, came back. "Mum's a brilliant cook, you'll be surprised. For supper today leek and mushroom crumble is on the menu accompanied by crisp, home grown, fresh salad, or newly-dug roasted root vegetables, delicious, you'll see," she flashed a broad smile at RK. *That remains to be seen. Dad's salad crops are still a few weeks away from being ready to eat and our winter grown root vegetables long finished.*

A short while later, down in the sitting room, RK found some of Tessa's children busily making Easter hats. Gil had, with solemn dignity, accompanied RK down the spiral staircase then joined Lily who was designing an Easter garden in a shoe box. RK who had a particularly endearing way with children gravitated towards Keir and Pansy with a smile. They beamed in return and offered RK some of the promised tea and scones. Then, quite unselfconsciously, they discussed the most effective way of presenting the flowers and items they had collected together, with their visitor. The late afternoon sped by in an enjoyable and creative manner and before they knew it, it was time for supper.

RK was quite apprehensive about Tessa's veggie dishes when offered them at suppertime. So it was a pleasant relief when after only one mouthful RK found the leek and mushroom crumble very tasty and gave Rosie a nod and conspiratorial grin.

"Do you know Mum's veggie dinners are very popular in the Village Stores? In fact they are just as successful as the ready meals range that Jilly Briggs and her team prepare," said the teenager proudly. With a full mouth RK could only nod.

"I help Jilly in the holidays and when I've completed my studies I hope to work in the Stores kitchen full time."

Rosie Jenner was full of aspirations for the future, and obviously saw herself as Jilly's right-hand man.

"You like cooking?"

"Oh, yes! I know, too, that Emma has further expansion in mind, possibly a tea shop, which is an amenity the village lacks, and I very much want to be a part of that." Her face glowed with enthusiasm.

"You seem to have inherited your mother's culinary skills," RK commented with a smile.

"And she is willing to learn under Jilly's tutelage, and take her NVQ, too," proudly interjected her father, Stuart, who had been listening quietly to the conversation.

"You're obviously a very busy person with goals worth aiming for."

CHAPTER THREE

Following the unexplained car accident that had taken the lives of their parents the previous Christmas, Emma Kemp and her sister, Alex, had become business partners and now ran the Village Stores and Post Office together. With the assistance of a number of the villagers the girls had pulled through those dark days of bewilderment and pain earlier in the year and gathered around them a good, reliable working team. While Emma divided her time between College studies and the Stores Alex concentrated on Post Office matters and looking after her home and family. They displayed a determination to succeed that would have delighted their father. His mind set was inherent in all their dealings in the running of the Village Stores. At times it was as if Mick was sitting on their shoulders nudging them to be always looking to the future and not be content to sit upon their laurels because things seemed to be going well.

Like him, they soon learned that the economic climate necessitated a steely approach to business matters as well as an open mind to utilising wisely the resources at their disposal.

To this end Emma and Alex spent many hours discussing the feasibility of turning Emma's flat into a coffee shop. The flat was a large Victorian space over the Stores, once the home of their great grandparents who first opened the village shop in this location, and offered to Emma by her parents on her eighteenth birthday. She enjoyed exercising her artistic flair without parental constraints and revelled in the independence it gave her but to some extent it was an extravagant luxury.

With this in mind Emma mentioned the possibility of using the flat to expand the business to Jilly Briggs, the cook at the Stores, and Rosalie, the long standing assistant in the shop, as well as other members of staff, including young Rosie Jenner, to gauge their thoughts. Their response was one of overwhelming enthusiasm and support but she was still undecided in her own mind if it was the right way to proceed.

Alex was unreservedly convinced it was a development that was needed so with the help of her husband, Graeme, drew up a business plan but even when she presented Emma with a list of advantages to both business and community her sister was still unsure if it really was an objective they should pursue.

"Why not ask Ben's advice," suggested Graeme. "He would give you an honest, unbiased opinion about the practicality of taking such a course of action."

"Good idea," agreed Alex, "with his expertise he'd assess and advise us what's possible and within our means. Don't you think so, Emma?"

"Mmm," Emma murmured uncertainly.

With this purpose in mind, their cousin, Ben, a qualified architect, was invited to be party to a discussion which met to look at all aspects of the proposal and thrash out all of their concerns. He listened carefully and made copious notes then commented, "Now that I know what your vision is for the flat, as well as your anxieties about embarking on such a project, I'd like to look more closely at the space available, if that's OK, Emma?"

She nodded and Ben continued, "I'll draw up some plans and along with my suggestions present them to you in a couple of weeks for your comments."

"Thanks, Ben," Alex flicked through her diary. "So, that will be the Tuesday of Holy week; 7.30 suit everyone?" Nods of assent filtered through to her so she pencilled in an evening appointment.

"Are you sure this is what Mum and Dad would have done?" Emma's throat clogged up.

"Oh Em," Alex looked across at her sister tears welling up in her eyes.

Graeme swiftly rescued them both by saying, "I'm quite sure your parents would see expansion, such as you are proposing, as a vital cog at the heart of village life."

The days following the meeting with Ben had kept Emma busy but doubts continued to assail her.

Torn between making the best use of the vast area that the flat offered and retaining her own personal space she decided to visit Uncle Roy Durrant, her mother's eldest brother, and chat over her reservations with him. As she sat on the pouffe by the side of his chair in front of the blazing log fire voicing her concerns he wisely listened and nodded his head.

"It may be selfish of me but I do like closing the door behind me after a busy day to relax in the peace and solitude of the flat. Through all the windows I have glorious scenes overlooking the village, across the heath land, over the harbour and out to sea. They change with the seasons so that I am woken on a summer morning with the rising sun from the east and in an evening I enjoy the splendour of its setting rays from the windows in the lounge. In the winter it's snug and cosy and being up the stairs I feel safe from the chilly winds and choppy sea.

"On the other hand I can see Alex's point of view. A coffee shop would be a great asset to the village for locals and visitors alike. We are fortunate to have a central position in the village so an obvious focal meeting point. We already have a kitchen in situ but where would we find additional personnel to staff it, and the coffee shop? Apart from Rosie, the other students who are doing their work experience with us will not be finishing their courses for another eighteen months to two years. Alex hopes we can be up and running long before that. It is a bit of a dilemma!" With elbows on her knees Emma sank her chin onto upturned palms, closed her eyes as if that would eradicate the perplexities furrowing her brow.

Roy did not attempt to speak. Knowing Emma as well as he did he knew there would be more to follow.

"Is it right to use money from the shop account to pay for the renovations? Would Mum and Dad approve? Should we borrow from the bank to make up the deficit? Do you think we'll take sufficient cash to pay extra staff – if we can find any, that is! Will my brother, Drew, feel he should be consulted about any proposals we have regarding the Stores? How will the elderly and those with buggies gain access? What about health and safety issues?"

"My, my, my, what a catalogue of questions you have!"

"But surely ones that need to be addressed."

"Have you prayed about the matter?"

Emma almost fell off her seat with incredulity. "Prayed about a coffee shop?"

"Yes! Why not? What did the Vicar say last Sunday morning about King David?"

Emma shuffled to regain her balance on the pouffe and looked up enquiringly at Roy.

"You remind me, Uncle Roy."

"Before he attempted anything he 'enquired of the Lord'."

"About everything?"

"Mmm, everything."

"Not just the bad things or difficult situations, then?"

"No, I believe this passage of the Bible teaches us that God is interested in all aspects of our life and wants His children to talk all things over with Him."

"To pray before making decisions, you mean?"

"Yes, not simply to ask His blessing on decisions we've already made."

In the ensuing days Emma gave much thought to Roy's words and followed his advice to pray about the coffee shop venture.

For a while college studies and shop issues became Emma's focus and on the day detailed to meet up again with Ben she was detained at her teaching placement by an end of term staff meeting, but Alex and Graeme kept the appointment with Ben. They carefully considered his proposals and were excited by the plans for the conversion of the major part of Emma's flat into a coffee shop which he set before them.

But, it wasn't until Easter Sunday when Emma was invited to share lunch with Ben, Rachel and their family that she had opportunity to pore over the plans Ben had drawn up for the alterations to her flat.

"As requested I've designed the coffee shop to the right of the existing stairs with a lift at the far end of the Stores as the main access to the upper floor. On the left of the stairs I've planned a simple living space for you in the remaining area available."

He stepped back to let Emma absorb the diagrams more closely and waited for her comments.

"I do like your ideas, Ben but..."

"Oh Emma," Ben chuckled, "you and your uncertainties!"

"...I must make sure it really is the right direction to be taking."

Ben got up, gathered together all the sheets of paper then grabbed Emma's arm, "Come on, we'll go and see what Alex and Graeme have to say about this." He marched her through the door and along the street and almost before she had time to catch her breath Emma found herself in the Castleton's sitting room.

As she listened to the conversation around her she learned to her astonishment that many of her queries had been resolved in unexpected ways.

"The shop quarterly statement shows that profits are up on previous years," said Alex.

Emma shook her head in disbelief.

"That's incredible considering how careful Dad was."

"In fact, you're holding a very healthy bank balance," assured Graeme who acted as the Stores' accountant.

"I guess that's all due to the tremendous support we've had from the villagers," commented Alex.

"They're anxious for you to succeed and the Village Stores to remain open."

"So will we need to borrow money from the bank for the expansion?"

"Yes, but not so much as you first feared."

"But what about extra staff and how to pay them?"

"Why not appoint Rosalie as shop manager..."

Emma's eyes opened wide. "What an excellent idea!"

"...and ask Christina if she would be willing to work an extra hour or two."

"I'm sure Aunt Bernice might come in more frequently if she were asked. She enjoys it so," offered Ben.

"Maxine already helps out on Saturdays and holidays and we've promised her full-time employment when she qualifies in a year or so's time," Alex reminded her.

"But how do we staff a coffee shop...and pay them?"

"The projected income figures are realistic so once the coffee shop is established I believe it will more than pay for itself."

"I see."

"I suggest you retain Jilly as overall chef in charge of the kitchen, baking for the shop and the restaurant, but I think by the time building work is complete Rosie will have completed her studies and be qualified. I would, therefore, make her pâtisserie cook and appoint her as assistant manageress of the coffee shop, whilst you retain general management."

"Yes, she really excels in that area, her pastry work and confectionary just melt in the mouth."

"And she certainly has a pleasant way with people."

"Build on the rapport Jilly has established with the college and offer to provide work experience places for students in all three areas, kitchen, shop and cafe."

"So, that's finance and staff taken care of," Graeme smiled across at Emma. "Now, what were your other areas of concern?"

"Drew?"

"Ah, yes!" Graeme looked across at Alex.

"I spoke to Uncle Roy about Drew's involvement and he asked, "Does Drew consult you over what changes need to be implemented in his Dental Practice? No, he doesn't because it has nothing to do with you. Similarly the Stores are yours and Emma's responsibility so all decisions rest on your shoulders.""

"I hope that answers that query. What's next?"

"Health and safety!"

"Oh that's easily dealt with – everyone will have to regularly attend Health and Safety courses and accept delegated areas of responsibility within the business."

"Access!"

"Ben has cleverly dealt with that aspect by relocating the storage area next to the kitchen and installing a lift from the path at the rear of the shop where the present store is. Everyone will have easy access to the coffee shop. The current stairs will be retained to comply with fire regulations and also to allow you access to the new self contained apartment."

"What about the back stairs and internal access between the two floors for staff?"

"In the plans you'll see Ben has incorporated a small preparation kitchen in his design for use in the cafe and recommends a dumb waiter be installed linking it to the main Stores kitchen."

All eyes looked eagerly at Emma as she absorbed all the information Graeme, Alex and Ben had offered as answers to all her concerns.

"Oh my, you have been busy. May I look at the plans again, Ben?"

"I'll make coffee, I'm sure you're all ready for some." Alex jumped up and made her way to the kitchen. She knew her sister well enough to know that on this issue she would not be hurried. As a youngster her impetuous nature had frequently landed her in scrapes but since the death of their parents Emma had become more thoughtful and reluctant to make hasty decisions.

For quite some time Emma pondered over the drawings laid out in front of her, piecing together the facts she had been given, with the proposals so clearly marked on the plans by Ben. As she sipped the mug of coffee Alex placed in front of her Emma carefully considered each aspect of the design. Eventually she became convinced of the rightness of the expansion and agreed with Alex that they should go ahead with redevelopment. They gave their consent to the plans, and confirmed that Durrant's, uncles Roy and Gordon's building firm, should be asked to carry out the work.

"This really looks an exciting project, Ben, but I think that in view of Matty's recent past history, Uncle Roy should be asked to keep a close eye on things."

"I think that's a good suggestion, Emma. Matty might be my brother but I can't condone his recent behaviour. It's causing upset to so many people's lives. I'm afraid Dad is as bad because he is all for keeping costs down and tends to turn a blind eye to shady dealing and cutting corners. Uncle Roy will ensure the work is done properly and to a high standard. You'll have tea rooms you can be proud of."

"Thanks, Ben."

How delighted young Rosie Jenner would be when she heard this news.

Chapter Four

After breakfast on Easter Monday morning RK set out to explore the area. Exiting through the door of the Mill Rosie slipped a small bag into RK's hands.

"Packed lunch," she explained.

"Why, thanks," RK smiled and accepted the parcel.

"All part of the Jenner service," quipped the teenager with a grin and she stood and waved as the Harley-Davidson roared out of sight.

At the same time as RK rode away from the Mill, along the narrow lane that wound between sea and river, another motorcycle approached from the opposite direction. As they converged each rider slowed down.

"Good morning," the oncoming rider called out above the roar of the machines and raised his hand in greeting. "Enjoy your day."

Recognising the police bike RK acknowledged P.C. Dan's friendly gesture before continuing the journey down the lane.

Well, RK pondered, as the motorcyclist accelerated away, *that policeman seems to be everywhere, though he does appear to be a very friendly young man.* Without giving Dan Prettyman any further thought RK proceeded to fulfil the plans for the day.

Fascinated by the architecture of the picturesque cottages and painted dwellings edging the lanes or tucked away behind trees and hedges RK stopped frequently to walk around them, more easily to appreciate the delights they offered, because they were built so differently to houses in Lincolnshire. The numerous breaks also gave RK opportunity to view the East Anglian landscape and climb the riverbank to enjoy the river, which seemed to have a life and ambience all its own. An abundance of waterfowl jostled for space on the water amongst the leisure craft and commercial traffic.

The sun was pleasantly warm and the breeze that blew over the water refreshing. Late morning RK sat down on a grassy knoll and watched the diverse activities, tacking yachts, as well as, mother ducks shepherding their offspring as they tumbled into the lapping water to take their first swim. How delightful it was to quietly absorb the sound and smell of nature and forget the provocation that had created the need to get away from home. *Dad is so pigheaded and uncompromising! His domineering attitude is something akin to that of a dictator! Business and bank-balance direct his life and his family but I want no part of it. It's people I care about and despite Dad's derogatory remarks about my work I'll continue on my chosen path.*

However, I won't waste this lovely day dwelling on that, decided RK with a quick shake of the head, *this setting is far too tranquil for such turbulent thoughts. Besides, the cycle of the seasons evident in the emerging foliage around me, the newborn lambs frolicking in the fields and chirruping fledglings nestling in the hedgerows, speaks of permanence and continuity. I think it is this that is important not the thrust and pull of a fragile economy Dad persistently focuses upon.*

The peace and serenity the scene afforded at that moment wrapped around RK like a comforting blanket and the gently flowing water had a mesmeric effect till rumblings in the stomach brought a reminder of passing time. Delving into Rosie's lunch pack RK discovered the contents were all one could have wished for; freshly baked rolls, full of cheese, a generous helping of mixed salad, fruit, and even a bottle of spring water, then, tucked in the corner a luscious pâtisserie delight that simply melted in the mouth.

Replete and rejuvenated RK zipped up the leather jacket and fastened the helmet then set out on the bike for further explorations. Heading down a twisting lane back towards Newton Westerby RK spied a quaint, thatched seaside cottage, with intriguing dormer windows in the eaves and walls painted in Suffolk pink. A 'For Sale' board by the garden gate aroused curiosity that simply had to be satisfied.

RK parked up the Harley-Davidson on the roadside verge turned to cross over the road but there, coming round the corner of the same cottage, walked Jansy and Dave. They seemed to be in the middle of a heated discussion and didn't at first see RK.

"I do think this is a really nice house," Dave looked up to admire its pleasing aspect and sturdy construction.

"Nice house in the wrong place," muttered Jansy.

"But, why? It's not far from the village."

"Too far from the hospital!" she snapped.

"Look, the main road to Norwich is just along the lane," Dave pointed out patiently.

"But think of all the travelling," Jansy's shoulders heaved with an exaggerated sigh.

"Oh come on, Jans, it's not that far. Wouldn't it be worth it to have such an attractively placed house?"

"Not really," was her glum reply.

"Don't you think it has potential to be a lovely home?" asked Dave persuasively.

"Maybe, but I don't want to live so far from the hospital," said Jansy impatiently. As she turned Jansy glimpsed RK a short distance away so waved and called out, "Oh, hi!"

Dave, with his back to the lane had not seen RK pull up so remained totally focussed on the house, quite unfazed by Jansy's ruse to use RK's unexpected arrival to deflect him from the matter in hand. He took up Jansy's hand and looked at her tenderly, and said earnestly, "Jans, my dearest girl, we've looked at numerous properties in so many places and you're still undecided."

"I can't help it, I'm just not sure," Jansy muttered petulantly.

"You know my feelings but I want you to be happy, Jans," said Dave gently. "Houses so rarely come on the market in the village this may be our only chance to buy our own home here. Our wedding day advances ever nearer so we must make a decis..." Dave stopped speaking when he, too, became aware of RK walking down the side of the building.

Jansy, glad of the diversion, reiterated her earlier greeting. "Don't mind us. We're trying to decide whether it would be best for us to live here in the village or in the city?"

"I'm really sorry, I had no idea you were going to be here," RK apologized, feeling dreadfully uncomfortable for barging in, prepared to backtrack and ride off, but Jansy purposefully drew RK into the discussion by asking for an unbiased opinion on the matter.

"Please, tell us what you think of this property?"

"Jans, that's so unfair!" Dave put his hand on Jansy's arm. She shrugged him off.

"Well?" she persisted looking directly at RK with piercingly blue eyes.

The cottage in question was in a particularly idyllic setting to RK's mind. "It's a pretty cottage in a delightful location and I think it offers the best of both worlds. It appears to be near to all the amenities of the village and not far from the main road into the city."

"That's my opinion, too," said Dave quietly.

"I've just been offered a Senior Staff Nurse post on the Paediatric ward at the hospital in the city," Jansy explained irrelevantly. She didn't add that it was another step on the ladder to the position of Sister to which she aspired. This had been her goal from childhood and now she found herself torn between achieving her ambition and pleasing Dave. Living in the city would be her choice but the sea was in Dave's blood. He loved the village and village life and would prefer to live in the familiar community rather than the anonymity of the city.

"But you know I would willingly give it a try, if it would make you happy, Jans."

"He's a stick-in-the-mud," Jansy complained to RK sarcastically with an impatient flick of her head, and proceeded to explain her view of the situation. "If we lived in the city it would be so much easier for me to get to and from the hospital when I'm on early or late shift. He can drive to Norwich when he's moored the boat here in the harbour and there are loads of places in the village where he can leave the car while he's at sea, for instance, my parent's or his. I really can't see the problem."

"I certainly wouldn't pass up the opportunity to live in such an idyllic spot. I suggest you grab this gem of a house with both hands. It seems solid, well-built and so attractive," RK commented.

"You've no idea how stressful this all is," Jansy shook her head as she wrung her hands in agitation.

"On the contrary, I know exactly what it's like to live under pressure," replied RK quietly.

Dave was shocked that Jansy shared such personal disclosures with a stranger. RK tactfully withdrew and left them to carry on their disagreement in private, thinking if they truly loved one another, where they lived didn't matter one iota.

Arriving back in Newton Westerby RK was attracted to the Village Stores by the eye-catching window display. RK peered through the window, surprised to see a well stocked shop in such an out of the way place, and even more surprised to find it closed when numerous potential customers appeared to be milling about.

Tramping across the Village Green RK noticed the open door of the church hall, remembered conversations from Sunday, and stepped inside. Teas were set out upon a long table to one side of the hall and an Easter bonnet parade was in progress on the platform at the far end of the building. The Jenner children recognised the newcomer who entered the hall and made a beeline for RK who admired their outfits, congratulated the winners and tactfully commiserated with those not so fortunate, then cleverly steered them towards the sumptuous tea table.

Pansy sidled up to RK and slipped her small hand into RK's large one and whispered, "I do like you. You're my friend."

"I like you too, pretty little lady," said RK and playfully tweaked the bonnet Pansy was wearing.

Pansy drew RK closer to her and spoke softly, "I think you're a girl," she said shyly.

"You do?" asked RK with pretended surprise.

"Oh, yes, you've got crinkly, smiley eyes and you laugh a lot," she replied with increased confidence.

"I see."

"Wow!" exploded Keir, distracting RK's attention. "Just look at all this food," he said, diving in with gusto and rapidly filling his plate.

Noting sausage rolls and ham sandwiches heaped amidst the cheesy offerings RK softly enquired, "Keir, are you allowed such a selection?"

"Oh, yeah, these are brill."

All the Jenner children followed Keir's lead and revelled in making a choice from the abundance displayed on the table as though they had not been fed for a week.

Rosie saw RK's look of concern.

"It's OK. We're allowed free choice when we're out. Mum has this theory that if we're not restricted we'll choose healthy veggie things, but if we're forbidden pork pies, sausages and other meat savouries, we won't know what the difference is and we'll eat them regardless. Dad's not wholly vegetarian, anyway."

"Right," RK conceded and followed the youngsters, filling a plate en route with some of the delectable buffet food on offer, to the table where the vicar's wife, Penny Darnell, was waiting to take their money.

"Hello again, enjoying your day?"

"Yes, it's been very interesting," RK smiled, pleased that the Vicar's wife remembered their earlier meeting at the Easter breakfast.

"That will be £2.50, please."

"And a cup of tea."

"Oh, it's all inclusive."

"Goodness that is cheap."

"We have to be realistic. The event's organized by the Women's Guild to raise funds for the church and they want people to come. If it's too pricey some can't afford it and it would prove expensive for families."

"Well, you certainly seem busy. Has it been successful?"

"Extremely! The ladies are thrilled at the response from day visitors as well as the usual enthusiastic support from villagers."

"We're just hoping for a lull in proceedings so we can sit down and rest our weary feet," said Pauline Cooper who was pouring out the tea.

"You look as though you could do with a cuppa yourself. Isn't there any one to relieve you?"

"We've sent the others home. They've had a long day having been here since early morning…"

"But so have you from what I hear. Look, why don't you have a break now. Rosie and I will hold the fort. Won't we?"

Before Rosie could reply, RK had everyone organized. The Jenner children were seated up to a table not too far from the serving table so Rosie could keep an eye on them, till her elder brother, Nathan came in with Dan Prettyman and assumed that responsibility. They both washed their hands, and then RK poured tea, made up a plate for Penny and Pauline and ensured they sat down to enjoy their break in relative quiet.

Within minutes Trixie Cooper emerged from the kitchen bearing clean crockery which she had just washed up. Her eyes lit up when she saw RK and Rosie handling the customers.

"Oh my! Reinforcements! Great!" were her comments as the crockery tray clattered down on the table.

RK looked round and saw tiredness etched on Trixie's face so took her by the shoulders, steered her to sit down with her friends, and supplied her with necessary refreshment.

More and more people came in, yet despite the busyness and the animated chatter of the children, RK caught snatches of the conversation between Trixie and her sister-in-law, Pauline, about Jansy and Dave's forthcoming marriage.

"How are the arrangements for the wedding shaping up?" Pauline enquired.

"Well, after much thought it's been decided to hold the reception here in the village hall and issue an open invitation to everyone from the village."

"Surely that's a bit daunting, all those people, how will you cope?"

"Thankfully, Jilly Briggs, with her incredible flair is going to prepare a wedding buffet and dear Emma, who's been Jansy's best friend since their first day at school, is going to decorate the hall in the style of Bettys of Harrogate," explained Trixie.

"That sounds a bit ambitious."

"Mmm," Trixie nodded "but surely, right up Emma's street?"

"Yes, I can see her pulling that off. Her window displays at the Stores have been amazing in the past few months. Obviously, she's inherited Mick's arty panache."

"Lizzie Piper, Jansy's young cousin from Newton Bridge, has been persuaded to play the piano throughout the proceedings."

"I'd heard she was giving a recital."

"Jansy's thrilled she's agreed and will alternate with Stuart Jenner. He quite publicly declares he is not really a piano man, just reserve church organist, but will help out so that Lizzie can have a break."

"That's good of him."

"I understand Lizzie's just won a scholarship to the Royal College of Music."

"Yes, she's such a talented young lady but my brother-in-law can't, or won't, see it."

"That's a shame."

"I agree. Lizzie's nimble fingers can sew a fine seam but their finest work is achieved when they run in cadences on the black and white notes of the keyboard but Joe feels his daughter should follow in her mother's footsteps. Her mum, my sister Maisie, as you know, is a skilled seamstress and currently making Jansy's wedding dress in between working on the furnishings for their boat business."

"Gosh, I wouldn't like to take on that responsibility."

"Actually, it's coming along quite nicely, so I haven't any worries on that score. The one thing that really does concern me is the discord between Dave and Jansy because they can't agree where to live."

"That is worrying."

"I hope they can resolve it while they're off-duty together before Dave goes back to sea," commented Penny.

"So do I," said Trixie with great feeling.

"I understand they were offered the cottage that was Alex and Graeme's home before they moved into the bungalow."

"Mmm. Turned it down flat!"

"No! I'd heard too, via the grapevine, that Lord Edmund offered them Gate Lodge, which is currently empty and also one of the recently modernized estate cottages. He feels so strongly that affordable housing should be available in the village for young people should they wish to stay, doesn't he?"

"You heard right."

"So, they have their pick of properties?"

"Yes, but Jansy is digging her heels in," said Trixie running her fingers through her hair in exasperated resignation. She gave herself a shake and looked towards the busy serving table.

"Well, this won't do. We'd better get on, can't leave the youngsters to do our job."

"They appear to have managed extremely well. Rosie's very capable and that young man seems to have everything in hand."

"Maybe," said Pauline dubiously.

"I wonder who he really is."

"Can't seem to go anywhere in the village without bumping into him."

"Anyway, the young folk have taken to him."

"He must be OK then," Trixie laughed.

CHAPTER FIVE

The following day RK walked along the harbourside enjoying the warmth of the continuing spring sunshine with a freedom of spirit that came from a relaxed body and mind. The liveliness and industry on this stretch of water was fascinating and repeatedly drew the landlubbing visitor like a magnet. Thus far, RK was totally unaware that the keen interest shown in the activity in the harbour was viewed with suspicion and being closely monitored by harbour master and local constabulary.

One of the longshore boats was preparing to cast off and set sail. A deck hand, who looked vaguely familiar to RK, manoeuvred the thick mooring rope from the stanchion on the quayside, tossed it aboard and jumped, following it closely on to the deck. *Now where have I seen him before?* RK scrutinized the young man as he coiled the rope into a neat pile while the boat slipped it's berth and seemingly, moved effortlessly through the water towards the harbour lights and out to the open sea, but simply couldn't place him.

The ever present gulls swooped and called as they accompanied the boat on the first part of its journey. RK watched the procedure enthralled but Titus Wills watched RK through binoculars with misgiving, contemplating the significance of RK's presence in Newton Westerby.

To the right a yacht was tacking, its white sails slackened then taut as they billowed to catch the breeze, and its mast reaching majestically to the sky. Alongside the quay, on the left, numerous craft of differing shapes and sizes were in the process of being kitted out, cleaned and painted, taking on board water, diesel or provisions, or simply 'pottered about in' by their enthusiastic owners.

Further along the bank, a lone fisherman sat patiently awaiting a catch, his rod baited and perfectly poised. Closer inspection would have revealed that beneath the large cap was Sergeant Tom Catchpole, incognito. From his vantage point he was vigilantly keeping an eye on the movements of RK.

Oblivious of the close scrutiny, RK leant on the harbour wall attracted by activity on the far side of the river, where a smidgeon of children were gathered on a floating pontoon, armed with their buckets, lines and bacon, engaged in gillieing. Gil Jenner had earlier in the day described in detail the art of gillieing or crab catching and proudly produced a trophy that he had won one year when he had come first in the gillieing championships. The intense look on the youngsters' faces showed how serious a pursuit it was and RK sensed the accompanying parents were equally absorbed by the activity.

In fact, the occupation was so engaging that RK almost missed the Catton family as they passed by on the landward side of the quay, until the excited voice of a young boy could be heard above the cacophony of harbour sounds assailing RK's ears.

"Why, hello there," RK turned and greeted the little family.

"You're the bike man, aren't you," stated Daniel jumping up and down.

"Yes, I do have a motorbike," agreed RK.

Daniel looked around mystified, "But... where is it?"

"I've left it in the car park at the Ship Inn. I'm going for a walk this morning and calling in to the restaurant for lunch on the way back."

"Oh," said the little boy disappointedly, the corners of his mouth curling down towards his chin.

RK crouched down beside him in order to speak with him at his level, "Now, we really can't have a glum clown face on such a bright day. You'll make us all feel sad." RK tweaked Daniel's crestfallen face, leant forward and whispered in his ear, "I shall be here for a few more days so I expect you'll have chance to see it again."

"Oh, goody," replied Daniel, his countenance changing rapidly. He beamed at the newcomer as he clapped his hands together in glee.

"Hello again," said Laura, drawing alongside her chatting son. "You obviously remember Daniel from Sunday morning when you met him at the sunrise service accompanied by my husband, Adam. This little lady is Kirsten and the sleepy head in the buggy is Poppy." Laura gestured towards her daughters.

"It's lovely to see you all. I'm just enjoying your splendid village." RK's infectious grin encompassed the whole family causing Kirsty to giggle.

"I hope it meets all your expectations," said Laura with a smile. "We've just been down to the pier head to wave off my Cousin Mark's boat."

"I thought it was unlucky to do that," remarked RK.

"Some would say so, but I don't agree with the old idea that it's bad luck to see a relative's boat out of harbour. That's superstition."

"I'd heard that fishermen object to it."

"Yes, it's true and my uncle would never allow it, but I like to wish Mark God speed and a safe journey when he sets sail and send him away with our prayers."

"Just another aspect of this rather captivating place, then?" said RK warmly.

"It all depends on what you are used to. For me, living in a village, by the sea, amongst family and friends, could not be better. We have fresh air, clear skies, interesting harbour, clean beach, long walks and a close-knit community who look out for one another. If that's what you're looking for then, that's Newton Westerby."

"So I'm discovering. This is only my third day and already it's been quite an adventure and I've met some interesting people."

"It's not always this tranquil but I tend to look for the best in every situation even when we have the howling winds and storms. God is so good!"

"I'm fascinated by the crab catchers."

"Oh, that's good fun," enthused Daniel.

"But we can only do it when Daddy's with us," explained Kirsten.

"I think that's very sensible." RK looked up at Laura. "How does one get to the other side of the water? I mean apart from swimming or by boat. I don't see a bridge."

"Oh, you mustn't swim. It's not allowed," admonished Kirsten solemnly.

"I won't try that, then, thankyou for telling me."

"There's a ferry," explained Laura. "It's about half a mile up river so that it doesn't impede vessels coming into harbour," she paused to point inland up the river. "If you look beyond the fisherman on the bank it's now reaching this side." With a craned neck RK looked in the direction Laura was pointing.

"How often does it run?"

"Oh, it sails back and forth all day and, when needed, in the evenings. It links the roads, which run down to the river on either side. I'm afraid you can't see them very well from here. It carries foot passengers, small cars, bikes, scooters, prams and mobility chairs. Larger vehicles have to do the twenty mile trip round by the main road."

"Where does it take you to?"

"The lane the other side leads to Newton Bridge and Newton Lokesby, a pretty riverside village that is also blessed with a railway station, a boatyard and a hotel."

"Ah, yes, The Station Hotel, fully booked because it's Easter," said RK rising to an upright position.

"You've obviously been in touch."

"Yes, but it sounds a place worth visiting. I might venture there tomorrow."

"Well, we're now off to the play-park where there are swings and slides and a climbing frame."

"That sounds like fun. Have a good time. I'm going to explore the coast line then plan to come back along the top of the cliffs."

Laura and the children waved goodbye and headed towards the park, Daniel chatting excitedly about seeing RK's bike the next day.

When they parted, Titus Wills and Sgt. Catchpole, who had observed the exchange from their different vantage points, met up and quietly conferred in the harbour master's office on their next course of action as they watched RK set out on the coastal walk.

Unfortunately, drug and people smuggling had become rife along some parts of the English coast. In recent days it had come to light that the tiny East Anglian ports were being targeted because the traffickers considered them an easy option to offload their cargo believing they were not as closely monitored so their illicit activities were less likely to be detected. However, the Newton Westerby men were scrupulously watchful, alert to unusual activity or strangers in their area, and acted accordingly. So that, unwilling to lose sight of the newcomer they sent a message to P.C. Prettyman instructing him to head in the same direction.

Meanwhile, further along the quayside, the Catton family were accosted on their walk to the park by a very distraught Mrs Jenner; seagulls had just messed all over her newly set hair.

"Look, the bird droppen's be on my coat and my face and in my hair. Oh dear, whatever shall Oi dew? Rachel has only just finished my hair. What a mess!" The old lady wafted her arms about helplessly.

"My dear Mrs Jenner, I am so sorry, what an unpleasant experience," Laura began kindly, as she rummaged in the buggy basket for baby wipes. Mrs Jenner had certainly worked herself into a state.

"Yes, but what'll Oi dew, Laura, you're the nurse, Oi don't want e'." Laura suddenly realized it wasn't just the mess that concerned Mrs Jenner but the very real fear that she might contract the dreaded bird flu because of the incident.

"I do understand your concern, Mrs Jenner. Here, let me help you clean up with these wipes."

"But e' be always in the news an…"

"Yes, I know, and I understand it is very prevalent in some areas but if you're careful I'm sure you'll be fine."

"But look at me, e' be everywhere," the old lady wailed.

"Look, we've got the worst of it off. I suggest you go home rewash your hair, sponge down your coat and thoroughly scrub your hands."

"Oi don't want to be ill, Laura," said Mrs Jenner, tearfully, grabbing Laura's arm.

"Then you need to take all the necessary precautions. If you're worried, take your coat into the Stores and have them send it to the cleaners, then call into the surgery on your way home, explain what's happened and they will give you some antiseptic hand wash. Use it."

"But my lovely hair-dew…"

"My dear Mrs Jenner, you must make the choice, but I know what I would do. Now off you go. The sooner you deal with it, the better. Come along children, the park awaits us." Laura binned the wipes, spayed her hands with antiseptic spray she always carried in the buggy, and stepped out briskly in the direction of the play area, Daniel and Kirsten eagerly following her lead.

Long legs enabled RK to cover a considerable distance along the beach at a relatively brisk pace, despite a number of stops, to watch the waves and pick up and marvel at the fascinating shells proliferate on the beach.

At the same time, P.C. Prettyman did his utmost to engineer an accidental meeting place. He had followed his quarry's progress, through binoculars, from a vantage point on the clifftop. He planned to overtake RK, hidden from view by gorse bushes that grew on the cliff, as RK rounded the promontory of the cove and ascended the steps that brought walkers onto the clifftop coastal path. To this end, as RK was climbing up the steps, the young constable ran fifty yards or so further along the path, passed the steps then, stopped, turned and slowly ambled back towards them. He struggled hard with the deceit of this situation but orders had been given and he was expected to carry them out.

In a short space of time RK appeared at the top of the steps just ahead of him on the clifftop path.

My word, how did she get up so quickly? Prettyman asked himself. *She?* Where on earth had that thought sprung from?

"Hello there! Mind if I join you?" Dan Prettyman's lengthy strides brought him swiftly to RK's side.

"Please do," invited RK amiably, continuing to scan the panorama before them in amazement. Then, with arms sweeping expansively to encompass the scene said, "What an incredible view."

"Yes, it is," Dan agreed, watching the movement closely. Oh *my goodness, she really is a woman*, he thought, *I'm going to have to tread carefully here.*

"Everywhere I look in this village I encounter surprise upon surprise."

"You're quite a surprise, too."

"Oh?"

"No bike and no leathers!"

"I've left them at the Ship Inn car park. Anyway, I do have a pair of perfectly good legs. I learned to use them at a young age, you know," RK grinned at him engagingly. The look completely disarmed him. *Why ever do the Sergeant and Harbour Master think this person is a threat to national security or is involved in smuggling activities?*

"But why the disguise?"

"Disguise?"

"Leathers etcetera."

"Oh, it's such fun to have an air of mystery about my persona. I love to watch people's faces as they try to figure out what I am."

"The way you look doesn't give much of a clue, in fact, quite the reverse."

"Depends who's doing the looking. Adults struggle but children have absolutely no problem."

"You're kidding?"

"No, the Jenner girls knew straight away. The boys, at first, took more notice of the bike than me and made the usual association."

"So, no real intent to deceive?"

"No, this is me. People must accept me for who I am."

"Not who they perceive you to be?"

"What do you mean?"

"Everyone in the village thinks you're a man." RK's rich laughter reverberated across the cliffs. Dan felt the sound must surely reach the harbour.

"That's the story of my life! My father wanted sons, he had four daughters. He gave us boys names, Philip, Michael, David and Keith and has treated us as such all our lives. Mum tagged on the 'a' to each name so we became Philipa, Michaela, Davina and me. I'm mechanically minded like motorbikes and dress accordingly. People make assumptions when they see the bike and leathers, and of course, I am taller than most girls. There aren't many people I look up to." Her eyes sparkled with playful humour as she looked up at the lanky policeman.

"Well, I'm 6'4", so you must be about 6'."

RK nodded, "6'1", actually."

"And your name?"

"Robyn Keitha Dickinson-Bond."

"Mmm! I see! Bit of a mouthful. I can understand RK being more manageable but I'm going to call you Robyn."

"You'll be my mother's friend for life."

"But why the short hair?"

"Long hair got in the way of the engines and it was too much of a bind to keep putting it up."

"And why did you come to Newton Westerby?"

"There was brief mention of it in a travel brochure which whet..." P.C. Dan put up his arm by way of an apology as his mobile phone interrupted their conversation and he moved a few steps away in order to answer it. RK sat down on a grassy knoll and from its clifftop vantage point watched the movement of the sea as the waves rolled in, one after the other, breaking continuously along the shore, an endless succession, always the same yet, always different.

"I have to go, an incident to deal with," Dan explained a few moments later.

"Right, I hope it's nothing serious."

"Someone's collapsed in the play-park."

"Oh dear!"

"I'll see you around. Just a word of warning, your presence and apparel are causing mayhem in certain quarters in our community, so, take care."

Before RK had chance to reply, P.C. Prettyman was gone. He raced along the cliff path to the lane where he had parked the police motor-cycle. Immediately he mounted the bike, Dan put on the siren and sped down to the play-park, a prayer in his heart for the family involved in the situation in the park.

RK was left in a quandary. She sat for quite a while wondering what the entire encounter, with Dan Prettyman, had been all about. His questions had been personal, yet, somewhat detached, probing while seeming trivial. She slowly shook her head. He was a likeable young man but RK had a sneaking suspicion that he had been surreptitiously interrogating her.

CHAPTER SIX

It was shortly after their arrival at the play-park on the Village Green, following the encounter with Mrs Jenner on the quay that, without any warning, Laura collapsed in a heap onto the ground. One moment she was pushing Poppy in a baby swing and the next she was unconscious on the safety surface beneath the swings. It all happened so suddenly but Daniel saw her fall as he stood at the top of the slide. He squealed in fright and flew down the slide. "Mu...um," he yelled as he got to the bottom and ran towards her. By the time he reached her side Kirsten was kneeling over Laura saying, "Mummy wake up." Daniel pushed his sister out of the way, shook Laura's arm hard and shouted, "Mum, open your eyes, it's me, Daniel."

Poppy started to fidget as the swing slowed down and because no one was paying her any attention she pulled herself up into a precarious standing position. Daniel caught the movement out of the corner of his eye. "Kirsty, keep shaking Mummy and talking to her, I'll put Poppy in the buggy."

With a presence of mind far beyond his years Daniel fastened his little sister carefully into her buggy then rummaged in his mother's handbag for her mobile phone. He dialled 999. When his call was answered he promptly said, "Come quick, Mum needs the ambulance man. She's deaded in the play-park on The Green."

"Where's The Green?"

"Newton Westerby, o'course."

As he was speaking Daniel's eyes unconsciously followed the line of houses that nestled around The Green. They stopped when Doctor Cooper's house came into view. Involuntarily his feet started to take him forwards so that he didn't properly hear the words spoken by the operator. In fact, so many thoughts were rushing through his head he was beginning to feel confused. Poppy's cries brought him back to the matter in hand and the need to get help for Mum. He turned back, made his way towards her, and did his utmost to pacify the little girl.

"Shush Poppy, there's a good girl, look here's your juice." Daniel placed the non-spill toddler cup into her hands.

He then turned to Kirsten and thrust the mobile phone at her. "Here, Kirsty, talk to this lady. I'm going to get Doctor John, OK?"

Daniel ran across The Green as fast as his legs would take him. He balled his fist tight and banged on the front door as hard as he could and shouted, "Doctor, Doctor." Trixie Cooper heard his frantic cries long before she opened the door. Surprised to see Daniel alone and so agitated she turned her head and called with urgency in her voice, "John, come quickly."

Turning back to her young visitor Trixie smiled warmly, "Hello, Daniel, do come in."

"No, Mrs Cooper, I can't. I need Doc John to help Mummy. She's fallen down."

"I see. Where are the girls?"

"At the play-park, Poppy's in the buggy and Kirsty's watching her, and trying to wake up Mum and talking to the phone lady."

"She's very busy, then. We'd better go and help her."

The news that Laura had collapsed as she played with the children in the playground, spread around the village like wild fire. The villagers were stunned. Talk in the Village Stores, Cooper's butcher's shop and the old codger's bench down on the quay, centred on nothing else for the rest of the day. It completely scotched the speculation that had been rife concerning the leather-clad motorcyclist.

"She fell down an' passed out so I heard."

"Did she trip?"

Heads shook uncertainly.

"A stroke, or some such, so they say."

"Is that roite?"

"Can't believe it, can yew, Pauline?" said Mrs Saunders as she reached out to take her parcel of sausages.

"It's certainly come as a bit of a shock and so unexpected," Pauline replied.

"Especially wi' 'er be'en' so young," continued Mrs Saunders.

"P'rhaps that's the reason for all those dizzy spells she kept having earlier in the year," commented Christina Ransome.

"Could be."

Across the road in the Stores conversation ran on similar lines.

"Fancy that child runnen' all the way to Doctor Cooper's," said Mrs Jenner, who had taken Laura's advice and brought her coat in to be sent to the cleaners.

"I say thank God he didn't pani…"

"… and thank goodness for mobile phones," interposed Rosalie as she finished writing out the docket for Mrs Jenner's coat.

"Good job they'd taught him 'ow to use one," remarked another customer.

"Always seemed a sensible lad, young Daniel," remarked Bernice Durrant coming to join the queue by the till.

"An' little Kirsty left a-watchen' the baby, calm as yew please in one so young," remarked Mrs Jenner.

Jennifer Pedwardine, standing a little aloof from the gossiping shoppers, suddenly asked, "Does anyone know what's happening about the children?"

Heads in the group shook; no one knew who was looking after them.

"I think someone mentioned they'd been taken to the Doctor's house," explained Rosalie.

"They'll be fine there, then."

"I say, Rosalie, isn't the young marrieds' house group due to be held at Adam and Laura's home this evening?"

"I believe you're right."

"I wonder, too, what they'll do about worship group practise tomorrow night. I think Adam's likely to be tied up, don't you?"

"I'll mention it to Emma."

So, in between serving customers, Rosalie drew Emma to one side as she came out of the office and explained their concerns.

"I'll manage here if you want to take time to pop up to the flat and let Ben know about Laura." Ben, as church lay reader and youth coordinator, could make any necessary re-arrangements for the group meetings. He was currently in Emma's flat, above the Stores, re-checking measurements for the plans he had drawn for the proposed renovation so it would only take a moment to acquaint him with the situation.

"What very upsetting news, I hope it's not as bad as everyone seems to think." Emma turned, "Thanks, Rosalie, I won't be long."

It was with mixed feelings that Emma made her way through the shop, passed the huddle of customers to the back stairwell, her thoughts very much on Laura and how her mishap would affect her little family.

As she climbed the steps she reflected that before long all this would be changed as the builders knocked out some walls, and reconstructed others, to implement Ben's innovative plans for a coffee shop. She pulled up abruptly, then stopped for a moment, and breathed deeply as remembered that this was the place on the stairs where she had last conversed with her father, the previous Christmas Eve. *Father God, thankyou for the strength You've given me to carry on since Mum and Dad died. Give strength now to Adam and healing to Laura in this their hour of need. Thankyou, too, for Your gracious patience, it curbs my hastiness and helps me control my temper. I am grateful for Your guidance. More than ever I'm convinced that Your blessing is on this new venture.*

With slow, measured steps she thoughtfully continued up the stairs. *I'm also sure Mum and Dad would approve these changes. I think they'd see them as progress. I can just imagine Mum's face as she concocted new dishes to serve in the coffee shop and Dad's delight at new people coming through the doors would know no bounds. How he loved to chat with all the visitors. He would revel in the possibilities that renovation will present and be excited at the challenge.*

Emma pushed her shoulders back and held her head high. *I'll do the same.* She reached the top of the flight, pushed open the door and approached Ben with the situation regarding Laura.

Meanwhile, back at the play-park paramedics had attended to Laura's immediate needs, and then swiftly conveyed her to the hospital in Norwich. Trixie, thankfully had no appointments scheduled for rest of the day, so took the Catton children home with her. She unearthed a box of toys from the cupboard under the stairs, kept for visiting children, and whilst Daniel, Kirsten and Poppy enjoyed delving in to find unexpected treasures Trixie quickly prepared a snack lunch for them.

With a heavy heart Doctor John picked up the phone in the hallway and contacted Adam at his Norwich office. Sensitively, he broke the news of Laura's collapse and pending arrival at the Norfolk and Norwich hospital and assured the young man of his children's well being.

"Give all your attention to Laura, my man, the children will be well cared for, so you have no need to worry about them. Our prayers are with you both. If there's anything at all, that you need, just give me a call."

John walked thoughtfully back into the surgery. Miranda, sitting at her desk in the reception area, looked up and saw that he appeared to be preoccupied so enquired, "Is everything alright, Doctor?"

John proceeded to quietly outline what was known to have taken place in the playground.

"Oh, Doc, I am so sorry." Miranda's tender heart caused tears to flood her eyes.

"Whatever will happen to the little ones?"

"At present they're with Trixie having lunch in the kitchen. We haven't yet had opportunity to discuss or plan beyond that, though I do feel the welfare of those children is of paramount importance."

Miranda blew her nose, wiped her eyes, and took time to compose herself.

"I see."

"Maybe together we can come up with some suitable arrangement. You're the world's best organizer, what would you suggest?"

She smiled up at the Doctor, "Now Doc, flattery won't get you anywhere."

"No, but your skill and common sense will, that's what I'm appealing to at the moment."

"Just give me a minute."

Miranda rose from her seat, stood stock still and appeared to be staring into space but John knew from experience she was simply sifting through information stored in her mind and calculating different permutations that could possibly solve the dilemma they had been presented with. John stood patiently by and waited.

After a short while Miranda shook herself, looked straight at the Doctor and said with self-assurance, "I've almost finished here, if I may ring Jackie and ask her to come across and discuss the situation, I will have completed the filing by the time she arrives, then together we'll work out a solution."

"You will keep me informed?"

"Of course. As soon as we've devised a plan I'll type up the schedule so that everyone, who needs to be aware of what's going on, has a copy. Does that meet with your approval?"

"Certainly," John turned to leave the reception area and head back into the hallway of the house.

"Doc, before you go can I ask what time scale you have in mind? Are we looking at interim locums or a long term situation?"

John slowly nodded his head, "I think it highly unlikely that Laura will be returning to work next week, or even the long term future, if at all," he finished in a murmur.

"You think it's that serious?"

"Quite possibly."

"Well, you don't need me to tell you the ideal solution to this scenario, do you?"

The Doctor raised his eyebrows quizzically as he looked at Miranda.

"Jansy."

Astonished once more at his receptionists unusual perception at dealing realistically with any problems that occurred John left her to get on with her work. Deep in thought he returned to Trixie and the children.

Jacqueline Cooper, middle daughter of Billy and Pauline, was acting deputy head teacher at Newton

Westerby primary school but since Jennifer Pedwardine's retirement from the headship, at the end of the last school year, a great deal of extra responsibility had fallen on her shoulders.

Jackie had joined the school in the nursery department on completion of her studies and she still had a preference for teaching the younger children but whilst they were understaffed she fitted in where the need was greatest. Currently, she was on school holidays preparing at home for the commencement of a new term.

By the time Jackie arrived at the surgery, in response to her sister's phone call, Miranda had completed the filing, made numerous phone calls and already had in place a possible rota of locums to fulfil Laura's duties over the next few weeks.

Miranda, long time receptionist to her uncle, Doctor John, was well renowned in the community as an able organizer. So that, within a short space of time, the sisters were able to devise a workable plan to look after the Catton children.

"It's naturally going to be an upsetting time for Daniel and the girls," said Miranda.

"Yes, but at least we're not strangers to them."

"Mmm, that's true."

Daniel and Kirsten were familiar with Jackie from their attendance at nursery and primary school, as well as, meeting her fairly regularly at services and other functions connected with church. However, Poppy was more comfortable with Miranda because Laura frequently brought her into the surgery to visit the staff. On occasions Laura asked Miranda to keep an eye on the little girl when she and Doctor John needed to discuss patient care. From time to time both sisters, too, had babysat at the Catton home.

"The children are going to find this all a little unsettling. We'll be able to explain what's happening with their Mum to Daniel and Kirsten but I think Poppy is going to be rather bewildered by the changes."

"I agree. I think whatever we decide is going to be a traumatic experience for them. They're not used to being without their parents for any length of time."

"Do you have anything planned for the rest of this week?"

"No, nothing... apart from the usual pre-term preparations and..."

"So, what do you say to us both going to stay at the Catton house?"

"That's a great idea; at least the children will be on familiar territory."

"It will also relieve Adam of anxiety for the children so he can give time and attention to Laura and her needs."

"Let's get our suggestions into some semblance of order," recommended Miranda as her fingers flew across the keyboard of the laptop.

When Doctor John returned from lunch Miranda presented him with two very detailed lists for his scrutiny.

"Splendid!"

"Have you heard anything further from the hospital, Doc?"

"Adam's just called to check that the children are OK. He was pleased that you were sorting that out for him but he was somewhat choked to learn how poorly Laura is."

"Are you able to say what it is?"

"The Doctors have indicated Laura has suffered a stroke and Adam has given permission to share that news so that idle speculation doesn't get passed around and people know what to pray for."

That evening, the house group, due to be held at the Catton's house, was switched to the home of Ben and Rachel Durrant. By the mysterious village grapevine the news, concerning Laura, had been telegraphed throughout the district, so that all present were aware of the meticulous contingency plans prepared by Miranda for the care of Daniel, Kirsten and Poppy as well as temporary nursing cover for Laura's position as practice nurse.

Uppermost in everyone's mind was the apparent severity of Laura's illness which had taken everyone by surprise. In hushed tones they spoke of the impact it would have on her immediate family and the implications for the wider community because of her nursing skills and involvement at the church.

"I'll miss her gentle gaiety."

"Yes, she always has a ready smile for everyone," agreed Jilly Briggs.

"Behind that quiet reserve she's a real joker and so full of life."

"And amazingly she has bags of energy despite running around three little ones all day," said Rachel.

"I don't know how she copes. It takes me all my time to look after one," said Alex with admiration.

"I know the feeling," grinned Sue Piper, ruefully.

"However will the Doc manage without her at the surgery?"

"More importantly, how will the children manage without her?" asked Rachel. "She has such exciting and original ideas to keep the children's imagination occupied. I know Mark and Rhoda love it when they're invited to play round there."

"Adam, too, will be lost without her. She's always been such a support to him," said Graeme.

"You're right there, Graeme," agreed Ben. "They're like chalk and cheese, but complement one another admirably, don't you think? Laura's calmness is the perfect foil for Adam's flamboyant impetuosity."

Around the room many heads nodded and others murmured in agreement with his words.

"I know it's going to be hard to focus our thoughts on our usual study," Ben continued quietly, "so I've chosen a Bible passage suitable for Laura and Adam's situation. Let's look at it together and then we'll spend time praying for our friends and their family.

"Rev Hugh has also asked that I mention the 24/7 prayer vigil he has set up. He envisages a continuous circle of prayer on behalf of Laura. If you want to be involved please contact him."

"What about visiting?"

"My understanding is that for the time being Laura is not allowed visitors, other than Adam, but we're putting in place a daily support system for Adam. He's going to need it. Rev Hugh will endeavour to go for an hour every day and would like others to commit to spending time with Adam, sitting, listening, praying, whatever Adam needs for about half an hour and certainly no more than an hour. It may be at home or at the hospital. There's a sheet on the church notice board and Penny Darnell will compile the roster."

"Is anyone with him at the moment?" Justin asked.

"I believe Rev Hugh has been with Adam since Laura was admitted."

"He must be exhausted. I'll go and relieve him for a spell."

Even as Justin spoke Hugh was preparing to sit all night by Adam's side so that he wouldn't be spending a solitary vigil at the hospital. The other side of the closed door a team of Doctors worked methodically in partnership to save Laura's life. In the Newton villages, clusters of friends prayed for her healing and restoration.

CHAPTER SEVEN

On Wednesday morning RK stepped unhurriedly down the spiral staircase taking great care not to trip over the hem of the long crinkle cotton skirt she had chosen to wear. Blue sky, coupled with brilliant spring sunshine, beckoned through the windows of the old mill in a most inviting way. As she meandered along the passageway towards the dining room, having decided to sample Tessa's vegetarian full English breakfast, RK anticipated the day's adventure with relish.

Earlier in the week she had read the timetable posted on the bus-stop outside the Village Stores. It indicated that once a week the 'Hopper' ran to the city picking up passengers in the villages along the way. RK decided to travel on part of the journey and explore the area around Newton Lokesby and Newton Bridge further inland along the river.

Stillness seemed to pervade the air giving the impression that either, RK was very early arriving for breakfast or, she was late and everyone else had eaten and already departed. Neither was the case as she discovered on entering the dining room. The weekend visitors had gone home but the remaining couple were seated at their usual table, as were the Jenner children, albeit in a rather subdued manner.

All eyes were on RK as she entered the dining room.

"Hey, you really are a girl!" exclaimed Keir.

"Keir!" admonished Rosie, "Don't be so impertinent."

"But she is," he persisted.

"That may well be so but it's rude to comment on it."

"I think you look very pretty," offered Pansy diffidently.

"Why, thankyou, that's very kind of you, Pansy," said RK as she took her place between the little girl and Lily then proceeded to help herself to fruit juice.

"Am I interrupting something? You all seem rather quiet this morning."

"We're just a bit sad," explained Lily.

"Why's that?" RK asked between sips of juice.

"Daniel and Kirsty's mum is in hospital to die."

"Oh?" RK raised her eyebrows questioningly.

"She fell down in the play-park."

"How did that happen?"

"I don't know."

"Well, I met them all on the quay yesterday morning as they were on their way to the playground and Laura seemed OK, then."

"You tell her, Rosie," Lily appealed to her older sister.

So Rosie explained what she knew about Laura's collapse and the Catton family's dilemma following this tragic event.

"I'm really sorry this has happened to your friends," RK told Lily, kindly. "Who will look after them now their mum is so poorly?"

"We heard that Miranda and Jackie Cooper have made arrangements for this week so that their Dad can spend time at the hospital," said Rosie, again acting as spokesman, "but I don't know how they will manage when school starts next week."

"Miss Cooper's my teacher," confided Pansy.

"That's nice, ducky," RK said quietly, thinking to herself that this news might put a different complexion on her plans for the day.

The Catton's predicament was also the main topic of discussion over the lunch time meal at Doctor John Cooper's house later that same day when the seriousness of Laura's condition became more widely known.

"It's quite obvious that for the time being Laura is going to be unable to fulfil her role as practice nurse," said Doctor John with considerable regret.

"What do you propose to do?" asked Trixie.

"She is an excellent practice nurse and it's going to be difficult to replace her but Miranda and I have been considering a number of options this morning."

Detecting mischief in her husband's voice Trixie smiled, "Oh, have you, and what are they?"

"Well, the most appealing is that we offer the position to you, Jansy," the Doctor said with a big beam on his face, as he turned towards his daughter.

"Dad!" said Jansy with an exasperated sigh, and turned the post down flat with an emphatic "No, no, no!"

However, Dave, who was lunching with the Cooper's, was delighted with the proposition and begged her to reconsider.

"Jansy, dear girl, we would be able to live in the village, near to family, which would greatly ease my mind about you when I am at sea. There wouldn't be any need for you to travel. It sounds ideal."

Jansy shook her head. She was devastated at this turn of events having set her sights on the Sister's position at the children's hospital in the city.

"Have they offered you the Sister's post?" her mother asked fully aware of her daughter's long-standing dreams.

"Not yet, but the position of Senior Staff Nurse would be a natural progression."

"I see," said Trixie dubiously.

Whilst already torn between her own ambitions and pleasing Dave, her father's dilemma added a further dimension to the equation. Jansy crossly clattered her cutlery onto her plate, folded her arms, and expelled an audible sigh. All eyes around the table focussed on her but Jansy was unrelenting.

"I don't want to leave my job," she pouted. "I've worked hard to get where I am today. I'm not giving up now I've almost reached my goal."

Silence pierced the air. Dave placed his elbows on the table and held his head in his hands. Trixie looked with consternation across to John.

"No one is suggesting that you give up your job, Jansy, just that you consider diversifying for a time."

Jansy shook her head vigorously as her mother was speaking. "Nothing will deter me from pursuing the career I mapped out for myself when I was still in school."

"If you haven't yet been offered the post you desire at the hospital can you make clear why you are so adamant about turning down the position Dad is offering to you?" Trixie asked her quietly.

"Because I then won't have cause to regret giving up the opportunities offered to me now in later life."

"Please explain, Jansy," said John patiently.

"What on earth is there to explain?" Jansy retorted with bad grace.

"It's unbecoming to be so rude, Jansy," her father admonished with restraint. "We would like to be able to understand the thinking behind your decision."

"I'm sorry, Dad," Jansy acknowledged grudgingly. "I've been thinking of Emma's circumstances and I really don't want to end up in the same situation."

"Jansy, you are talking in riddles. What on earth has Emma to do with you becoming practice nurse pro tem? You're going to have to explain more explicitly than that."

Jansy gave another over exaggerated sigh before expanding on the reason for her decision.

"I believe Emma will ultimately come to regret her decision to give up her career, in order to run the Village Stores, following the tragic deaths of her parents. I don't want to find myself in the same predicament because I make the wrong decision now," she concluded forcefully.

Dave raised his head and looked at Jansy through eyes loaded with sadness.

"Helping out the Practice would be a wrong decision?" Dave murmured sorrowfully.

Jansy deliberately turned her head away from him and ignored his question.

"When did you last speak with Emma about this issue?" her father quietly enquired.

"Not for some time now. We met up on the Norwich bus quite by chance a few weeks ago. I noticed how tired she looked and thought all the work must be proving too much for her."

"I suggest you make time to go and see her. I think you will find Emma has a very positive approach to her responsibilities and what she believes to be her goal in life."

"I find that very hard to believe considering her outburst at Christmas," said Jansy, disbelievingly.

"I can't speak for Emma, but again, I urge you to speak with her," her father gently advised.

"I'll see," she replied in a non-committal manner. "But I'm not going to change my mind about the job. I've always wanted to be Sister-in-charge on the paediatric ward. For years I've worked towards that goal. Now I am so close to realising those plans I don't want to jeopardise my position."

At the conclusion of the meal John assisted Trixie in the clearing away of the dishes leaving the young couple to continue their discussion in the sitting room.

"Much as we'd like to solve their problems for them this is one thing they've got to sort out for themselves," said John gently holding Trixie's arm and guiding her towards the kitchen.

"Even when they seem to be making bad decisions?"

John nodded before he replied, "Hopefully they'll come through this experience stronger people. All we can do at the moment is pray for them. They've got to learn to trust and believe our Lord has their best interests at heart."

"Where did our bubbly girl go?"

"I think, my dear, for a time, she's allowed self to be the centre of her life. When she gets back her perspective, things will run on an even keel, but I think it may take some time and prayer."

"You don't think it's wedding nerves, then?"

"No, I think it goes much deeper than that."

"We used to be so close but at present she won't talk to me about anything of a personal nature."

"I rather suspect that's part of the problem. We know her too well. She doesn't want to get too close to us at present because she's fully aware of what we would advise her to do. She doesn't want that. Jansy wants her own way. We impede that."

"Ideally then, she needs to speak with someone not so emotionally involved?"

"Yes, I think Emma would be perfect but, it seems, they haven't seen much of one another of late. Both too busy, I guess."

In the sitting room the conversation between Jansy and Dave was not going too well.

"What possible future is there in fishing?" asked Jansy sullenly.

"The fishing industry is changing," explained Dave guardedly.

"Floundering more like," retorted Jansy scathingly.

"No, these days it requires a different approach," he calmly replied.

"Why don't you leave the sea and take a land job, then?" Jansy demanded curtly.

"Jansy!"

"You could possibly work in the city, like me. We could also live there. That would solve our problems." Jansy crossed her arms defiantly across her chest and glared moodily at Dave.

"Jans, you've been wheedling me to this position for a number of weeks, hoping your pending promotion would sway me in your favour," Dave shook his head sadly. "I really don't want to work in the city. I can't be cooped up in enclosed spaces. The sea is my life. Don't you know me, Jansy?" he pleaded.

"It just isn't fair," Jansy whimpered sulkily, "I had such great plans and now they're about to be ruined."

"No, they're not," protested Dave.

Jansy's eyes narrowed as she looked at him in disbelief.

Dave attempted to lighten her mood by jovially suggesting, "We could always be like the nomads and live in a tent and move from place to place as our shifts dictate."

Jansy wasn't amused. "Don't you dare to joke about this!"

"Well, it is a possibility."

"You don't care, if you really cared you wouldn't talk like that," Jansy began to raise her voice hysterically.

Dave said quietly, "Jansy, calm down." He reached out to take hold of Jansy's hand but she abruptly pulled away and continued barraging him.

"Most of all, I'm angry with you for not understanding how important this is to me and I thought you knew me so well!"

Dave sat back in his chair and put his hands behind his head. "Jansy, I understand you well enough to know there isn't any reasoning with you when you're like this. You're being childish and deliberately misjudging me."

Jansy jumped up and yelled, "I can't stand this and if you continue to swing on the back of the chair legs you'll have my mother to answer to!" She flung at him irritably.

Dave rose slowly and stood in front of Jansy. "I care a great deal about what's important to you, Jans."

Jansy dismissed his words with a flick of the wrist, responded with more irrational, cutting remarks and hurled angry accusations at him. It seemed impossible for Dave to diffuse the situation and reach a compromise that was acceptable to Jansy. He sat down as calmly as he could while she continued to harangue him.

"You're a stubborn old mule and I refuse to discuss it with you any further!" Jansy sat down again, folded her arms and, with a toss of her head, dismissed it out of hand. As a consequence, her attitude eventually led to further moments of intense disagreement. "I won't, I won't, I won't be coerced into changing my mind," she declared dogmatically, thumping a balled fist into the palm of her hand.

Once again, Dave gently reminded her that, although he wanted to settle in the village, he willingly considered properties in the city because her happiness was important to him,

She rose angrily. "You're arrogant, selfish and stubborn, Dave Ransome," Jansy finally flung at him petulantly.

"Shouting won't solve anything," he called to her retreating figure as she flounced out of the room and slammed the door hard.

Dave slumped down in the chair; his head drooped in exasperation, mingled with sorrow, "Dear God, whatever happened to our Love?"

Jansy strode angrily across The Green with no particular purpose in mind. She fully expected Dave

would come after her, anxious to make up, and ultimately give in to her wishes. When he didn't appear she sulked and stomped aimlessly.

Not looking where she was going Jansy bumped into Penny Darnell, as she approached the vicarage gate, and almost knocked the vicar's wife over. Penny instinctively sensed by the dispirited look on Jansy's face that all was not well. When she had regained her balance Penny slipped her arm through the younger woman's and steered her through the gateway and said cheerfully, "Hi, there, Jansy, I'm just about to put the kettle on. Would you like to come in for a cup of tea?"

Before she had chance to refuse Jansy found herself in the homely vicarage kitchen as though it was a quite normal occurrence for her to be there. Penny turned on the kettle, set out the mugs and chatted about inconsequential everyday things. In a haze Jansy pulled out a chair and sat down by the kitchen table.

Jansy wouldn't look directly at Penny which gave the older woman opportunity to study her after she had poured out the tea. Something was very obviously wrong. Penny didn't know what. In fact, she couldn't even guess what was troubling Jansy but clearly she was tense. The effervescent aura that was the hallmark of Jansy's lively personality was distinctly lacking.

Penny was a no-nonsense person. As vicar's wife she had learned through the years to deal with all sorts of people and all manner of problems. At all times she was kind and caring yet always direct in her dealings with a person and saw no reason to change now.

"Out with it, Jansy," she demanded.

Jansy looked up and frowned at her.

"Out with what?"

"Well, that's just it, I don't know. But something is wrong. I can tell."

"No, I'm fine." Jansy lowered her eyes and fiddled with the handle of her mug.

"So, you're so fine it's normal for you to stomp across The Green and barge into someone as though they were not there, is it?"

At that remark Jansy did look up. Penny's kind, but honest face was before her. It didn't take long to admit, at least initially to herself, that something was wrong. Horribly wrong!

"You'll never believe me if I tell you," she at last managed to blurt out.

Penny smiled encouragingly, "Just try me."

Those few words were all that were needed to open the floodgates. In the next few minutes Jansy poured out her heart to Penny. Everything tumbled out; her vexation with Dave, her irritation that he wouldn't agree to work in the city, the stress created by the indecision over which property to make their home, her annoyance with Laura's fall coming at this time, her anger at her father's suggestion that she become practice nurse, her feelings of betrayal by the injustice of God in the Kemp accident at Christmas, the frustration that was building up inside her because she was being pressured to make choices that conflicted with achieving her life goals. All the muddled thoughts about events in the recent past, and how they complicated her decisions about issues in the present, gushed from her in a steady stream.

As Jansy spoke Penny sat still and listened. When there was a break in the torrent of words Penny enquired quietly, "Have you prayed about the situation?"

Jansy hung her head and mumbled, "No."

"Why?" she asked, surprised that Jansy hadn't already done so. When there was no response Penny let the silence hang in the air for a time.

"You've always been one of the first to pray in the past."

"I can't pray," Jansy responded.

"Why do you think that is?"

"I feel out of touch with God," Jansy reluctantly admitted.

"For any particular reason?"

"I suppose I was influenced by Emma's situation at Christmas."

"Why was that?"

"Well, the death of her parents was distressing and I was troubled by the way it affected Em and her faith. I thought maybe she had a point. Where was God in a tragedy like that? My faith took a bad knock. Who can you trust," said Jansy scathingly, "if God let's you down like that?"

Penny pointed out the positive way Emma was coping with the tragedy but Jansy had seen very little of her friend in recent weeks and even then there had been little opportunity for in-depth conversation so was unaware of any change in Emma's attitude.

"I can only remember that awful day and visualize her initial reaction to the news of the accident."

"Believe me, Jansy, Emma has moved on since those early days of trauma. You really ought to chat to her about it."

"That's what Dad said."

"Then why not do it and set your mind and heart at rest concerning your friend's well being rather than speculating on what you think she's feeling and making that the basis of your own feelings."

"But…"

"Be honest with yourself, Jansy. Aren't you using Emma's experience to mask your own shortcomings and faithlessness?"

"I don't think so." Penny sensed a trace of uncertainty in Jansy's reply.

"Come on, Jansy, this is all about you, your work situation and your relationship with Dave and the place you give the Lord in your life, not about Emma." Penny paused for a moment to let Jansy think about what she was saying.

"Are you sure you're in love with Dave and not with the idea of being in love?" Penny asked Jansy, gently. Jansy looked at her blankly.

"Of course I love him!"

"It's always been assumed by everyone that you and Dave would marry one day. Have you drifted into this decision because of these assumptions? Has your relationship become a comfort zone because it's familiar?"

"Of course not, Dave's just being unreasonable."

"Oh Jansy, it's all very well having goals for the future but the here and now is also important; your here and now."

"Oh, I agree, that's why I want to do what I want to do before it's too late."

"Then why are you so unhappy about that decision?"

"I'm not."

"Jansy, your whole demeanour indicates you are."

Chapter Eight

Disappointed she was unable to get her own way with Dave Jansy became intent on pursuing her nursing career to the exclusion of all else. Her anger fuelled the conviction that, because Dave had not rushed immediately after her when she stormed out of her parent's house, he no longer truly cared for her. She determined to obliterate him from her life. Jansy couldn't face the distraught look on her mother's face or the reproachful eyes her father cast upon her; nor cope with the soulful pleading in the texts, notes, telephone calls and messages Dave constantly sent to her. She convinced herself they were just a sop to make her feel guilty and acquiesce to what she considered to be his selfish demands to live in the village and accept the position of Practice Nurse offered by her father.

So, after her discussion with Penny Darnell, Jansy decided it might be best for her to cut short her leave and return to the nurse's home near the hospital in Norwich, thus distancing herself from the tension that was building; tension she couldn't handle; tension she blamed on Dave and her father. She stubbornly refused to countenance that the friction between them was any of her doing.

The following morning the postman brought a missive to the Cooper home containing the formal offer of promotion she craved. As soon as she had read it Jansy whooped with delight and punched the air. She held in her hand confirmation that she was moving up the ladder; the post of Senior Staff Nurse on the paediatric ward was hers. Surely, here was proof that she was right to pursue her own goals.

Straight away she penned her acceptance. Her feet barely touched the ground as she ran across The Green and down the lane to post it back to the hospital board believing this position would put her one step nearer to achieving her goal of becoming Sister of the ward. She made hasty preparations to rearrange her plans and depart from her parent's home as soon as possible.

When gentle, loving Dave heard of the curtailed visit he became withdrawn. The hurt caused by Jansy's refusal to talk things over with him and her resolve to return to live in the city in order to continue nursing at the hospital settled like a lump of lead around his heart. He saw it as a rejection of himself and a sign that Jansy did not want to resolve the rift between them.

Over the next few days Dave persistently called her mobile phone but Jansy wouldn't answer. He phoned the Cooper's house, "I'm sorry, Dave, but Jansy won't come to the phone," said Trixie apologetically.

One morning, when he couldn't bear the stone wall of rejection any longer, he walked up the lane and crossed The Village Green to knock on the Cooper's door. Doctor John threw open the door and put his arm around Dave's shoulders, "She's gone. I'm so sorry, my boy. Come on in." But Dave unable to speak shook his head, and with tears in his eyes, and a pain so piercing it was difficult to breathe, retraced his steps. *Dear Lord, why is she behaving like this? Whatever is going on in her heart and mind?* That really bothered him but he was completely in the dark. *For years we've always shared our plans and dreams. Isn't that part of loving?*

In the days that followed Dave continued to be deeply affected by the falling out with Jansy. His heart was heavy and he felt sick to the pit of his stomach. He wanted to be with his dearest girl, to hold her hand, to look into her lovely blue eyes, to assure her of his love but knew that the wall she had erected between them was at present insurmountable. The oneness that had been a characteristic of their dealings with one another had evaporated so rapidly Dave doubted that it had been genuinely meaningful on her part. Jansy's ambition to be a ward sister seemed to have completely taken over her life to the exclusion of all else including a future with him. Dave struggled to make sense of it all.

In this deeply troubled state of mind he called into the office of his brother-in-law. Ben listened as Dave, hesitatingly, requested a moment of his time to talk. "It's about Jansy," he said awkwardly.

Ben noted the strained expression in his friend's eyes. His normally bronzed, rugged face also displayed an unhealthy pallor that was etched with pained tautness. Dave's usual upright stance evidenced an uncharacteristic slump of his broad shoulders.

Straightaway, realising the importance of Dave's need to share with someone, Ben quickly made him a strong, sweet cup of tea and said, "Look, Dave sit here, have this drink, give me five minutes and I'll be with you." Dave collapsed heavily into the chair that Ben indicated. Ben found it most disquieting that Dave appeared to have aged ten years overnight and his entire behaviour spoke of dejection.

In the past the two men had shared many deep meaningful discussions together. They were comfortable with one another and each held the other in high regard. Both were keen walkers and so when Ben had wrapped up his business he suggested to Dave, "Let's go out on the heritage coastal path, we'll have privacy and a chance to chat without interruption."

Ben was a natural listener but Dave was not a natural talker particularly about something as personal as his relationship with Jansy. For some time they walked in companionable silence but gradually Ben encouraged Dave to speak of the hurt that was causing him such heartache.

Squawking seagulls hovered above them, numerous rabbits scampered along the hedgerow beside them and relentless waves pounded at the foot of the cliffs beneath them but Dave saw none of these. His voice thick with emotion he haltingly spoke of his sadness and despair at the gulf that had unexpectedly come between him and Jansy.

"What did I do wrong, Ben?" he implored of his brother-in-law. "It all happened so suddenly. I keep asking myself, why? We knew each other so well. We'd been going out together for such a long time. Did I take her for granted? Didn't I make it clear how much I loved her?"

"Don't blame yourself so, Dave," said Ben quietly. "The workings of a woman's mind are vastly different to ours. Once we realise that, it still takes a lifetime to understand it. It's quite a challenge, I know from experience, but well worth the effort." Ben paused for a moment.

"But, we'd always planned things together. We spoke at all times about everything before making a decision," explained Dave defensively.

"From what you've told me, I think Jansy had a different agenda to yours for the immediate future."

"What do you mean?" Dave asked, puzzled.

"Your marriage has always been something to plan and prepare for in the future. Suddenly it's imminent." Dave nodded. "Career wise, Jansy's aim since childhood has been to become Sister-in-charge on the paediatric ward. All at once that objective is in view."

"I know that and I've always supported Jansy in her ambition but I don't see why there should be this conflict."

"Marriage and a Sister's post are no longer aspirations for the future, they are here now and they've arrived together. I guess Jansy feels she is being pulled in two opposing directions."

"But why sacrifice one for the sake of the other?"

"Only Jansy can answer that," commented Ben wisely.

"I'm sure we could have resolved the issue of where to live if only she had been willing to discuss it rationally."

"There has to be compromise on both sides."

"I realise that," Dave shook his head and uttered with a deep sigh, "I'd live in a tent in the hospital grounds if that would make her happy. I do miss her so."

"What do you miss?"

"Her smile, her laughter, her company, the joy she generated, her presence, the sharing and praying together." Dave stood still, as though he was looking out to sea, but the manner with which he spoke the words suggested he was reaching out in desperation to grasp something precious that he had lost.

Ben gently touched his arm, "Would you like us to pray together, now?" With pleading in his eyes Dave nodded.

Ben caringly committed Jansy and Dave and their situation to the Lord. He prayed for guidance and a willingness to accept God's will for their lives, whatever that might be.

As a result of their conversation a renewal of faith and deep trust in God about the future with Jansy came about for Dave. Ben also reminded him of a verse that had been discussed recently in Bible study that spoke of the presence of God completely surrounding a person.

"Oh yes, I remember," Dave recalled, "from the Old Testament, wasn't it?"

"Yes, Psalm 139 verse 5, 'You hem me in, behind and before.' "

"That's a reassuring thought."

"It certainly is. God's presence is constant and all-embracing."

Dave nodded in agreement. "You know, Ben, I still believe it is the will of God that Jansy is the wife for me."

"Are you prepared to let her go till she finds this out for herself?"

"Mmm. I'll do whatever it takes."

"That same psalm goes on to speak about the Lord knowing all things."

"I find that a great encouragement so I'm going to leave all this in His hands."

"It's not going to be easy," replied Ben.

"Yes, I'm very conscious of that, Ben, but I feel Jans needs a bit of space to sort out her own commitment about the future."

"So, what will you do in the meantime?"

"I'll need to chat it through with Dad but I'm thinking I might sail south for a spell."

"Oh?"

"Well, if I'm not around I won't be causing unnecessary pressure for Jansy, will I?"

"I suppose not. Have you spoken with Rev Hugh?"

"Yes, and he graciously agreed to postpone the wedding date, indefinitely."

Thus, after talking to his brother-in-law, Dave decided to go for a time to Brixham, in Devon, to fish. He was concerned for his father, because the sea was also his livelihood and he was more used to fishing the North Sea waters, so after explaining his position Dave asked him, "What will you do, Dad? Will you come with me?"

"No, m'bor, Oi'll be glad to 'ave some time ashore. Give yourn Mother a break from the fish stall, too, 'specially now she be doin' more hours in the Stores. Oi'm sure you'll find one or two of the lads down the quay will readily mate for you."

That same evening the worship group and music team met as usual in the Church for the weekly rehearsal. In Adam's absence Justin Durrant took charge of proceedings. He had earlier in the day visited Adam at the hospital so, when everyone had assembled, he shared the up to date news concerning Laura, in answer to the many questions put to him on arrival.

"I'm afraid the report about Laura is not very good," Justin began. "The surgeons operated again today, to stem leaking blood in Laura's brain, but they are unable, at this stage, to say how successful it has been."

"Do they know what's wrong with Laura?"

"The Doctors gave Adam to understand they believe Laura has suffered a haemorrhagic stroke, which I understand is a bleed in the brain. She was unconscious when she was admitted but they are unsure if this is as a result of the stroke or whether she banged her head when she collapsed. She hasn't been able to communicate and the children were too frightened to notice whether the swing caught her on the head or if Laura hit her head on the ground as she fell. But, she's in the care of a skilled team and we have a great God so, let's pray for her, Adam and the children, believing for a miracle."

The friends drew closer together and bowed their heads in prayer, as one by one, a number prayed aloud, earnestly pleading for Laura's healing. Unspoken prayers, too, ascended from aching hearts on behalf of Laura and Adam.

For a short time following the prayers the group spoke with affectionate concern about their friends.

"How is Adam bearing up?" Emma asked.

"He's obviously very distressed but also incredibly calm," Justin explained.

"What about the children?" enquired Annette Andaman.

"Adam doesn't want Daniel and Kirsten to see Laura at the moment. He feels it would distress them to see her in an unconscious state and the many tubes to which she is attached might frighten them. I did bring him home while she was still in recovery so that he could spend time with the children and explain as clearly as possible what was happening to their Mum. Poppy is obviously too young to comprehend what's occurred but I think Daniel and Kirsten have a fair understanding of the situation, that their Mum is rather poorly."

"Will Adam continue staying at the hospital?" asked Emma.

"As you can imagine he is very torn and doesn't want to be apart from the children for longer than is necessary, but on the other hand, he can't bear to leave Laura, at least, while the situation is so critical."

"That's understandable," Emma affirmed.

"How will we know where to link up with Adam?" asked Stephen Cooper.

"Rev Hugh's rota is going well but there are still one or two times not covered so if you are able to fill the gap give Penny a ring. She, too, will keep you abreast of Adam's whereabouts."

"I hear the programme of care for the children, Miranda and Jackie have put in place, is working out quite well," commented Annette.

"Yes," replied Justin, "Adam was quite overwhelmed at the way so many have pulled together to ensure he can be with Laura, yet at the same time, the children be well taken care of."

"But then, that's what we've come to expect from those two," said Alex with warm appreciation.

"What will happen next week, though, when Jackie has to return to school? Miranda can't be expected to hold the fort on her own because she too has responsibilities at the surgery," Annette observed.

"True," agreed Justin "but I have some surprising but positive news. The motorbike chap whom we simply know as RK is in fact a girl..." There were gasps of surprise from some quarters, "No...o!"

"Anyway," Justin continued when the hubbub died down, "it appears that our motorbike friend is well qualified in childcare and has impeccable references. RK is currently between jobs so has offered her services to Adam, as Nanny to his children, for as long as she is required. Adam, as you can imagine, is mightily relieved and has accepted the offer, subject to references." As Justin concluded this revelation there was further astonishment.

"I thought RK worked in the nurseries on her father's flower farm," Emma remarked.

"So did Adam and I. We both jumped to the wrong conclusion about her nursery involvement and the subject of work never cropped up again in our conversation," confirmed Justin.

After the music practise the young people engaged in more general talk particularly about the Spring Bank Holiday car treasure hunt that Adam and Laura usually organized for as many of the village and surrounding district who wanted to participate.

"I suggest we make alternative plans for the treasure hunt," said Justin.

"So many people are already planning to take part we can't possibly cancel it," said Graeme.

"But who on earth is likely to be available to organize such an event at short notice?" asked Annette.

"Miranda, whom we all recognise as the best organizer around, is already tied up with the wellbeing of the Catton children so we can't really ask her to take on something else," explained Ben.

"What about approaching Miss Pedwardine," Alex suggested tentatively.

"Alex! You've got to be joking!" A number, at first, greeted her suggestion with disbelief.

"On second thoughts I think it could be a possible answer to our problem," agreed Justin.

"Most of the young folk are tied up with work, college or families, but Jennifer Pedwardine, as recently retired headmistress, is freer in the daytime than anyone in the village," explained Alex.

"She may even be glad to participate in a village activity that has nothing to do with school," remarked Emma.

"As proposer I nominate Alex to go and ask Miss Pedwardine," said Stephen cheekily.

"Thanks very much for your vote of confidence," retorted Alex with a laugh as she playfully punched Stephen on the shoulder.

"Friends," intervened Justin, "before we share the Grace together and make our way home Ben would like a word."

"Thanks, Justin. It concerns Dave and Jansy. I'm not breaking a confidence when I tell you they have spoken with Rev Hugh and Mrs Darnell and decided to postpone their wedding."

"Oh no," Emma gasped and burst into tears.

Her reaction quite jolted Ben. "Dear Em, I'm so sorry," he said quietly. "I thought you knew."

Emma shook her head and glanced over at Stephen, Jansy's younger brother.

He nodded his head. "It's true, Emma."

Regretting the bombshell he had just dropped on his cousin, Ben said, "I understood they had already spoken with all those closely involved. I would not have hurt you like this for the world, Em."

"It's OK, Ben," sniffed Emma, "though it is rather a shock." She took a moment to blow her nose and regain her composure before adding, "On reflection, I'm not surprised."

"Oh? What makes you say that?"

"When we met up a few weeks ago Jansy was somewhat vague and offhand when I asked about the wedding plans but very focussed on her forthcoming job promotion."

"You've hit the nail on the head. However, they both need our support and prayers. For a time they will be separated by the miles, Jansy in Norwich and Dave in Brixham but, thankfully distance is not an issue with our Heavenly Father."

CHAPTER NINE

It was with some trepidation that Alex rang the front door bell at Jennifer Pedwardine's home on Saturday morning.

I do wish the very thought of seeing her didn't still make me feel like a naughty little schoolgirl waiting outside the headmistress's room, Alex thought as she waited for a reply. She stood for what seemed quite an age, with one hand on Bethany's buggy ready to make a quick retreat, only too aware how sharp-tongued Miss Pedwardine could be. *I should have insisted Emma or Justin do this they would have been more assertive.* How her knees quaked!

Then, Alex recalled the words of her father last Christmas Eve morning when he stated that, "Before long we shall see a change in Jenny Ped now she's relinquished her position of authority."

Now Alex, she sternly reprimanded, *think positively, maybe retirement has mellowed her as Dad predicted it would.* Tentatively Alex reached out to press the bell for the second time.

She can refuse my request or she can say yes but she can't bite my head off. Alex stepped back from the door, lifted her head, stood tall and waited.

It was an intriguing house, painted white, with a squarish bay window to the right of the solid wooden front door, two quaint inverted v-shaped windows upstairs under the thatched eaves and one similar on the left of the front door. They all had tiny panes of glass in them, divided into diamonds by leaded lights.

Alex's eyes followed the line of the building, to the left of the small window, which had once been the bakery and shop. She remembered the tantalising aroma that teased her taste buds as she had skipped along the adjacent footpath every morning on her way to primary school; the tiered shelves behind the window full of loaves of all shapes and sizes and she knew that inside, displayed in a cabinet, were all manner of delicious cakes. Mum always bought fresh bread each day and very occasionally allowed her to choose something out of the cabinet. While Alex enjoyed the heel of the loaf spread lavishly with butter and Mum's homemade jam her tongue relished the exploration of the scrumptious, colourful, gooey delights kept behind the glass protection.

The hedge now obscured that window and sadly all that remained were her memories and the name 'Bakers' for at some point since its closure the old bakery had been cleverly incorporated into the cottage creating a spacious home. Further observation and daydreams were curtailed when the back gate, adjacent to the side of the house, was opened and a voice boomed out, "Yes, can I help you?"

Alex hastily turned round.

"Good morning, Miss Pedwardine, I've come on beha..." she began, and then stopped. Before her was a dishevelled lady who in no way resembled the prim and proper retired headmistress Alex knew.

"Oh, it's you Alex. No Post Office this morning?"

Hastily recovering from her surprise Alex replied, "Yes, Melvin Andaman is covering for me." Miss Pedwardine's brusqueness belied her appearance but it confirmed for Alex that this truly was the lady she had come to see.

"Well, don't just stand there, girl, come in." Jennifer Pedwardine opened the gate wide and, brandishing a pair of lopping shears in hands encased in gauntlet type gardening gloves, waved Alex through.

"It must be time for coffee." Clad in a holey jumper and baggy trousers, her normally immaculately styled hair was sticking out untidily from under a flat cap. Muddy smudges streaked her cheeks and forehead but, despite her appearance and abrupt manner, the warm smile of welcome cheered Alex's heart.

As Alex pushed the buggy through the gateway the vista before her took her breath away. She could hardly believe what she was seeing. For a moment she simply stood and gazed at the many pergolas and trellis fencing, festooned with early clematis and the promise of an abundance of roses later in the summer, stretching as far as the eye could see.

"This is so lovely and unexpected," exclaimed Alex overcome with admiration.

"Thankyou, Alex," was the clipped response. "Feel free to wander or sit and enjoy," invited Miss Pedwardine, indicating a rustic bench. "I'll switch on the kettle."

Alex pressed the brake on the buggy into place, left the sleeping Bethany by the open back door, and followed one of the crazy-paved pathways to explore the hidden treasures of this hitherto unseen enchanting garden. Neatly clipped evergreen hedges seemed to frame numerous individual garden rooms. Some were waist high whilst others only reached up to her knees and one was just beyond her eye line.

The first one Alex peered into contained perennial shrubs edged with a hint of colourful spring bedding. Another area had budding rose trees surrounded by, what promised to be, fragrant lavender. The next one the winding path led to, revealed a lush, oval shaped lawn, with an embryonic rose entwined arbour to one side, behind a pristine cut privet hedge. Beyond delightful early clematis laden trellis Alex spied a greenhouse which was bulging with growing plants. There also appeared to be blossoming fruit trees in the distance, whilst new seasons growth on a plethora of oak, copper beech, horse chestnut and sycamore on the perimeter of the garden gave the impression that the whole garden was embraced by a wooded frame of trees.

Before Alex had opportunity for further exploration she heard a bell and the call of "coffee", so she turned round and ambled back towards the house. She thought she had retraced her steps but when she saw to her right a superb rockery flanking a potentially delightful lily pond she knew she had taken a wrong turning. Thankfully, she heard the bell again enabling her to regain her sense of direction.

"Lose your way?"

Alex nodded.

"Coffee is in the summer house. You can hear the baby from there."

Alex didn't think she could take any more surprises but Miss Pedwardine led her to a beautifully designed

Victorian summer house furnished with elegant wrought iron garden furniture. The table was graced with a silver tray set with Crown Derby china and buttered scones.

"Sit here, best view of the garden," commanded Jennifer Pedwardine as she plumped up a floral chair cushion.

"Thankyou, Miss Pedwardine."

"And the name's Jennifer, not headmistress anymore," that lady instructed as she poured coffee from a stylish silver coffee-pot.

"Like the garden?"

Alex nodded as she sipped her coffee. "It is amazing!"

"A bonus, then?"

"Yes."

"Why did you call?"

Gosh, thought Alex, *she might not be headmistress any longer but she is still direct and to the point.*

Alex decided it might be wisest to answer in a similar vein.

"I came on behalf of the young marrieds' house group, to invite you to organize the May Bank Holiday Monday car treasure hunt," her voice was clear and distinct but her heart was pounding rapidly against her ribs.

"Problem, no car," was the immediate response. "Gave it up when I retired. Use public transport."

Alex looked at her hostess in dismay. This was an obstacle she had not bargained for.

"Why me?" Miss Pedwardine demanded.

Alex started to explain the situation regarding Laura and Adam which precluded their involvement this year when Miss Pedwardine interrupted, "Yes, yes, I'm well aware of the Catton's situation. So, why me?" Patiently,

Alex pointed out the unavailability of the young and married residents to make the necessary preparations during the daytime because of study, family or work commitments and mentioned Emma's comment that Miss Pedwardine might welcome the opportunity to participate in a village activity unrelated to the school.

"I see, mustn't let the old girl vegetate, give her something to get her teeth into!"

Alex diplomatically ignored Miss Pedwardine's light-hearted sarcasm and said, "I've brought a copy of last year's schedule and clues to give you an idea of the usual procedure," as she handed over the file.

"Meticulous, as ever, I see," Jennifer complimented and again treated Alex to one of her warm smiles.

"Give me a few days to digest this and then I'll give you my answer. Is there room for flexibility?"

"I'm sure there is. Everyone will gladly accept what you are able to offer, grateful the event can go ahead. You know where to contact me if you want to discuss it further. Here is my home phone number or leave a message with Emma at the Stores."

Dawn broke on Monday morning to reveal blue skies, a gentle sea breeze, a rising sun and the prospect of a warm day. Jennifer rose early. She had spent an interesting time going through the treasure hunt schedule the previous day after a solitary lunch following the morning service and relished the challenge the project proffered. Ideas continued to jostle in her mind throughout the night. The new day brought with it a desire to share those thoughts so it was with impatient enthusiasm that she waited for the opportune moment to contact Alex.

Emma also rose with the dawn and went downstairs to the Stores early. She checked the thermometers of the fridges and freezers, tweaked a few things into place in the window displays, and then ensured the shelves and baskets containing the popular early morning snacks and fruit were replenished. She could hear sounds coming from the Stores' kitchen so guessed Jilly was already preparing fresh rolls, sandwiches and pastries.

It was the first day of a new school term and Emma knew from experience that it would be a hectic morning. Like her father before her she wanted to ensure that the shop was spick and span and ready for the rush of early morning customers who would soon be arriving in droves. They were always in a hurry to make their choices before getting on the bus that would take them into the city for the activities of their day. While she was making sure there were sufficient bottles and cans in the drinks cabinet the back door opened.

"Good morning," called out Rosalie, her assistant.

"Hello, Rosalie, are you ready for the onslaught?"

Rosalie laughed as she put away her outdoor clothes and slipped on her overall. "As ready as I'll ever be for a first day back. It's hard to think we're at the start of the summer term."

"I can't believe people are so unprepared."

"Good for business, though, as your Dad would say. Did you remember the pens and pencils? We sell more of those in the first week of any school term than we do for the rest of the year."

"Yes, I've tried to make sure we are as geared up as he was to meet people's needs."

"You've done exceptionally well, Emma, balancing study and the shop. Your Mum and Dad would have been proud of you. I hear your exam results came through this week, congratulations."

"Thanks. It's in no small part due to your willingness to work extra hours to leave me free to carry on at college."

"Nonsense, you're more than welcome. When's your graduation?"

"May 26th then afterwards, all being well, I'll be more available to fulfil my responsibilities at the Stores."

"Will Roger be able to attend?"

Emma rapidly shook her head to swing her hair forwards in order to cover up her blushing cheeks forgetting that she'd tied it back as she always did when on duty in the shop.

She put a hand up to the side of her face and blurted out, "Hopefully, if he can re-organize his time off duty."

Rosalie smiled knowingly then, to spare Emma further embarrassment, changed the subject, "Have you heard anymore about your application for the teaching post?"

"Not yet but it's..." The door from the Stores' kitchen swung open and Jilly came through with a heavily laden tray.

"Hi, Em, I've got the pasties, sausage rolls, filled rolls and sandwiches here. Where would you like them?"

The women quickly arranged the fresh food in baskets on to the shelves nearest to the counter knowing that those coming in to buy them would be in a hurry to catch the buses to school, college and the city.

"These look good, Jilly, mouth-wateringly appetizing, as Nicky would say."

"Our aim is to please," Jilly laughed as she made her way back to the kitchen. "By the way, Emma," she called back over her shoulder, "those new food labels are a vast improvement. They're neat, colourful and contain all the necessary information and they actually stick onto the poly bags!"

"Yes, they do look good. Nicky and his mates designed them as a college project."

"My compliments to them for a fine job. I hope they got good marks!"

Emma and Rosalie nodded in agreement.

As they worked Rosalie asked quietly, "Have you seen Jansy, Emma?"

Emma shook her head, her hands busy.

"We haven't been in touch lately. I saw her briefly during the Easter weekend but I've been tied up with the shop and college and I assumed Jansy's spare time was taken up with wedding preparations."

"You can't throw any light on the situation, then?"

"No, I'm afraid not. Doctor John spoke to me after Church yesterday and explained that for a time Jansy and Dave have gone their separate ways."

"So I'd heard."

"Jansy's apparently staying in Norwich. That's all I know. I don't know what's gone wrong. They were so in love with one another. Has Christina said anything about Dave?"

"Only that Dave has decided to go fishing elsewhere and his Dad is staying ashore for a spell. He's so upset."

"I'm so very sad that this has happened."

Someone knocked impatiently on the large plate glass window. Simultaneously Emma and Rosalie looked up. Stephen and Nathan gave them a wave.

"First customers are here already!" Emma unlocked the shop door.

"Good morning, lads, you're nice and early."

"Morning Emma, Mrs Andaman," greeted Stephen cheerfully. "We wanted to get first pick of the pasties for lunch."

Emma pointed to the newly stocked basket on the counter. "There they are, all straight from the oven this morning."

"Brill! Jilly makes the best veggie pasties around. The ones at college taste like sawdust," grimaced Stephen.

"Perhaps they are," joked Nathan. "Maybe the cleaner sweeps up the shavings from your workshop at the end of the day and passes them on to the cook."

"Ugh! That sounds gross, Nat," said his sister Rosie nudging him to one side.

"I'd be careful what I say if I were you, ole boy, or Rosie might introduce similar fillings when she's on duty in the kitchen here," teased Nicky with a quick grin to Rosalie, his mum.

"No chance! Jilly's set very high standards and I intend to help her keep them, so there," declared Rosie emphatically.

"That's right, Rosie, you stick to your guns. Don't let these whipper-snappers intimidate you," laughed Annette Andaman, Nicky's twin.

"I hope you've left some pasties for Annette and me, Stephen." His cousin, Hilary Cooper, pushed her way to the front of the counter. She, along with Annette, preferred the veggie products made by Jilly in the Stores' kitchen. The trio had embarked on a school project together in year eight which resulted in them experimenting with their palettes and as a consequence deciding to become vegetarians. Hilary quickly made her choice as more young folk jostled to get to the head of the queue. His height enabled Stephen to reach out first to be served.

"I hear congratulations are in order, Stephen," Emma said as she wrapped his purchases.

"Yup, thanks Emma, now I've got the level 3 diploma in carpentry and joinery under my belt I can concentrate on my English finals."

"There'll be no stopping him now, Emma," chuckled Nathan. "You know, have drill will hammer."

She looked at them both and smiled. "I may well need your services soon, Stephen."

"Oh?"

"Hey, Steve, is it true about your sister?" a voice yelled out across the crowd. Stephen turned and quietly replied, "I'm afraid it is."

Their day had begun!

Throughout the day gossip was rife in the village. In fact, many customers came into the Village Stores chiefly to speculate on the break-up of Dave and Jansy.

"Can't believe it," said Mrs Saunders.

"Do you think he's found someone else?" asked Annelie Durrant who'd popped into the shop to buy milk for the office morning tea.

"'Course not," was the emphatic reply.

"Then why's he gone so far away?" Annelie persisted.

"For work, o' course, good fishin' in the southwest, so Oi've 'eard."

"Well, they were very close Easter Sunday morning. Something drastic must have happened since then," Annelie commented.

"Oi 'eard they couldn't agree where to live," put in Mrs Peek, the verger's wife.

"That's a trivial reason to split up," said Annelie contemptuously.

"Speaken' o' Easter Sunday, that wretched motorbike chap still be abaht. Roaren' down the lane half-past six this mornen', 'e be. Shouldn't be allowed. Tom Catchpole ought t'dew somethen' abaht that noise," grumbled Mr Bracewell.

Some of the customers nearest to him murmured in agreement, but Annelie remarked, "Oh I'm sure it's not that bad."

"How dew yew know? Yew live the other side o' the village," he retorted angrily.

"Now, now..." Rosalie soothed before tempers became too frayed.

"He's not a chap, RK's a girl..." called out Rachel Durrant as she pushed Rhoda's buggy down the aisle towards the chatting shoppers having just taken Mark into school.

"No!" the group around her gasped in surprise, "...and is looking after the Catton children," she concluded.

"Surely not!" This news left them speechless. Once the import of what Rachel had said penetrated they all spoke at once.

"But the bike..."

"Those leathers..."

"Too tall for a girl..."

"...and what about the deep husky voice."

"I just don't believe it!"

"You must be joking, Rachel," Annelie said as she approached her sister-in-law.

Rachel shook her head. "I assure you it's perfectly true."

Clustered as they were at the bottom of the aisle the customers failed to see Jennifer Pedwardine slip into the shop hoping to discreetly catch Rosalie's attention.

It was Monday morning and Emma was busy in the office. It was the time she allocated to contacting suppliers, placing weekly orders and preparing invoices and bills. She was anxious to have them ready for Alex so that she could attend to the monthly accounts when she closed the Post Office at lunch time. Rosalie was standing by the till having just served Mrs Jenner.

Miss Pedwardine moved towards the counter.

"Good morning, Rosalie. Is Alex in today?"

"Yes, she's serving behind the Post Office counter."

Miss Pedwardine marched down the aisle passed the cluster of gossipers to go through the arch that led into the Post Office.

At that moment Michelle Cook took opportunity to sidle up to Rachel and quietly ask, "Any news about Laura?"

"Not much change, I understand."

"Thass a tragedy, poor Adam."

"It certainly is. How are you managing?" Rachel asked kindly, well aware that Michelle's husband, Joe, had recently been sentenced to another term in prison for a number of offences including the attack on Rev Hugh's wife on Christmas Eve. Her eldest son, Josh, was also in a Young Offender's Institute for his part in the same burglaries and attacks on a number of persons in the village, so life was not very easy for Michelle at the moment. The pending trial of possible perpetrators of the crash which had taken the lives of Val and Mick Kemp at Christmas was also hanging over her head as most villagers had already accused, tried and convicted her husband and son for the accident.

"O'roite," Michelle replied in a whisper.

"Seen the poster about the treasure hunt?" inquired Rachel, changing the topic.

"Goen' ahead, then?" asked Michelle.

"Seems so."

"Well, Adam and Laura won't be doen' it, will they?"

"Hardly."

"I say, have you heard, Jenny Ped's doing the treasure hunt?" called out Annelie mischievously as that lady passed by them.

"Really?"

"That's different."

"I'll say!"

"Not at work, today, Annelie?" Miss Pedwardine asked, choosing to ignore the young woman's facetious remark, knowing full well that Annelie had no real notion of her possible involvement in the arrangements for the treasure hunt.

"Of course, Miss Pedwardine," replied Annelie sheepishly, "I'm just collecting milk for the coffee break."

"Don't waste time, then, time means money."

"Yes, Miss. Have a nice day," she replied cheerily as she made her way to the till. Miss Pedwardine winced at the Americanism.

Michelle turned back to Rachel, "Are yew a-goen'?"

"I expect so, usually good fun, especially for the kids, what about you?" Rachel asked.

Michelle slowly shook her head and said ruefully, "no car."

Rachel could have kicked herself for her thoughtlessness. "Oh, Michelle, I'm so sorry."

But Jennifer smiled to herself convinced her proposals would more than meet the criteria.

CHAPTER TEN

Unaware of much of the activity taking place in Newton Westerby, Dave continued to stay down in Brixham, sailing in the fishing grounds of the southwest. Spells at sea gave him ample opportunity for reflection and at times his mood was tempered by the inner anguish of his heart. He missed home and felt out on a limb in the unfamiliar place so busied himself with work.

He heard not a word from Jansy. The texts, notes and phone calls he sent to her remained unacknowledged. His heart was heavy when he remembered the unresolved issues between them. *How had the question of where to live escalated into such a big problem? I would willingly live in a tent or caravan just to be with her. I miss her, her smile, her warmth, her friendship, her cheerful spirit, her very presence.*

Nevertheless, Dave retained contact with home through his brother-in-law, Ben. "I'm not much of a letter writer but I will text you," he promised, and they spoke at length when Ben phoned him every Friday evening when he was on shore.

"Have you been able to visit a Church fellowship in Brixham?" Ben enquired after Dave had been working there for a few weeks.

"Well, shortly after arriving here I linked up with The Fishermen's Mission."

"Oh, that's good. How do they treat you?"

"Quite well, actually. I go to their canteen for most of my meals when I'm ashore, as well as, for company," Dave explained. "They seem friendly enough although I think the girls find me sulky because I'm quieter than the other chaps."

"I shouldn't let that worry you," said Ben.

"No, I don't," replied Dave thoughtfully. "One morning when I went up to the Mission's canteen for breakfast Heather and Kelly invited me to the Sunday evening cafe Church, which I understand is held in the upstairs meeting room."

"Will you go?"

"I just might."

"How are you getting on with the resident fishermen?"

"Not great, because they can't understand my accent so look on me as an interloper and as such resent my presence in the harbour. Consequently, I keep to myself which causes the locals to consider me sullen and moody so they in turn keep their distance. The other fishermen are jovial, friendly though somewhat raucous, and accept me as I am. Ironically, some of them have more pronounced accents than mine."

"Perhaps when they get to know you they'll realise it's your nature to be quiet and reserved."

"Maybe, but I'm happy with the way things are at present, they don't question my mood or background and it's a relief not to be pestered for any explanations."

In fact, if the truth were known, most of his fellow fishermen had discovered that Dave was good at his job even though he went about it in a silent manner, and weren't too bothered about his personal history, accent or disposition.

At the outset, Dave had looked in Newton Westerby for a deckhand to accompany him to the southwest. Young Brett Saunders had said he would 'give it a go' but after the trip down and a couple of spells fishing out at sea he was so homesick that he elected to return to the east coast. Thus, Dave was forced to rely upon the availability of casual deckhands from the local workforce which, on the whole, worked reasonably well. Dave was a good skipper; fastidious but fair.

In his free time ashore Dave tended to stroll on his own around the intriguing Brixham harbour, with its red rocky outcrops, so vastly different to the sandy shore of Newton Westerby. He deliberately ignored the steep flights of steps built into the cliff face, such a contrast to the sloping scores back home, but he enjoyed casting a practised eye over the pristine yachts in the marina quite distinct from the leisure craft that frequented the river that flowed through the Newton villages. Walking along the breakwater, looking beyond the lighthouse towards Torquay, the wide sweep of Torbay also fascinated him.

On one such occasion he had the distinct feeling that as he left his boat he was being followed. Dave didn't pay much attention at first because he was quite absorbed by the scene and activity around the harbour but after a while it became apparent that when he stopped to look at the yachts or watch the cormorants spanning their wings on the jetty the shadowing footsteps also stopped. When he recommenced his walk so too did the footsteps behind him.

By the time he reached the breakwater Dave found the tail a little unnerving so he deliberately came to an abrupt standstill, crouched down on the pretext of adjusting his boot lace turning as he did so to confront his followers. His movement caught them unawares and they almost fell over him. He noticed there were three of them. Their attire placed them as fishermen, two were unfamiliar but the third he recognised as the deckhand from 'Seagull,' Mark Bemment's boat, which normally sailed out of Newton Westerby.

"Why, hello Billy, I didn't expect to see you down here."

"Hi, Dave," Billy Knights responded dourly.

"Is the 'Seagull' fishing off the southwest as well?"

"Nah, Mark's still in the North Sea. Oi juss fancied a change."

"I see, well have a good trip." Dave nodded to Billy's silent companions then continued on his walk, thinking he must have been mistaken in believing he was being followed.

Another time while stretching his legs along the waterfront Dave met the superintendant from the Mission who extended his hand with a warm invitation to attend a service. "Hi, I'm Jack Pridmore. We'd be pleased to see you any time you're on shore."

Dave accepted the firm grasp and introduced himself, "David Ransome."

However, some weeks passed before he was able to respond to the invitation. After a number of trips out at sea Dave was eventually in harbour on a Sunday and decided to attend the cafe Church at the Mission. It was low tide but the stone steps leading from his mooring onto the quayside were still wet and slippery. He negotiated them with care holding onto a rope thread between rusted rings attached to the harbour wall with his free hand. He had just reached the top of the landing stage when his arms were seized and yanked behind his back sending the Bible he was carrying into the air, landing with a thud on the concrete pier. His two assailants dragged Dave along the unforgiving surface, through a door they kicked open, into the deserted fish market.

Before his eyes had chance to adjust to the gloom of the empty fish warehouse Dave felt sharp blows on his face and chest, as well as, repeated kicks in his stomach. "Ouch!" he cried out but sticky tape of some sort was inexpertly fastened across his mouth to keep him quiet as the brutal assault continued. His knees buckled but he was grasped roughly by the throat to keep him upright, a face thrust into his and a voice hissed menacingly, "Shut yourn face, if yew know what be good fer yew. If yourn arsked, yew niver saw me."

A siren sounded in the distance, his attackers dropped him abruptly, kicked him aside and without a word left the desolate wharf.

Dave, breathing heavily to cope with the painful aftermath of his attack, waited a few moments till the footfalls died away, then gingerly peeled the tape from his mouth and slowly raised his hurting body from the ground. Movement was tentative. He cautiously stroked his aching jaw and held his throbbing head. *What on earth was that all about?* He was completely bewildered by the actions of Billy Knights and his companions. Dave had never really had any dealings with Billy but simply knew him as a lad from Newton Common who worked as a deckhand on various boats out of Newton

Westerby. *His actions tonight suggest his presence in Brixham is not entirely above board and he's obviously very anxious that I don't tell anyone I've seen him here.*

Dave slowly brushed himself down, smoothed his hair as best he could and walked painfully out of the warehouse. With great care he bent down to gather up his torn and battered Bible which the thugs had deliberately trampled on. It took him a considerable while to get upright again, a stabbing pain across his chest slowing his actions. Sweating profusely he stood for a moment to catch his breath cogitating what to do. Should he return to the boat or carry on up to the Mission? He felt uncharacteristically vulnerable and longed for the safety of home. *I think company will be preferable to being on my own in the boat at the moment.* The deckhands he employed lived ashore in between fishing trips which generally suited Dave but following the attack he would have welcomed the presence of someone on board. So, having made his decision, Dave limped slowly in the direction of the Mission building.

When Jack greeted him, as Dave hobbled uncertainly through the Mission meeting room door, the Superintendant was surprised to see Dave sporting a bruised, swollen face and a tattered Bible under his arm but wisely refrained from commenting on it. *You're going to need attention, son.*

"It's good to see you, David, welcome." Gingerly Dave returned his handshake but winced as his hand was grasped. Dave glanced about him. Thankfully there were quite a few faces that he recognised from the Mission canteen, some waved in acknowledgement while others smiled, so he didn't feel as intimidated as he had anticipated. He moved awkwardly towards the nearest chair and grimaced as he tried to sit down. Realising it was an action he was finding difficult to perform Dave stood for a moment pondering his next move. Prompted by Jack, Heather approached Dave quietly with a glass of water and a couple of paracetamol. "You might find these helpful," she whispered. Dave gratefully accepted her offering as well as assistance to sit down on an adjacent vacant chair that sported arm rests.

When the service commenced Dave was glad that the hymns, too, were ones that were familiar to him. By the time the Missioner came to open the Word, Dave felt more at home in the unfamiliar surroundings though sitting was getting increasingly more and more uncomfortable. He shuffled to relieve the pressure on his emerging bruises.

"We've reached verse 24 in our study of Jude, 'To Him who is able.' " Jack Pridmore opened his Bible and carefully read through the whole chapter again to refresh the memory of his listeners. Dave tried to follow the words closely in his own Bible but the swelling around his eyes was getting bigger and made focussing on the print difficult. Instead, he adjusted his position on the chair, cautiously leaned back, closed his eyes and concentrated on the words spoken by the Mission Superintendant.

"We've learned that Jude's letter challenges us to grow in faith, pray in the spirit and remain surrounded by God's love...." Dave's thoughts began to wander. His faith had certainly been challenged during the past few weeks and he doubted that it had been growing. He acknowledged that he had allowed the rift with Jansy to affect his prayer time and relationship with the

Lord and just lately he hadn't always been aware of the all-encompassing love of God. *Please forgive me, Father God.*

"...let doubts and uncertainties cause confusion but, and this is the crux of the matter, to Him who is able there is trust, confidence and certainty." The voice of the missioner brought him back to the present.

Dave forced open his swollen eyes and carefully sat more upright in his seat. A wonderful sense of peace washed over him. *I don't have to worry! I don't need to worry about Jansy, about the future, about fishing or about where to live. I'm not expected to solve my problems alone. Thankyou, Heavenly Father, for the assurance that I can have confidence in you for the future. Where I cannot see, I'll trust that you are able to.* 'To Him who is able.' Dave nudged the chap next to him and indicated that he would like him to underscore the verse in his Bible.

Frequently, over the next few days as his vision improved Dave referred back to it. 'To Him who is able.'

His injuries made fishing impossible so he had plenty of time for thinking and reading and praying. His body ached and was very stiff from the battering it had taken which meant he couldn't venture very far from his boat. Jack Pridmore called in daily to check up on him and on his first visit was accompanied by a local GP who gave Dave a thorough examination to assess there were no internal injuries, other than a couple of broken ribs, and gave him a prescription for medication to cope with the pain and external abrasions as Dave declined a trip to the A&E department of Torbay hospital.

Dave remained sore for some days and movement was quite restricted so a cooked meal was sent down from the canteen once a day till such time as he was able to make his own way up to the Mission for meals.

Perturbed by the unprovoked attack by Billy Knights and his companions Dave rang his brother-in-law, Ben, to explain the situation. "I can't understand Billy's aggression. He very obviously doesn't want it known that he is in Brixham. I can only guess at the reason. I don't want to make false accusations but his behaviour does seem very suspicious."

"I'll have a word with Wills and Dan Prettyman about your concerns. I do know the local force is carefully monitoring movement in and out of the Newton Westerby fish dock in connection with the drug smuggling and people trafficking clampdown. Maybe their counterparts in Brixham are involved in a similar campaign. Leave it with me and do take care."

"Thanks, Ben, I appreciate your support."

Even though he was away from Newton Westerby Dave's heart was back home in the village. He longed to return and prayed for the day when that would be possible. Believing it would happen someday he had instructed Adam Catton's firm of solicitors to act on his behalf in the purchase of the pretty cottage he and Jansy had been viewing when RK had stumbled across them. Dave thought it was so right for them and, although their wedding was not taking place in the near future, he was unshaken in his belief that it would occur, ultimately. Moreover, he saw the property not only as a sound financial investment for the future but also as the place he and Jansy would one day want to make a home.

"Please let Lord Edmund know who wants to purchase it. I don't want him pushing the price up by bidding against me," Dave instructed the solicitor, well aware of Lord Edmund's practise of buying properties in order to keep them available for local people. "Would you also inform Trixie Cooper that the property will be available to let for this holiday season only?"

In the meantime, Jansy remained in Norwich, apparently totally immersed in her work. She rarely made contact with her family. It seemed as though she had deliberately cut-off all links with home, family and friends. She also chose not to have any involvement with a Church fellowship and as a consequence neglected her personal prayer and Bible study in her endeavour to prove her self-sufficiency. It was surprisingly easy to get out of the habit of Church. *I'll show them I can manage without God and men!* Her constant busyness gave the impression that she was doing everything possible to eradicate Dave Ransome from her life. She refused to answer his calls and threw his notes, which her mother faithfully forwarded on to her, unopened into the bin. She was still very angry with him for not coming after her following their disagreement over where to live when they were married and agreeing with her wishes not to become involved in her father's practice. Nursing at the hospital became her life and she thrust herself into it wholeheartedly.

Her absorption with her work and relationship with the medical team, with whom she was most closely associated, was total and almost merged as one. The desire to achieve her goal drove her relentlessly from day to day. She developed an aptitude for putting on an act so that it was impossible for any of her colleagues to gauge her real thoughts and feelings. Daily she exhibited an excellent show for staff and patients. The children responded to the sparkling personality and ready smile she presented. None more so than Riley.

"Hi Staffy," he greeted her each morning as his chest laboured and he gasped for breath.

"Good morning, yourself," Jansy said as she tended to his needs, "How's my best boy, today?"

"Champion," he replied with a toothy grin, a phrase he had picked up from his grandfather. "I could play for Man U today, if they pick me," he wheezed.

"Right, we'd best get you sorted in case the call comes."

One of the reasons the children loved her was her sense of fun and the light banter she engaged in with them as she attended to the more serious aspect of their illnesses. Doctor Jeremy Stead admired her calmness and skill when dealing with her young charges. He'd observed that Staff Nurse Jansy was thorough and firm, her manner crisp and precise yet so alive it brought a flicker of light, albeit briefly, into the wan faces of his sick patients. Her innovative tactics were tremendously effective. She persuaded them to take their medicines by instigating award stars.

Also, her careful planning and cajoling motivated the patients to do things for themselves and partake in activities designed to stimulate them, where previously lethargy had instilled static acceptance of their condition. She had the ability to generate reassurance in child and parent with consummate skill. Her very presence on the ward seemed to energize all with whom she dealt. Jeremy Stead's roving eye appreciated Jansy's natural dainty demeanour as well as her efficiency as Senior Staff Nurse except when she was roused to fight on behalf of her patients or incensed by injustice. Then sparks would fly and all within her path would be recipients of a tongue lashing.

Doctor Stead had kept a close eye on Jansy ever since she came to work on the ward and now that she had been appointed Senior Staff Nurse he believed she would serve his purpose well.

One morning, once the ward handover report was concluded, Doctor Stead kept a careful eye on Jansy's progress around the ward as she dealt with the children on her list. He waited till she was cannulating a sick child to send a junior nurse to request keys to the drug cupboard ostensibly to administer necessary medicine to a patient he was attending. As she was not in a position to attend to the matter herself Jansy reluctantly relinquished the keys. It was not until the lunch time drugs round that Jansy realised the keys had not been returned.

Along with his effusive apology Doctor Stead invited Jansy out for a drink and her willingness to acquiesce to his invitation was coloured by her intent to win his favour. His view might sway the decision regarding her promotion to ward sister. His nearness excited Jansy in a way that perturbed her so to cover up her emotions she presented a veneer of energy and a sense of fun. In order for her true feelings not to surface she immersed herself in busyness. Thoughts of Dave were firmly suppressed.

So much so, that she and Doctor Jeremy Stead became inseparable, both on and off the ward. Jansy naively believed that the liaison would further her career.

However, it was with some trepidation that she prepared for her first evening out with Jeremy Stead. A vision of Dave flashed briefly through her mind. Jansy shook her head and pursed her lips together. *I'll enjoy my evening with Jeremy. Yes, it will be different, but I'm going to have a good time.* She peered in the mirror and practised a smile. *Dave is honourable. Can you trust Doctor Stead?* She quickly smothered that thought before it surfaced any further.

When the door bell rang she went readily to meet her escort.

Later, at their venue for the evening, when pressed for which drink she preferred, Jansy requested an orange and lemonade. Stead insisted she have something stronger but Jansy remained firm, "No, I'm on earlies tomorrow and I need a clear head."

Reluctantly, Stead gave in to her wishes but when she woke in the night and was violently sick Jansy knew she had not imagined the odd taste to the drinks she had been given.

Doctor Stead had carelessly flung an arm around her shoulders after he had placed the drinks on the table, and then moved closer to her in an intimate fashion. Jansy inched away. Working to keep the conversation light she tried to draw Jeremy out by asking about hobbies and his family. However, he would not be drawn but persisted in inane chatter quite unlike the competent Doctor on the ward. *Maybe this is the way he unwinds.* But the more he drank the more he joked and fooled around. Although she nervously laughed at his ludicrous witticisms Jansy grew increasingly uneasy at his inappropriate behaviour towards her.

Half-way through the evening they were joined by Doctor Steve Hollis and a staff-nurse from the orthopaedic ward with whom Jansy was only slightly acquainted.

As the evening progressed, the two doctors and Hollis's companion became more and more inebriated. Jansy grew perturbed at the lateness of the hour and was anxious to leave and return to the nurses' home. Work, particularly the quality with which she performed it, was important to her and a good night's rest prior to her shift was essential if she was to give her best to her young charges. She desperately wanted Stead to have a high opinion of her but his constant poring of her and slurred entreaties to quit harping on about going home left her torn between staying and leaving.

Finally, when it became apparent Stead was no longer aware of her presence Jansy slipped out, hailed a taxi and returned home.

The following day Stead was fulsome in his apology to Jansy for his loutish behaviour and promised better manners if she would agree to go out with him again.

Jansy looked directly at him and briskly shook her head.

"Please, Jansy," he pleaded.

When challenged concerning an addition to her drink he reluctantly admitted he had added something to her orange and lemonade though refrained from enlightening her as to what.

Fired up Jansy tore into him, "Don't you ever do that to me again, Doctor! Don't you realise how dangerous that can be especially to someone unused to alcohol?"

"You mean...?"

"Yes, never touch the stuff. I told you – I want a clear head to enable me to work at my best."

Although Jansy eventually accompanied him again she restricted their time together to evening meals in restaurants or visits to country parks and stately homes on their days off duty. The demeaning episode was never repeated and their acquaintance became friendship, of a sort, though Jansy was guarded in her response to the more intimate closeness he frequently tried to initiate. She was anxious to keep their relationship controlled whereas he felt it was imperative to liven it up. When Jansy was animated Stead found her company scintillating but she could only present such a facade when she felt in control. Above all else she was anxious he see her as the right candidate for the top post when it became vacant later in the year.

CHAPTER ELEVEN

Back home in Newton Westerby, Jansy's mother, heartbroken by her daughter's cavalier attitude towards them, and Dave in particular, plunged herself into work. Trixie Cooper was a chiropodist. She normally ran two clinics at the surgery each week and visited the less able who lived in the sheltered housing complex in The Close for treatment at home once a month. To Doctor John's dismay she took on more clients and also busied herself with extra duties in the village.

One morning after breakfast he lovingly put an arm around her shoulders as her busy hands put instruments into the sterilizer and gently said, "Trixie dear, I hardly ever see you these days, please slow down."

Trixie glanced at him with raised eyebrows and pursed lips.

"Don't work so hard, my dear, you'll wear yourself out."

Reaching out automatically to switch on the machine Trixie looked up at him imploringly. "I need to stay busy it keeps my mind off Jansy and Dave's situation."

"Oh, my dear," John shook his head, sadly, "have you forgotten about taking your burden to the Lord and leaving it there?"

"No, of course not, but I feel if I keep occupied I don't give myself opportunity to dwell on their state of affairs."

"Just stop for a minute, Trixie, I want to share something with you."

Trixie shook her head disconsolately.

"Please," John pleaded gently, took hold of her arm and tenderly guided her to sit down, picked up his Bible, then proceeded to reveal what was on his heart. "I was reading Psalm 94 early this morning and the words came as a sharp reminder that when we are held secure in the love of God we are supported and strengthened in every circumstance. Not some, but all! The psalmist said of the Lord, 'When anxiety was great within me Your consolation brought joy to my soul.' "

Tears welled up in Trixie's eyes as she replied, with a quiver in her voice. "You're right, John dear, I'm not trusting as I ought. Please read that verse to me again."

"'When anxiety was great within me, Your consolation brought joy to my soul.' Those words have been a source of strength to me over this issue with our daughter. I pray that you will find them equally as helpful."

"Thankyou, John, I will try to," Trixie answered in a subdued tone. John was always such a tower of strength she hadn't given thought to how the split between Jansy and Dave had affected him. His revelation brought her up with a jolt. *How selfish I am, please forgive me, Father God, I've been anxious about so many things. Teach me to trust You for every situation and to be a more perceptive wife.*

Trixie looked up into the kindly face that was viewing hers with such concern.

"There are some things I have promised to do, so I must fulfil them, but I give you my word, John, that I will ease up from my futile busyness." John brushed a hand though his hair raised his eyebrows and then with his head tilted to one side smiled lovingly at his wife of thirty years. Trixie took a deep breath. *How well you know me, dear John.*

"Truly, I will."

"My dear, you say that now but so many of your projects involve the wellbeing of other people that I think you'll find it hard to let go."

"I can't let people down, can I?"

John slowly shook his head as he pondered the many lives his wife's caring manner touched each day.

"Maybe you could just slow down a little," he gently suggested, "or delegate? You're really not expected to solve everyone's problems single handed."

"Mmm…" Trixie responded vaguely as her mind floated over activities of recent weeks when she had increased her involvement with the Ladies Guild and WI and in view of Laura's recent illness she had readily offered to help the family with anything that was needful. She had also raised a number of vibrant issues with the Parish Council which they in turn nominated her to carry through.

One of the subjects to gain her interest was the matter concerning empty or derelict property in the Newton Westerby area being grabbed by outsiders as second or holiday homes. They stood unoccupied for three-quarters of the year while young people from the village were unable to get on the property ladder, or find a house to rent, so that they could stay in their home locality.

Lord Edmund de Vessey had broached this matter most vociferously at a Parish Council meeting some five years earlier. As a consequence he bought up properties when they became available to prevent what he termed 'second home snaffling.' He then arranged for them to be renovated and made available to villagers at a fair rent. Any currently unoccupied were then offered as holiday lets.

Trixie had been appointed by the village housing committee to manage the lets on their behalf in conjunction with Graeme Castleton, who as accountant administered the financial side of things, and Christina Ransome who assisted with practical matters, such as cleaning and furnishings. The money raised by this venture was ploughed back into maintaining the properties to a high standard.

Driven by her anguish for Jansy and Dave, Trixie had pitched in with the scrubbing and cleaning of the cottages with extra vigour in readiness for the forthcoming holiday season, even though it wasn't her responsibility. It was as if the harder she scrubbed the more the deep hurt would go away.

John broke the silence, "There is such an irony to our conversation, my dear."

"What do you mean?" Trixie rubbed a hand vigorously across her brow as though to banish the thoughts dancing in her mind.

"Well, it was my intention to chat with you about the overgrown eyesore opposite brother Billy's shop that was broached briefly at the last PC meeting but the ideas I have would probably add to your workload not reduce it," John smiled wryly.

Trixie returned his smile and leaned forward expectantly. "Now that does sound intriguing."

John glanced at his wrist watch as he rose from his chair. "I really do have to get on. I have a full list today. Perhaps we could discuss this matter over dinner one evening soon. I'll book a table at the Station Hotel." He leaned over and kissed Trixie goodbye. "Please take it easy today and don't worry unduly about the young folks. I believe in time, all will be well."

"Yes, dear John, I'm sure you're right," she murmured as the Doctor departed for the surgery.

Yes, Lord, all will be well. But, dinner out? That is so un-John like!

Nevertheless, following her chat with John, Trixie was able to approach her tasks in a more optimistic manner. So much so that Christina picked up on the change in her as they cleaned windows and rehung curtains together in one of the holiday cottages, later that morning.

"You're cheerful today, have you had some good news?" she asked.

"In a way, I've realised again how valuable prayer is. So often it changes things," Trixie explained.

Christina inwardly sighed. *Oh no, not more of the religious squit!*

"Oh, I thought you'd had positive news about Dave and Jansy. Much good prayer's done them!" she mumbled cynically.

Trixie smiled and replied cheerfully, "It will, I fervently believe it will."

"Humph!" Christina snorted, disheartened by their children's break-up and her son's departure to the southwest. *I very much doubt it!*

"You heard the grumbling in the village?" Christina briskly changed the subject not wanting to be drawn into Christian talk.

"What about?" asked Trixie as she fitted curtain hooks into the slots of the rufflette tape.

"Some of the villagers are still up in arms about the motorbike noise so early in the morning. Prayer hasn't worked a miracle for them, either," she said sarcastically.

"Oh, you mean when RK travels to get the Catton children up?"

"Yes, they're saying if RK can't live in then she must live nearer."

"That's easier said than done," commented Trixie, handing a curtain complete with hooks up to Christina who was standing on the steps.

"Yes, I know, but those most affected by it are fed up with the noise and want something done about it."

"It's a bit of a hike from the Jenner's in Marsh Newton to the Catton's in Newton Westerby."

For a time, the two women worked in companionable silence, each concentrating on the task in hand yet mulling over the very real problem caused by RK lodging at Jenner's Mill.

After a little while Trixie said, "One possible solution comes to mind."

"Oh?"

"We could offer RK Ferry Cottage. It's not ideal but it is within walking distance of the Catton's house."

"But Trixie..." Christina grimaced and looked at her aghast.

Trixie nodded her head. "I know, at the moment it's in an appalling condition but it might fit the bill, pro tem, and get the grumblers off RK's back."

Christina shook her head, "I wouldn't want it. Too much work needs to be done merely to make it habitable."

However, when she heard about Ferry Cottage RK accepted the offer gratefully, without even viewing it.

"It's one that is not used regularly because it's earmarked for renovations so is in need of a thoroughly good clean," explained Trixie. "We'll come and give you a hand in the morning."

For the time being, thoughts of easing up seemed to have escaped Trixie's mind. She handed RK the key. "Maybe, you'd like to take a look when you've finished at the Catton's this evening. If you change your mind I won't be the least bit offended."

RK was quite unperturbed by this less than rosy report on a possible new home and on her return to the Mill that evening eagerly relayed to the Jenner's news of the offer of a cottage.

"I understand it hasn't been used for some time so will need a good clean. I plan to go and have a look this evening to see what is required."

"If you like we'll come and give a hand," suggested Tessa.

"Thanks. I'll meet you there," RK answered.

As soon as she had eaten her evening meal RK changed and then set out on the offending machine to view the property and see what was going to be necessary to spruce up the cottage.

The Jenner's were sorry to learn she would be leaving them. The children particularly enjoyed RK's company and zany sense of humour but understood the reason for the move. So, at the conclusion of supper they scurried around to complete their normal evening chores, then under Tessa's direction, the family piled into the people carrier armed with all manner of cleaning utensils and prepared to help RK make her new quarters habitable.

"This is gross," protested Gil as he stumbled down the shallow stone step on the threshold of the front door, through cobwebs, into the grimy living room of Ferry Cottage.

"You can't live here, RK," declared Lily, "It's awful!"

"It stinks!" shouted Keir pulling a face.

"You're right it is pretty disgusting, so let's get to work. Together we'll make it a pleasant place for RK to live in," decided Tessa who then proceeded to detail everyone a specific task. "Chop, chop, off you go now and do the very best you can."

"Mum," Gil shouted down the stairs a few minutes later, "we can't find the bathroom."

Tessa looked at RK and raised her eyebrows.

RK nodded in the direction of the back door, "Outside, on the left."

Rosie went out to investigate and returned in haste. "Oh, Mum, it's dire, absolutely revolting. RK really can't be expected to use that."

"Stuart, please investigate," said Tessa decisively.

The speed with which her husband returned confirmed Tessa's worst fears, "Housing referral?"

"Yes, ASAP! I'll call Lord Edmund, now."

By bedtime, the cottage windows sparkled, walls and floors scrubbed clean, dust and cobwebs eradicated, tatty curtains taken down, the suite hoovered and sponged, dining chairs and table polished, the bed stripped and the mattress left to air, and the wheels were in motion for an emergency meeting of the village housing committee.

"Come on everyone, time for home," Tessa called and her weary troupe of workers tumbled thankfully into the vehicle, glad to be finished.

"Thankyou all for your hard work," said RK with heartfelt appreciation. "I'll see you presently at the Mill and then come back tomorrow to finish off the cleaning and check to see what additional equipment I might need."

"Don't you go buying anything," Tessa firmly insisted. "Just make a list of your requirements. Let me or Trixie Cooper have it and I'm sure by the end of the week you will have everything that is necessary, from one source or another," she instructed.

RK waved them off, dusted down her hands then rubbed them together with glee as she strolled from room to room surveying what was now her own domain. After a while she stepped outside, locked the front door and with a smile on her lips turned to view her new home with a keen sense of satisfaction before returning to the B&B for what would probably be the last time.

On Saturday morning Stephen Cooper was working on a commissioned coffee table in a confined space in the Cooper's garage when the front door intercom buzzed. His parents were out so he knew it was up to him to attend to the caller. He turned off the sander, removed his goggles, pressed the button and spoke through the grill. "Hi, how can I help you, today?"

"Good morning, is that you, Stephen? Hugh Darnell here. I was hoping you could help me tomorrow with…"

Stephen guffawed, "Oh, Vic, you've got the wrong guy. Preaching sermons is not my thing. Hang on a mo'." He placed his tools safely, wiped down his hands and opened the garage door. Still laughing loudly at the thought of himself gracing the pulpit on Sunday morning he walked towards the house porch where the Reverend Hugh was standing.

"Well, young man, sorry to interrupt your work but I'm glad I've brightened your day," Rev Hugh greeted Stephen heartily as he moved towards him.

"That's OK, I'll be glad of a break if you'd like a coffee. It will have to be in the kitchen." Stephen grinned and shrugged his shoulders, "Mum won't allow me in anywhere else in this clobber."

"That's fine, my boy," said Hugh graciously as he followed Stephen through the garage past the wood-work corner and into the kitchen via the inter-connecting door.

Stephen filled up the kettle and switched it on. "I hope you're kidding about the sermonizing. I can hammer and saw, sand and turn, even paint and read a bit but the preaching I leave to folk like you."

"You're right we're all gifted in different ways. I couldn't produce the fine work that I know you achieve with the tools you mentioned. Actually, I had no thoughts of inviting you to take over the pulpit, what I came to ask of you was of quite a different nature. Would you be willing to come with me to visit Josh tomorrow afternoon?"

"Aaah!" Stephen gulped and almost spilled the coffee as he poured hot water into the mugs he'd set out on the kitchen work-top. This was not what he was expecting the vicar to request.

Hugh pulled out a chair from under the kitchen table, took the mug Stephen offered and sat down.

"I know it's a big undertaking but I would appreciate your help."

"Uhm, well..."

"I've been a couple of times to see him but Josh was sullen and uncooperative. He seems to have built a hard shell around himself which I find difficult to penetrate."

Stephen chuckled, "Sounds as though he's setting you a teaser, Vic."

"You could be right. The only response I get is nods or monosyllables."

"That's Josh, alright," Stephen nodded. "He's posing a puzzle which one of you will lose and it certainly won't be him."

"You seem to understand what makes him tick, Stephen, that's why I think you, as one of his mates, might have a better rapport with him."

Stephen took a slow sip of his coffee as he considered Hugh's words.

"He might talk with you," Hugh added.

"OK," replied Stephen reticently, unsure what the inside of a youth prison might be like. "I'll give it a go."

At the conclusion of Sunday lunch the next day Stephen travelled with Hugh Darnell down the coast to the Young Offenders' Institution at Hollesley Bay. His first visit was not an entire success.

"What yew a-doen' 'ere?" Josh demanded gruffly as he slouched towards Stephen with his hands in his pockets.

"Come to see you, mate."

"Yew could hev saved yourn time," he said moodily and turned towards the door.

On the next visit Josh yelled at him from the doorway, "Yew needn't a-bothered, mate, I hent a-comen'."

"Stop that squit! I'm here now so come and sit down, Josh, I want to know how you're doing."

"What a joke," he sneered. "what dew yew think? Looks like the Ritz, doan't it?"

Despite his mood Josh did eventually sit at the table across from Stephen.

"Got any smokes?"

Stephen shook his head.

"Some mate yew are!" and he thumped his fist on the table. " 'Ow abaht them tools o' yourn or a Big Mac."

Stephen laughed and shook his head. Josh scowled. "Bet yourn 'ad a good ole Sunday lunch, ent yew? Roast Beef 'n Yorkies, eh?"

"Nut roast, actually."

"Oh, yeah, f'got yew hev that veggie muck." He continued to thump a beat upon the table.

At least he's speaking to me.

On the following visit Josh spent the whole hour venting his resentment at being confined in the institution and the restrictions it placed upon him.

The bell rang. "Shall I come again?"

"It's up to yew."

Thereafter, Stephen faithfully accompanied Hugh Darnell most Sunday afternoons. Josh never said anything about his visits but Stephen got the impression that Josh looked forward to their time together as the highlight of his week.

On one occasion, many weeks later, it emerged that Josh was intensely jealous of the achievements of his group of friends.

"I started the breaken' an' enteren' 'thing' to prove I could be good at somethen' particularly if I could achieve it without be'en' caught.

"Ryan be a whiz at mechanics an' knows engines inside out. Nat be brill with animals an' farmen'. Nicky be a real charmer an' gits on with everybody but such a Holy Joe. An' then there be yew. Yew're a book-worm but can soon turn yourn 'and to anythen' when yew've got a fistful o' tools in 'em.

"Me? I'm good fer nothen', hopeless at everythen'."

"That's not true, Josh and you know it. Look at the skill it required to do the breaking and entering."

"Oh yeah!" Josh tossed his head back in disbelief.

"Yeah! You just need to channel that skill more constructively."

"Doan't yew juss like to joke, mate!"

"Stop putting yourself down, Josh. You've got a good brain, mate – use it!"

"Doen' what?"

"You were good at IT at school, what about developing in that field?"

"Nice try mate but I doan't 'ave a laptop so where do yew suppose I start? Can't nick one in 'ere."

"At this stage I shouldn't worry about your own PC." Visiting time was rapidly running out. Stephen thought wryly. *This is the first time we've discussed anything other than Josh's anger at being confined. Whatever can I say to him?* He didn't want to dampen Josh's spirits and would prefer to leave him with some positive thoughts and possibly a plan of action.

"Why don't you ask what classes or study sessions are available while you're in here."

"Ask who?" Josh feigned ignorance omitting to mention to his friend that though part of his sentence specified participation in educational study or a course to prepare him for work when he was released he had so far refused to attend.

"No idea, but I'd start with the chap who let me in here. If he doesn't know he might suggest someone else who does. Or you could write to Mr Mitchell at school."

"Naah! He'd tell me off for a-throwen' my chances away and a-wasten' his time."

"You don't know that until you ask. Try it and see. You've got nothing to lose."

Chapter Twelve

At a candlelit table Trixie sat across from John enjoying the cosy ambience of the Station Hotel restaurant. For midweek it was quietly busy and the piano music playing softly in the background created just the right atmosphere John felt Trixie needed as a respite from her constant activity. He was pleased to see his niece, Lizzie Piper, enchanting the diners with her skilful playing of Chopin. When she concluded a piece and glanced up, he gave her a wave of appreciation.

"I'm glad that young lady stuck to her guns, she has remarkable talent."

"Mmm! It took tremendous courage to defy her Dad and accept a place at the Royal College of Music."

"Yes, it goes against the grain to flout a parent's wishes but I understand she's surpassed all expectations in her entrance exams."

"Indeed, but Maisie says that even now Jack won't acknowledge his daughter's ability. He would still prefer Lizzie to train as a needlewoman and work alongside her Mum in the family business."

"What a shame to stifle such a gift."

"He says piano playing won't pay the bills."

"And I suppose he thinks sewing upholstery for the boats will, even though it's a dying craft."

"What do you mean?"

"The popularity of holidaying in boats on the river or the Norfolk Broads is diminishing."

"Getting too expensive, I suppose."

"Well, certainly beyond the pocket of the ordinary man in the street."

"Oh, look there's Kaitlin and Donald."

John inclined his head in greeting as a young couple came through the door into the restaurant.

Both were Doctors at the Norfolk and Norwich hospital and had spent some time at Barts in training with their son, Roger. Kaitlin was a gynaecologist whilst Donald's skills lay in surgery. Kaitlin smiled across at the Coopers as Donald carefully guided her to their table. Following their marriage the young couple had settled in Newton Lokesby and Kaitlin occasionally acted as locum for John when he and Trixie embarked on one of their infrequent holidays.

As their young friends were seated at a table on the far side of the restaurant Trixie's eyes drifted back to their own table.

"This is such a pleasant evening, John, thankyou for suggesting it."

"You deserve it, my dear. You work so tirelessly for others I felt you ought to have a treat yourself."

"Well, it's certainly that. It's a real delight to be waited on." Trixie smiled up at the face that was so dear to her, conscious of the flecks of grey that were beginning to pepper John's dark brown hair.

"I do appreciate your thoughtfulness."

"The pleasure's all mine. I'm so pleased you are easing up in your busyness. I just want you to relax and enjoy the evening."

"Oh I am. I've nothing pressing at the moment. The problem of accommodation for RK is on the way to being solved…"

"That is good news."

"…the alterations at the Catton's home are well in hand ready for Laura's pending discharge…"

"That shouldn't be too long now."

"Christina is also ahead with the preparations for the Holiday Cottages Summer lets. I haven't any outstanding concerns relating to either PCC or PC matters and I haven't had to prepare the veg or set the table this evening and I won't have to do the washing up."

"Don't be too sure about that. If I haven't sufficient funds…" He playfully patted his pockets.

"John, you're such a tease. It's good to see you so relaxed."

"Well, the company is very special and the food really quite delicious. I must confess I was a little dubious whether it would come up to par because you are such a superb cook."

"Oh, my dear," Trixie reached for his hand. "Thankyou for such a pleasing compliment but the chef here does have a good reputation, you know. I believe he trained with Jilly Briggs who's now helping out Emma using her prowess in the kitchen at the Village Stores. He certainly has some very innovative ideas."

"Oh, I agree. In fact I thought the starter was a rather unusual combination of flavours…"

"… but quite appetising," Trixie finished off for him.

John nodded thoughtfully, "Yes, you're right."

"I wouldn't have dared to put ginger and apricots with salmon, as well as, what tasted like a hint of aniseed but I'm really enjoying what has been prepared for us. It's nice to have something different."

"I'm glad you like things to be different because that thought nicely brings us to the reason we're here. I have some ideas you may think are very different but I would appreciate your honest opinion on them."

"That sounds a little ominous, John."

"Oh, no, my dear, just different," he smiled.

"I see."

"It concerns our three children..."

"Well, they are certainly all different," Trixie said emphatically.

"Excuse me, Doctor, may I clear?" the young waiter hovered, waiting for a nod from John.

"Yes, please do."

The plates were quickly removed and Trixie looked at John expectantly.

"So?"

"I think we're agreed that the situation regarding Jansy is not at all what we expected but we'll deal with it as we've already discussed – prayer and trust." John paused and reached across the table to gently squeeze her hand. Trixie nodded so he continued, "I propose we put the funds we earmarked for the wedding expenses and their wedding gift into a separate account. It will then be available as and when it is required."

"You seem so very sure that those two have a future together, John."

"Yes, Trixie, I do, but all the difficulties they are encountering at the moment are issues only they can sort out. In the meantime I want to be prepared for all eventualities."

"Yes, I agree. It sounds quite a sensible idea to set an amount aside but why does it need to be in a separate account?"

"My second suggestion is to offer Roger a junior partnership in the practice when he concludes his year at Barts but..."

Trixie gasped in surprise but John continued, "...obviously, he will not have sufficient savings to buy into the partnership so it will be our gift to him. However, he will need to scrutinize the practice accounts before he signs a formal contract. I feel that the monies we've allocated to Jansy and Dave's nuptials needs to be equal to that gift and kept distinctly apart till such time as it is required."

"Dear John, I think that's a splendid idea. Have you intimated your proposal to Roger?"

"No, I wanted to get your views first. Similarly, I want to ensure we have an amount set aside when he and Emma get married."

Trixie laughed. "Do you have inside information on that matter, too?"

"No, I just believe it's a question of time." He smiled his lopsided grin. "You'll see." His eyes sparkled with mischief.

"Oh, John!"

"We...ll, who comes home at every opportunity to see a certain young lady? And who has a personal invitation to her graduation?"

"You are most observant, my dear."

"Just so!" John nodded wisely. "It's a skill I've learned over time."

"Is that right?"

"That leaves Stephen. Now that he's got his diploma I feel we ought to do something to help him get established."

"In work, you mean?"

"Yes. We didn't give him a gift for his eighteenth and his twenty-first is coming up next year…"

"But we paid for the barbeque for the whole village and we're providing his funds for the UEA."

"Yes, I know, but what I'm proposing as far as he is concerned will not only help you but hopefully secure his future, too, as well as be of benefit to our community."

"John, that sounds more like a riddle."

"I'm thinking of books, books and even more books. Our house seems to be overtaken by them."

"Tell me about it. It's impossible to get into Stephen's room without falling over all the volumes he has piled on the floor. There are masses of boxes in the loft, too, and the spare room is gradually becoming equally inundated. I can't hoover and I mustn't move them."

"Right! So, we need to find them another home and I have just the place in mind."

"Really? I've been longing to find a solution to that little problem for such a long time."

"I believe the derelict eyesore opposite brother Billy's shop to be the ideal solution."

"John!" Trixie's involuntary shout caused the waiter to jump as he was setting the dishes upon the table. She was horrified at her husband's suggestion.

"Ooops! I'm so sorry," She patted the arm of the young man as he tried to fix the food that had spilled. "Please, not to worry. It was my fault entirely." Trixie quickly righted things. "See, not too much damage," and she proceeded to serve the side orders onto each of their plates.

"You know, John, some of those books are first editions and others are quite valuable. We can't dump them on wasteland simply to get them out of our way."

"No, no, that's not what I intended. Our son must make them earn their keep."

"How?"

John slowly savoured the fork full of food he had lifted to his mouth. "Oh my! This is absolutely delicious."

"John!"

"Do try it, my dear; it is so succulent and tasty."

Trixie looked at him with exasperation. "Stop teasing, John, and explain how that overgrown wilderness can possibly solve the problem of Stephen's books or contribute to his future success."

"Please eat, Trixie, while the food is still hot."

"Only if you'll explain the conundrum you have set before me."

"You'll be the loser; your food won't taste quite so good if you let it go cold."

Trixie caught the glint in John's eye, sighed resignedly, and commenced to eat her meal.

John let the silence hang between them for a time as they appreciated the texture and flavour of the meal set before them. He was well aware that between each mouthful Trixie was peeking at him through the corner of her eye for his mischievous manner.

After a while she said, "Don't keep me in suspense any longer, you tease."

John wiped his mouth on his napkin, deliberately taking his time.

"Have you ever really looked at that plot of land opposite Billy's shop?"

"No, I can't say that I have. It seems to have always been there, part of our growing up. At times the trees and shrubs hang over the roadway and some of the roots stick up making walking that side of the road somewhat difficult particularly when you're pushing a buggy or are accompanied by a small child. It is beginning to look a little unsightly, though I think the council, or someone, comes occasionally to cut the worst of it back."

"Have you ever looked beyond the undergrowth on the fringe?"

Trixie shook her head. "As children we always referred to it as the dark wood and kept well away."

"Yes, I recall as a youngster that there were gaps between the hedges that looked like gaping black holes and we dared other lads to run into them or pay a forfeit."

"You're right. It always seemed a scary place."

"I am quite convinced that at the heart of that neglected woodland there are some dwellings."

Trixie perked up, "Really?"

"I don't want to draw undue attention to the plot because unscrupulous speculators so quickly jump on the band wagon. In fact, I'm surprised that some builder hasn't already seen its potential and snapped it up, unless they've viewed it as green belt land and left well alone."

"Have you spoken with Durrant's about your theories?"

"Not yet," John slowly shook his head. "Ben and Roy would hold their own counsel if I shared my ideas with them but..."

"...Gordon and Matty would struggle to keep the news to themselves."

He nodded. "Sadly that is all too true. They would blunder ahead with the scheme, without forethought or planning, focussed solely on what was in it for them."

"What has this to do with Stephen and his books?"

"I would like to purchase the property for him ..."

"Whatever for?"

"...as a place for his books and..."

"John!" Trixie rolled her eyes to the ceiling and gave an exasperated sigh. "You have a rare imagination if you can visualize storing books in an overgrown jungle."

"...I think it has potential to be developed into a book shop and wood workshop."

Trixie shook her head in disbelief, "But it's woodland, John!"

"So it would appear but I'm convinced the trees and undergrowth are peripheral and that at the heart there are buildings of some sort. The shrubs may have protected them over the years or they may be in a sorry state of disrepair and decay but I'm certain there's something there and I want to find out what it is."

"How can you be so sure there is any sort of structure amongst that entire tangle?"

"Because I remember on the occasion when I was dared to run into the gap in the undergrowth I tripped and fell against something solid. It felt like a wall of some sort."

"But how do you expect Stephen to turn that into a viable business?"

"My dear, I've told no one my thoughts, but you, because of the reasons I've already given but I'm sure if we got the area cleared and had a good look at the heart of the plot we would find a structure of some sort that could be renovated for Stephen's use."

"That sounds a tremendous undertaking."

John nodded thoughtfully.

"Mmm, but not insurmountable. I am currently looking into the ownership of the property so that I can make an offer. I've looked through the PCC records and there's not an entry there that suggests it belongs to the Church so I suspect that it was at sometime in the past acquisitioned by Lord Edmund's father or even his grandfather. I have an appointment with the de Vere estate manager tomorrow morning and hopefully between the two of us we'll be able to get to the heart of the matter."

"I see."

"I will put in a bid, with your approval, then take Adam Catton into my confidence and ask him to act on our behalf."

"If that is what you think will be best I'll go along with your decision, John. But, what if there is nothing there but scrub land?"

"Excuse me, sir, can I get you a sweet?"

John looked questioningly at his wife, "My dear?"

Trixie began to shake her head but the Doctor forestalled her, "They have got your favourite."

"They have?"

"Crème Brulee with raspberries," he said enticingly.

"Oh John, I shouldn't really."

"Why not, just this once? We don't eat out very often and this is a treat," he cajoled.

"Oh, alright," she acquiesced with a smile, "as long as you make it right with my doctor if my cholesterol readings go sky high."

"Two, please," John requested of the waiter, "and we'll have two coffees, thankyou."

"Yes, Doctor."

John looked across at Trixie. "If, when the area is cleared, I'm proved to be wrong there will be opportunity to develop the land as we wish."

"You're getting quite animated about this project, aren't you?" Trixie smiled at her husband's boyish enthusiasm.

"Yes, I suppose I am. I've been thinking it over for some time but wanted to be sure in my own mind that I had covered every aspect before sharing with you my intention and setting the wheels in motion."

"So where do we go from here?"

"Dependant on the outcome of my appointment with Scholes in the morning, I'll notify Adam, then as soon as the sale goes through we'll tell Stephen."

"He'll be so excited. He's been desperately searching for property suitable for a woodwork studio. His enterprise has outgrown the space allocated to him in the garage."

"Well, if this all goes ahead I'm sure those problems will be solved for him."

"I guess it will then be all systems go?"

"You're spot on. The work will be a challenge but what a reward, if I'm right," he said eagerly.

"How long should it take?"

"The sale, about five weeks or so, I should think if all goes well. The land clearing," he shrugged, "as long as it takes!"

"Then we shall have our house back and Stephen will have space of his own to develop his two passions."

"Yes and I believe there will also be opportunity to create jobs for other village youngsters."

"Such as?"

"I don't know yet but I feel the site has so much potential which I'd like to see being utilised for the benefit of our community rather than remaining a blight at the heart of our village."

It was well known that the village shop or the school gate were first-rate places to go to glean news or gather gossip. So, as parents, mostly mothers, dropped off their children at school on the Tuesday morning following Doctor and Mrs Cooper's evening out at the Station Hotel, a stranger mingled amongst them. She attached herself to first this chatting group and then hovered behind others. She nodded and said 'hello', joined in the general chit-chat, as appropriate, and gave the impression that to all intents and purposes she was one of them. Then, she fluttered between them like a restless butterfly, as in twos and threesomes they meandered along the lane towards the Village Stores. But by the time they reached the shop she was gone.

"Who was that?"

"I don't know."

"I'm not aware of a new family in the village."

"Nor me."

"She complained about the lack of parking…"

"Not a local, obviously!"

"…and grumbled about the wood."

"Called it an eyesore and a waste of space and berated the council for not doing something about it."

"I shouldn't think the council is the least bit interested in our trees."

"It's lovely in spring when the fresh green leaves burst open and a real picture when they change into those brilliant autumn colours."

"The roots can be a nuisance, though and the leaves are a funny ole mess when they drop in the autumn but on the whole I think it's a nice attraction in the centre of our village."

"It's a haven for wildlife but a trap for litter when the wind blows."

"Those brambles be mighty laden back-end o' the summer an' make delicious jams an' pies."

"Well, it's been there all my life and long before me, as far as I am aware, and I guess it will outlive my children. I need to cross over to the butchers, must get something for dinner. I'll see you later, 'bye."

"It will be so good when Emma opens the coffee shop. We'll have somewhere to meet and chat when we've been up to the school."

"Not long now."

"Can't come soon enough for me."

The bell jangled as Rachel Durrant pushed open the door and entered the shop. "Morning, Aunt Rosalie."

"Good morning, Rachel, morning Sue, RK," Rosalie affably greeted her customers.

"We were just longing for the day Emma opens for coffee."

"Surely you're too busy to spend time chatting over coffee."

"Don't you believe it, we'd make time," Rachel quipped.

They all laughed.

The young women went in different directions down the aisles in the shop to select the grocery items each had come in for.

RK searched for something for the Catton children's tea and then hovered over the delicatessen counter to choose a fish dish for her own evening meal.

"Does it feel good to be stocking up your own store cupboard, RK?" Rachel leant across to select a pie for her family's meal.

"Mmm! Incredibly good!" RK replied with a grin that stretched across her face.

Rachel laughed, "You look like a cat that has found the cream."

"You may laugh but it is so wonderful to have a place I can call my own."

As far as the clandestine purchase of Kezia's Wood was concerned not one word leaked out. The quiet talks behind closed doors remained private and contained. Even the speculative stranger's presence only triggered ripples of interest in the village for a day or so and certainly didn't link in any one's mind with definite plans to change the well established woodland. For Doctor John negotiations went more smoothly than he could possibly have anticipated and a week the following Friday morning he received a phone call from Adam Catton.

"I'm finalizing all the legal aspects of the purchase but I do require your signature. Could you come into the office? Say, Wednesday at 10.30?"

CHAPTER THIRTEEN

Within a few days RK was settled happily into Ferry Cottage. Relief flooded through her that finding somewhere suitable to stay was sorted out so quickly. Discord was an uneasy bedfellow and one that had caused her to retreat to Newton Westerby in the first place. She paused by the doorway and viewed the room before her with pleasure. *I do hope this arrangement will appease those villagers who objected most vociferously to the frequent noise of my motorbike.*

Glad of the space the cottage gave, RK delighted in setting out her meagre possessions to her satisfaction. She walked to the kitchen window and fingered the curtains Christina and Trixie had hung up for her after the big clean-up. If she wasn't mistaken it was a Crowson fabric, delicately patterned with meadow flowers and butterflies, and led the eye straight into the garden. *Davi would just love this* she mused as thoughts of her country-loving sister fluttered into her mind.

For the first time in her life RK had her own home and revelled in the freedom and independence she felt as she walked along the lane towards the cottage door at the end of each working day. She appreciated the hospitality so generously extended to her by the Jenner family but the accommodation at the Mill was geared primarily to short stay visitors and, whilst she enjoyed working with the Catton children, entering the cottage every evening and closing the door behind her, brought a sense of peace and contentment.

From the kitchen window, through the garden, there was a clear view across the beach to the rolling waves of the sea. To satisfy her insatiable appetite for the sea RK repositioned the table and chair, so that, when eating her breakfast and evening meal she could look out of the window and enjoy the changing patterns of sunrise and the dusk of evening as each danced on the restless water.

True to their word, Trixie and Tessa had ensured that, by the end of the week, RK had all she needed to make the cottage comfortable and cosy. She was amazed that in so short a space of time the two-up and two-down began to feel like her home. RK wrapped her arms contentedly around her chest and breathed a deep sigh of relief. *No more kowtowing to the whims of my sisters or giving in to the demands of my parents. I can please myself. Maybe invite some of my new friends for coffee or a supper evening.* That thought gave RK tremendous pleasure.

Throughout her childhood and teenage years inviting friends home to the farm had been actively discouraged by her parents. Tasks about the farm always took precedence over all else. "Chores first then you can play," was her father's adage but he kept them so busy there never was time for social activities. So, she looked forward to repaying the kindness so many of her new friends had willingly offered to her since her arrival in Newton Westerby.

Even the primitive plumbing arrangement, which the Jenner children had found so archaic and disgusting, didn't trouble her. RK knew when she accepted the cottage that it hadn't been occupied for some time because it was on the list to be upgraded. Nevertheless, the villagers rallied to meet her personal needs with numerous offers of shower and bathing facilities. RK eventually elected to accept the one from Jennifer Pedwardine, of all people, "because her house is within easy walking distance of the cottage." After all, RK had no hang ups from Miss Pedwardine's schoolmarm days, she only knew her as a retired lady resident of the village.

"There's vacant space in the garage, too, if you care to use it to store your motorbike," Jennifer generously suggested, "keep it out of harm's way."

Consequently, early one evening, P.C. Dan passed RK wheeling the Harley-Davidson along the lane to Miss Pedwardine's house. He braked, parked up the police motorcycle and jogged back to join her. Just like the children of the village Dan found the tall, dark haired young woman with the captivating smile, a fun person to be with.

Dan had mentioned his fascination with RK to Adam and Justin, one evening when they were leaving the Church following choir practise. They'd both advised caution and reminded Dan of the Biblical concept of being 'unequally yoked' to a non-believer and RK's persistent affirmation that Christianity was not for her.

"Guard your heart, Dan," Adam wisely counselled. "Don't mistakenly think that human love can bring about another's salvation. That's the Lord's prerogative. By all means pray for her and offer friendship. She needs it. But don't presume that you can change her."

Dan respected Adam's judgement. No one could doubt his sincerity and the depth of his love and commitment to Laura. It was obvious their closeness stemmed from a personal relationship with the Lord Jesus. That oneness was of paramount importance in their lives and evident in their dealings with each other, the people belonging to the church fellowship and their fellow residents in the village. It was the foundation upon which they had built their family life and the anchor that was now holding them steady through the difficulties of Laura's illness.

"I believe a shared belief is a necessary prelude to a successful marriage," commented Adam. With this in mind Dan took care not to present the wrong vibes whenever he and RK met.

"Hi there, can I give you a hand?" Dan enquired pleasantly as he strode to RK's side.

RK shook her head. "No thanks, I can manage."

"OK, Miss Independent," he said with a smile, "but here's a card with my phone number on it; assistance available anytime, should you need it."

"Now, why would I need that?" She turned to look at Dan her merry brown eyes twinkling impishly as she reached to accept the card.

"You may not realise it but you're in a rather vulnerable position down at Ferry Cottage," Dan explained carefully.

"It's a lovely spot and I'm sure I can watch out for myself," RK confidently assured him with a bold, wide smile.

"Maybe," agreed Dan against his better judgement, "but should the isolation get to you just give a call."

"I'm sure you've got more important things to occupy your time than concerning yourself about me," asserted RK coquettishly.

Meanwhile, at an emergency meeting instigated by Trixie Cooper, the village housing committee agreed to the proposal to have interim improvements made to the outside lavatory at the cottage. Durrant's, the builders, were invited to submit plans to brick up the outside doorway, install a modern toilet suite and cistern and open up access via the living space next to the back door. However, when Ben Durrant was taking measurements for the building work he also intimated that, by portioning off the small area from the toilet wall in front of the back door, an indoor porch could be created.

"The toilet facilities would then not lead directly off the kitchen area. Also, it will give added insulation to the rear of the property, as well as, much needed protection from the cold, east winds and possibly provide storage for outdoor shoes or boots and the like. The new wall could provide a useful space to put up hooks for coats."

"You think of everything, my boy," commended Lord Edmund warmly.

"Well, sir, it's my opinion that if the job's done properly now it can remain, and be a valuable asset, even when further renovation takes place."

"Increase the value of the property, too, I imagine," Lord Edmund commented dryly.

Closing the bedroom curtains in the twilight one evening, when she had been in residence almost two weeks, RK saw shadowy figures lurking on the beach near the crumbled rear wall of the cottage garden. Many people enjoyed an evening stroll along the beach so it was not an unusual occurrence but it was the furtive movements of this group, in particular, that caught her attention and she stood glued to the window staring at them.

However, in the next instant, RK caught her breath and clapped her hand across her mouth as she watched them clamber, one by one, over the wall into her garden.

They moved towards the cottage and as she looked out into the gloom RK recognized one of them as the deckhand from Mark Bemment's boat. The other two were people with whom she was totally unfamiliar. Small packages were passed between them and the stealthy manner with which it was done perturbed RK. The men looked cautiously around them. Before she knew it eyes from below were locked on hers. RK gulped and quickly stepped back from the window.

"Hey!" a voice barked.

Hairs on the back of her neck bristled as fists hammered on the back door. RK leaned against the bedroom door afraid the unexpected visitors could hear the pounding of her heart. She held her breath, as goose bumps snaked down her spine, recalled P.C. Dan's cautionary words, and listened.

"Thought you said this place was deserted," hissed a voice angrily.

"It was, bin empty a couple o' years. Must be a squatter," spat out the irritated reply.

"Don't be stupid, someone's living here."

"How could they? Look at it. It's derelict." He viciously kicked the dilapidated lavatory door to prove his point and something unidentifiable scuttled out of the debris into the evening shadows.

"Would you want to use that?"

"There's definitely someone up there. I saw them," he retorted furiously, "and, you can be sure, whoever it was saw us."

"Oh Doc, keep yer hair on. What did they see? Three mates getten' together."

"What if we're recognized?"

"Who in the village knows yew?" His companions shook their heads. "Precisely! No one. If they recognize me they'll assume yew're fishen' pals of mine. Ten to one it's not even a local in there. They wouldn't be seen dead in the place."

"I still think we need to be cautious."

"OK, OK, but it's hardly the same as the ole shopkeeper. He was too nosey, at least we silenced him." The deckhand was beginning to get riled with his companions.

"I don't know why you thought it necessary to meet out here, again. What was wrong with our usual venue?" The disgruntled speaker looked suspiciously over his shoulder.

"Not safe; getten' too hot; spies everywhere in the city," came back the clipped reply.

"I thought we were always discreet."

"'ard to know who to trust, these days."

"Don't get careless and don't take risks," warned the second voice, menacingly.

"Thass why we 'ad to switch location."

RK hardly dared to move. She waited.

"We need to lie low…"

The taller of his companions grabbed him by the scruff of the neck and pushed his face into that of his captive. "Don't drag us down with you," he threatened.

The deckhand shook off his attacker. "Cool it, Doc. Who would think yew city gents and me were mates?"

They shrugged their shoulders.

"Thass right, no one. So, I'll go this way an' yew go that way an' I'll be in touch." He leapt back over the wall and was gone.

RK held her breath and waited. Eventually all seemed quiet. She listened till she thought the nocturnal visitors had moved away, then very cautiously crept down the stairs, not daring to put on the light. RK felt her way along the wall into the kitchen and across the length of the worktop to where she had placed her mobile phone. *Now, where did I put the card that P.C. Dan gave to me?* She fumbled about until she found it in her jacket pocket. She tiptoed to the farthest corner away from the window and by the dwindling light dialled Dan's number but there was no response. Her battery was flat. She sighed. She'd forgotten to put it on charge. Frustrated she ascended the stairs and prepared for bed.

The following morning the sky was overcast and the grey clouds reflected RK's sombre mood. After her unpleasant experience the previous evening she had spent a somewhat restless night but slowly, understanding had dawned on her so, as soon as possible, she made a point of seeking out P.C. Dan Prettyman. Putting on a cheerful face she briefly related the incident to him.

"I suggest the harbour master and your police sergeant investigate in that direction regarding the smuggling episodes instead of targeting me." RK grinned at him as he looked at her with disbelief. "I think they might have more success." During the night she had sussed out the reason for the dogged police presence wherever she went and recalled where she had encountered the deckhand before. He was the obnoxious youth who had offered her drugs in the Ship Inn on her first day in the village.

"When you catch him, ask about the nosey shopkeeper that was silenced. Also, he referred to one of his friends as 'Doc' and called them 'city gents'."

Dan, for once, was speechless. Before he recovered his senses RK was half way down Ferry Lane. "Robyn," he called after her but she had turned the corner, presumably to go into the Village Stores, and didn't hear him.

Dan pulled out his mobile phone and pressed the buttons that would link him to the police station.

"Sarge, I think I have a lead on the smuggling incidents."

"Fire away, m'bor, Oi'm a list'nen."

After an intense conversation with Sergeant Catchpole, Dan made his way with haste to the Village Stores. He was anxious to speak again with RK and enlist her help in police enquiries. As he entered the shop he spied her half way down one of the aisles. He pulled her to one side and quietly explained his assignment.

"My sergeant would like to send a SOCO team to carry out a thorough search of the area around the cottage and in your garden."

"SOCO?"

"Excuse the jargon, Scene of Crime Officers."

"So, they do believe me then?"

"They consider the information you passed on to be a valuable lead and wish to investigate further, with your permission, of course."

"You sound very formal, Constable."

"Sorry, but in the circumstances, I'm afraid, rather necessary."

"Then, I can hardly do less than comply."

"Thanks. Rain is forecast for later in the day so they would like to make an immediate start."

"Right, I'll just pay for my groceries then go straight back home to wait for their arrival. Does that meet with your approval?" Dan nodded as RK lifted the wire basket onto the counter then he turned and exited the shop to ride hurriedly away on the police motorbike.

Rosalie looked up at RK with concern in her eyes as she swiftly passed RK's shopping through the checkout. "Is everything alright?" she enquired kindly.

RK, with tightly compressed lips, nodded. She packed her bags in silence.

Laden with shopping RK made her way back to Ferry Cottage her heart thumping with apprehension as she approached the front door. With the shopping bags balanced round her wrist she fumbled with the key in the lock. It fell to the ground. Anxiously RK bent down to pick it up. She tried again and this time succeeded in opening the door and stepping inside her home. She had barely finished putting away her groceries when a police car pulled up outside Ferry Cottage.

One officer hovered in the kitchen to ask RK questions regarding the incident of the previous evening while his colleagues set about their task in the garden. Sometime later, when the policemen had all finished and were on the point of leaving the property, one of their number turned and said to RK, "Someone will be in touch about attending an identity procedure." Sensing her apprehension by her body language he added, "Now don't you worry about a thing, Miss. You'll be shown some photographs and asked to indicate if you can identify anyone as last night's intruders."

RK merely nodded and watched through the window till their car passed out of sight then spent the rest of the day in an unsettled haze.

When the new day dawned, despite an uneventful night, RK was glad to be going to work at the Catton house. The episode in the garden had shaken her more than she cared to admit to others. She felt as though the nocturnal trespassers had robbed her of the joy of her new home. Her footsteps barely touched the ground as she sped to commence care of her charges. The needs of the Catton children would keep her occupied in mind and body.

Although RK had not mentioned her experience to anyone the sight of the police car outside Ferry Cottage fuelled speculation among the gossips in the village. Huddles of parents by the school gate and shoppers along the aisles in the Village Stores tossed around all manner of possibilities for the police presence at RK's new home. As Emma checked the fresh food display she couldn't help but overhear their conversation.

"I wonder what she's done."

"Yourn guess be as good as mine."

"But who knows anything about her?"

"She do seem to appear from nowhere, doan't she?"

"Perhaps she be in hiden'."

"Ooh! Maybe we be harbouren' a criminal."

"Stands to reason she's bin up to somethen'."

"No wonder she pretended to be a man."

"'Spect it be that wretched bike noise."

"Noo...oo, can't be that. She hardly rides it these days."

"Then I guess they've caught her a-thieven'."

"We'll 'ave t' watch our purses."

"Why were the police a-trampen' round the garden then?"

"A-searchen' for the loot."

"Hope those children aren't at risk."

"Don't be silly. Adam Catton be a stickler for the law. She'd 'ave to be checked out by the police, CBR check or somethen' afore..."

"Good morning, ladies, how can I help you today?" Emma called out as she strolled down the aisle. Immediately the conversation stopped. *Aah! Red coat and Purple coat from Newton Common! I might have known it would be you two casting aspersions on someone's character. Poor RK hasn't much chance when she's up against the acid tongues of Irma Morton and Dot Knights.*

"I have a few of today's pasties left, if you're interested." Emma walked slowly back to the counter, breathed deeply to keep her temper in check. She didn't intend to reduce the price because it was still early in the day but she did want to distract their attention away from crucifying RK. After all they had no idea what was really going on and were letting their imaginations run away with them. To blacken RK's reputation so was quite dreadful.

I do wonder how I can help RK if she really is in some sort of trouble. I'll give Mirry and Justin a call. Perhaps we could have an impromptu house warming this evening. Emma was concerned for her friend. She stood for a moment looking out of the large shop window. Her eyes drifted across the village towards the lane that led to Ferry cottage as she tried to recall the conversation she and Rosalie had shared last evening. *I think Rosalie mentioned RK being upset about something when she came in the shop for her groceries yesterday and that Dan Prettyman chased in after her and had some strong words with her. So there might be some truth in the gossips tittle-tattle.*

"Good morning, young lady." Emma turned with a start from her reverie at the smarmy voice addressing her. Leaning over the counter was a stranger. She eyed him up and down and didn't particularly like what she saw. She estimated he was fortyish trying to be twentyish. He was wearing a light grey suit with an overstuffed briefcase under his arm, hair jelled and spiked to within an inch of its life and above his smirking lips he was sporting a Hitler style moustache. What she disliked most of all was the manner in which he was leering at her in a most suggestive way. *You're obviously a rep hoping to impress.*

Hearing a new voice in the shop the eyes of the gossiping customers lit up with interest. They hushed their talk, picked up their shopping baskets and bustled along the aisle towards the checkout to stare at the new arrival.

"Good morning, can I help you?"

"I'd like to speak to the proprietor."

"What about?"

"That's between him and me," the smooth talker replied tapping the side of his nose.

"Well, I'm afraid you'll have to make do with me."

"If he's tied up at present I can wait." He stepped back and looked derisively across the entire shop. "You don't seem to be very busy so I wouldn't have thought he has that many things pressing for his attention. Just go and ask him if he can spare a moment for our little discussion, there's a good girl."

Emma began to seethe. *Come on, girl, keep calm. Don't let him get to you. Stand tall and take a deep breath.*

Emma did just that and looked straight into his shifty eyes. He couldn't hold her gaze.

"If there is anything to be discussed you'll have to discuss it with me," she said decisively, wishing this wasn't Rosalie's day off.

The stranger waived Emma away dismissively. "No, no, no that won't do at all. I can't discuss such important issues with a chit of a girl like you."

"Then you're going to be disappointed."

Red coat and Purple coat edged nearer to the counter sensing something interesting was beginning to develop.

"Oh, look you have customers," he sneered. "Not much choice here, is there ladies?" He looked into their sparsely filled store wire baskets and pulled a face. "A supermarket would be a better option, don't you think? Especially if there's also a car park."

They looked at him blankly.

"Competition would be good, wouldn't it?"

"Good for whom?" Emma was struggling to remain gracious and kindly in her attitude towards the offensive stranger who was so obviously decrying her monopoly.

"Bit pricey in here, isn't it, ladies? Be good for your pocket to get more for your money, eh?"

Other shoppers stopped their browsing and gravitated to the checkout counter, ears a-wigging.

"What be he a-talken about?" whispered Mrs Saunders. Mrs Peek shook her head, "I've no idea."

"Oh, you're busier than I thought. I'll leave you to get on. I'll find the boss myself. Office down here?" The stranger blundered through the cluster of customers towards the back of the shop leaving the ladies by the till staring after him open mouthed and Emma flabbergasted at his audacity.

"Did he say this a-goen' to be a supermarket?"

"Emma be yew a-sellen' the shop?"

"No, most certainly not. I'm not sure what he was talking about."

The shop door bell jangled and Bernice Durrant came through the doorway. Emma breathed a sigh of relief.

"Aunt Bernice, could you hold the fort for a little while, I have a serious matter to sort out?"

"Of course, my dear girl," Bernice slipped off her coat, pushed it into her basket and tucked them temporarily underneath the counter.

"Now, who's first?" Bernice clapped her hands to catch the attention of the chattering shoppers.

CHAPTER FOURTEEN

❖

"Come yew on, Mrs Durrant, do hurry yew up," Mrs Saunders grumbled as she jostled impatiently from foot to foot while waiting her turn at the checkout. She couldn't wait to get across to the butcher's shop and share the snippet of news that had the customers in the Village Stores all agog.

"I bet they won't be callen' on yourn services when this place is a supermarket." Patience was not Mrs Saunders' strongest virtue.

"Oh, surely not," dismay flitted across Bernice's face. "I'm sure Emma doesn't plan changes of that sort to the Stores."

"Yew weren't in 'ere when that chap said that be what a-gorn to 'appen," explained Mrs Peek.

"I 'spect that be what Emma's discussen' with him right now," said Mrs Saunders with a flick of the head towards the office.

"I wouldn't place too much credence on what a stranger says," Bernice advised.

"We'll see," said Mrs Saunders as she packed her bag, paid her money and hurried out of the door. She crossed the road to Billy Cooper's butcher's shop with a spring in her step. What news she had to share!

But the stranger had been there before her so robbed the dear lady of her anticipated moment of glory. As she listened to the ongoing chatter Mrs Saunders learned she had completely misunderstood his intent.

"He's planning to open a supermarket in competition to the Village Stores," explained Billy.

"Hopen' to put Emma out of business, I expect," mumbled Mr Bracewell.

"Thinks we'll be won over by building us a car park," laughed Pauline sarcastically.

"Thass the last thing we need a-spoilen' the village."

"You be right, we want less traffic not more."

"Where's he a-plannen' to build it all, then?"

"On the waste land opposite the Stores."

"Kezia's Wood?" asked Mr Bracewell thoughtfully.

"So he said," confirmed Billy.

Mr Bracewell shook his grizzled head, "Can't do that. It's entailed land."

"Oh?" Billy raised his eyebrows questioningly.

"What be that, Mr Bracewell?" asked Mrs Saunders. "I allus thought that be common land."

The old man pondered for a while. "I don't know all the ins and outs o' the matter, it was all way afore my time, but I recollect my Grandmother a-sayen' that land be all tied up with the Kemp family inheritance. Can't build on it."

Billy looked at him quite shocked. "Are you sure? I'm certain Alex and Emma aren't aware of that."

"Oh, yes, I be quite certain. I expect ole Capps-Walker's got all the paper work in his arffice."

Before the day was out rumours of all kinds were circulating around the community. When it reached Doctor John's ears he was astounded because only days before he had finalized the purchase of the land under discussion with Lord Edmund's estate manager and Adam Catton. As far as the Doctor was concerned the land was now his. He was looking forward to breaking the news to Stephen when he came home for the weekend.

"Can there be any truth in the rumours?" Trixie asked anxiously.

"I wouldn't have thought so. Adam did a thorough land search but I will contact him in the morning to see if anything could possibly have been overlooked."

However, as soon as the idle speculation reached Adam's ears he contacted his boss, Jocelyn Capps-Walker. Afterwards, he rang Doctor John.

"Doc, the Chief suggests you call a Parish Council meeting ASAP. If it could be this evening he will be there at 8pm. There could well be something significant that I totally missed because I was unaware that it existed. I'm so very sorry, Doc. Mr Capps-Walker has called in a junior to go up into the loft at the office where there are boxes of files kept from his grandfather's day. They are sifting through them as we speak."

"Not your fault, my boy, you investigated in your usual meticulous manner. I'll do my utmost to get a quorum together for this evening."

"Thanks, Doc. The Chief insists it is imperative that Lord Edmund is present at the meeting as he's the assumed vendor."

"Right, I'll see what I can do."

"The Chief's also learned from Heath and Black, fellow solicitors in the city, that representatives from a multi-national superstore have instructed them to act on their behalf in the purchase of the site. Believing it's all cut and dried, bar dotting the i's and t's,

I understand contact has also been made with Durrant's builders to undertake the necessary work, therefore Mr Capps-Walker advises that Roy Durrant also be at the meeting to speak for the company, as well as Graeme Castleton to represent the Kemp girls interests."

"This is serious, then?"

"Yes, sir."

"Not rumour?"

"It would seem not. As far as Mr Capps-Walker is aware no one else knows of your intent to purchase the site, Doc."

"I sense there is a need for urgency if we are to stave off a takeover by a national company."

"That is also my understanding, Doc."

"I'll get on to it immediately. Goodbye, Adam."

John turned to Trixie but before he could speak she said, "I heard it all. You had the speaker phone on."

"I'll get on with these arrangements."

"I think, dear, as any decision making is going to involve Alex and Emma they ought to be allowed to hear what is being said about this issue."

"I don't know what the PC ruling is on that score."

"I think if two thirds of the quorum is in agreement a non-member of the PC can be invited to attend if their being present has any bearing on the outcome."

"It would seem in this instance that is likely to be the case."

"Mention to Graeme, when you invite the girls, that I will go and babysit Bethany, if necessary. Their presence at the meeting seems to be far more crucial than mine."

Lights blazed in homes around the village till the early hours of the morning. The villagers were worried. They talked and talked about what they had heard earlier in the day and how it might affect them and future life in the village. Those not in attendance at the PC meeting sensed that there was something gravely amiss. Those actually present at the PC meeting were stunned to silence when Mr Capps-Walker read to them the contents of ancient documents that had been unearthed in his office attic.

They confirmed that the land did indeed belong to the heirs of Kezia Durrant, nee Bemment, whose mother had been a Kemp. The situation regarding any dwellings on it, if they were still standing, was uncertain as there had been insufficient time to search for and study relevant papers to authenticate such a suggestion.

"A family tree was appended to these documents about twenty years ago and if my reading of it is correct the majority of people living in the village today are descendents of Kezia Durrant or more specifically, Ada Durrant, her mother-in-law, through her marriage to Benjamin Durrant.

"Others in the village are related through Ada's first marriage to Ted Woodhouse. Thus, in a sense the land belongs to the whole village. It could become legally very technical. Tonight, you need to decide how you wish to proceed in order for us to draw up a document that is legally binding and which the lawyers of the superstore will not be able to overturn."

Doctor John was the first to break the silence that followed the lawyer's words. "Lord Edmund, it would seem that the superstore is unaware of the true ownership of this land and assumes, as I did, that it belongs to the de Vessey Estate."

"That is also my understanding of the situation Mr Capps-Walker has brought before us. I was unaware that parcel of land, known as Kezia's Wood, was the property of someone else. I would also like it putting on record that I have not been approached by anyone other than your good self, Doctor, with an offer to purchase the land."

"So the plan of the supermarket chain to engage Durrant's to carry out building works is somewhat precipitous and bumptious," Roy Durrant shook his head in disbelief.

"Quite!" quoth Mr Capps-Walker with legal authority.

For some time conversation buzzed across the room as opinions were expressed and ideas were presented following these revelations.

"Mr Capps-Walker may I ask you a question?" Emma ventured tentatively not knowing if she should by protocol go through the Chair.

"Yes, certainly."

"If the documents you have just read to us had remained unfound would the bill of sale between Lord Edmund and Doctor John been legally binding?"

"Yes," came the clipped reply.

"And the lawyers for the superstore could not have had it overturned?"

"No," he said brusquely.

"I understand Doctor John's plans for the site are for the benefit of the residents of the village so if the documents were to go permanently missing no one would be any the wiser and the locals would certainly not be the losers."

There were gasps from some of the people sat around the table at Emma's bold suggestion but more than a nod or two from other quarters in agreement with her proposal.

"But would that be ethical?" asked Doctor John.

"I would be very loathe to destroy these documents. They are legally binding as well as being a valuable record of the social history of this community," replied the lawyer in an irritated tone.

"I wasn't suggesting they were destroyed just that they go permanently missing and the parcel of land revert back to the de Vessey Estate," Emma responded defensively. She was beginning to feel hot under the collar and wished she had not voiced her opinion as the piercing legal eyes of Mr Capps-Walker held her gaze.

"Young lady, are you advocating the estate holds it in trust for the village?" he barked impatiently.

"Yes, something like that."

"Doc, can you clarify what you propose to do with the land?" interrupted Graeme, anxious to calm the heated exchange.

Doctor John carefully explained his vision for the parcel of land that had stood neglected for such a long time in so prominent a part of the village.

"That sounds a fascinating project, John."

"I can't be more specific at the moment. Our findings, when the scrubland is cleared, will determine what may be possible. I hope to find a vestige of the original buildings, upgrade them, provide a job for our son, and maybe others, a service for the local community and an attraction for visitors."

"I think, we would all agree, anything would be an improvement on the unsightly mess it has become but certainly not a supermarket or a car park."

"The havoc those huge delivery lorries create doesn't bear thinking about."

"We've narrow lanes and very few footpaths, a child's life could be in danger."

"I agree! I would consider donating the field we use for visitors parking on bank holidays as a permanent car park rather than give way to multi-national concerns."

"That's very generous of you, Lord Edmund."

"Not at all, it would enable us to retain control of vehicular access to the village."

The discussions continued until late into the night when Lord Edmund as chairman of the PC called a halt to proceedings. "We are all tired, have many commitments in the morning, can I suggest we bring our deliberations to a conclusion."

Mr Capps-Walker looked across to Adam, "Do we have sufficient material to work on?"

"Yes, sir, I do believe we have."

"We will trawl through the de Vessey Estate deed of settlement, and any other documents held in the archives, Lord Edmund, to ensure there are no legal loopholes. However, as they are written in such archaic script and language it will take some time, but it shall be done and the rights and objectives of the villagers will be upheld."

Nods of approval from around the table seconded his words.

"I think, too, it is of paramount importance that we locate a copy of the will which states how property has been left to descendents in order to ascertain to whom the land has actually been bequeathed."

After everyone had dispersed Mr Capps-Walker walked across The Green in company with Adam to where he had parked his car at the Catton home.

Together they discussed legal strategies and possible ways to surmount any difficulties. As he prepared to drive away he wound down his window. "Write down what is foremost in your mind at the moment, then sleep on it, and come back to it fresh in the morning. I'll do the same and we'll compare notes tomorrow when we meet in the office. Good night."

Adam was grateful that RK had agreed to a last minute arrangement to babysit the children and stay the night. It enabled him to focus on the legal document he was required to prepare without worrying about the needs of his family.

The buzz throughout the village the next morning centred on the possible closure of the Village Stores and the development of Kezia's Wood. More people than was usual strolled around the perimeter of Kezia's Wood. They looked at its tangled mass intently, finding it hard to visualize the area as a supermarket with a car park.

At one point Emma noticed the shop was so heaving with chattering customers it was impossible to get down the aisles. RK and Rachel found a niche by the delicatessen counter to air their views until the queue by the till had quietened down.

"Not much left in here today, is there?" Rachel said as she leant over the display cabinet to make a choice from the meagre selection remaining.

"I think most of the villagers will have heard about Emma's visitor and his scaremongering so turned out in force to show their support for the Village Stores."

Rachel nodded, "I'm sure no one wants to see this shop close. Emma and Alex have worked jolly hard to make it a viable concern in these hard economic times."

"You're right. Where else could you go to get this kind of personal service and choice of fresh produce at such reasonable prices?"

"I agree. A supermarket would be hard pushed to better the quality of freshly made products on sale here every day."

Rachel held up a fish pie. "Just look at this. One of Jilly's best. My children love it."

"From your Dad's catch?"

"No, he doesn't go out fishing so much now that Dave is down in Devon. I guess it's from Mark Bemment's last trip out and the vegetables will be from Jenner's market garden or the Beckingsdale's farm."

"Can't get fresher than that, can you?"

"And we know the provenance and carbon footprint of all the fresh food that's sold in this shop without scrutinizing a label."

The queue began to go down by the till but before the two young women moved on Rachel put a hand on RK's arm. "How are you, RK? I hear you had a bit of a scare the other night."

RK shrugged her shoulders, "It was rather unpleasant but I'll be OK."

"Sure? You're welcome at our house, anytime."

"That's really kind of you, Rachel, thanks. I didn't sleep at home last night because Adam was at the PC meeting. He anticipated it would go on until late so I stayed over at the Catton house with the children. I'm hoping I'll be fine tonight."

"Remember the offer's there should you need it."

RK nodded as she picked up a packet of Jilly's fish cakes for the children's tea and joined Rachel by the till.

"Hi, Mum, it's busy in here this morning. How's Emma coping with the rumours?" Christina was serving at the checkout and greeted her daughter cheerfully.

"It's good to be busy and Emma's taking the gossip in her stride. The chap who came in yesterday knocked her for six, at first, but she soon gave him short shrift. He couldn't accept she was the owner."

"Good for her. Thanks, Mum," Rachel said as Christina handed her change to her and turned to the next customer.

"Well, good morning RK and how are you? You must have had a right commotion at your cottage last night. Have you got someone in to fix your windows?"

RK stared at Christina blankly.

"Windows?" she asked when she found her voice.

"Yes, windows! I noticed all your windows were smashed when I came to work early this morning."

"Smashed?" RK said faintly.

"Mu...um!" Rachel shouted. "Have you called Sergeant Catchpole?"

"No...oo!"

"Then do so now, please." Rachel took hold of RK's arm. "Come on RK."

"But... she hasn't paid..."

"POLICE, Mum!"

"Right..." Christina's voice trailed off. She was astounded that Rachel should shout at her. Rachel never raised her voice to anyone. *Oh dear! It must be serious.*

When Rachel and RK reached Ferry Cottage they couldn't believe their eyes. Someone had wreaked havoc on the cottage. Large stones, obviously taken from the beach, had been hurled through all the windows.

"What a blessing you weren't here last night, RK. By the amount of rocks and pebbles on the floor someone wished you harm."

RK kicked angrily at the shingle path and pummelled a balled fist fiercely into the palm of her left hand. "Why? Why? Why?" She yelled.

Rachel reached up to put her arms around her friend's shaking shoulders. "Revenge for the other night, maybe? I guess someone's afraid you might recognize him. I'll stay with you till Tom comes."

"But what about Poppy and Rhoda? They're due out of pre-school and nursery soon."

"I'll ring the school." Rachel quickly retrieved her mobile phone from her pocket, pressed a button, and within seconds was connected to the school secretary. "Hello, Mrs Scholes, it's Rachel Durrant. There's been an incident at Ferry Cottage. I'm waiting with RK for the police. Could you keep Poppy and Rhoda at school till I'm free to pick them up? ... Right ... Oh, good ... That will be fine ... Thankyou."

"There, that's fixed. They're going to give the girls lunch and keep them at school till we're able to collect them."

The police, when they arrived, came in force. Inspector Capps took charge of the investigation, delegating his men to specific tasks. When SOCO had finally finished Ben oversaw the repairs to the cottage and Trixie Cooper organized a bevy of cleaners to restore the property back to RK's home. Rachel ensured RK had a bed for the nights she had to be away from Ferry Cottage and Tom Catchpole guaranteed a visual police presence in the vicinity to make certain her safety. For a short while the incident served to fuel again gossip concerning the nature of RK's presence in the village.

Three weeks later P.C. Dan Prettyman called at Ferry Cottage to drive RK to Norwich to participate in an identity process that had been set up.

On the way there she inquired, "Do you think the windows of Ferry Cottage were smashed by the same men who came into the garden?"

"Possibly," was Dan's noncommittal reply.

At the police station RK went through the photographs placed before her. For a few nerve racking moments she had to relive that awful night once again. Quite quickly she picked out Billy Knights as the nocturnal intruder and also identified him as the young man who had offered drugs to her in the Ship Inn on her first day in Newton Westerby. She also recognised another picture as one of his companions but was uncertain about the third in the group.

Afterwards everything seemed to return to normal.

"If there is such a state as normal," RK laughed as she walked through the village one morning with Rachel having dropped the children off at the school. Rachel thought it was high time gaiety returned to RK's demeanour and outlook. It was a joy to see sparkle in her eyes and wit in her conversation. They stood for a moment watching the workmen as they worked on Kezia's Wood.

No one knew who had commissioned the work because the PC had kept their deliberations under wraps pending the outcome of the legal findings but most of the residents were glad that the overgrown 'jungle' was being tackled by someone. They were curious to know what was going to happen to the site. The two strangers had created a sense of unease amongst the villagers. Their brief visit to the village had caused bitter wrangling between neighbours. Some were totally opposed to any modernization or construction work taking place in the village.

"We'll need to set up a protest committee."

"Before yew know it we'll 'ave double yeller lines on the ruds, traffic lights an' keep left signs all uvver the place."

"We'll lose our peace and tranquillity."

"As well as our quaintness and beauty."

"And there'll be accidents galore."

Others welcomed the prospect of a supermarket.

"More choice and everything under one roof."

"Could be cheaper, too"

"And a car park is essential, for visitors."

Ostensibly, the work was being carried out on behalf of the de Vessey Estate by Chit Beckingsdale with a team that had been at Easton Agricultural College with him but also included present day students such as Ryan Saunders and Nathan Jenner. However, behind the scenes much consultation was taking place between Lord Edmund and Doctor John, Stephen Cooper and the two Kemp sisters. Stephen could hardly contain his excitement when his father related to him what he had done with regard to the site. So that, whenever he was not at College he was working on the site driven by the expectancy of what might be hidden behind the undergrowth.

As soon as the extensive research and painstaking deciphering in the Capps-Walker office had been completed it had been agreed to uphold the original gift of deed held by Ada Durrant. A document had been unearthed which stated that, with some buildings attached, it had been given as a Deed of Gift to Annie

Kemp, mother of Ada, for services rendered to Lady Marion de Vessey. Annie's will left the property she owned to Ada. It was decided, therefore, that the de Vessey Estate would continue to hold it in trust for the villagers, as so many of them were her descendents.

The lawyers deemed the Kezia Kemp bequest to be something quite separate and referred to property not land. They advised waiting to see what was uncovered on the site. So, Doctor John's cheque was frozen pending the outcome of the methodical clearance of Kezia's Wood but he and Lord Edmund agreed to share the cost of the initial land clearance. When anything further was discovered negotiations would take place to resolve ownership. All the parties immediately involved agreed this appeared to be the most sensible way to proceed so, Adam and Mr Capps-Walker drew up a citation to this effect in order to protect the property and land from developers.

Strangely, nothing further was ever heard from the smooth talking stranger about the construction of a car park or a supermarket but he and his associate had cleverly engineered an atmosphere of discord and unpleasantness which persisted for some time amongst the villagers.

CHAPTER FIFTEEN

At the end of May residents and visitors turned out en masse to participate in the car treasure hunt organized by Jennifer Pedwardine; some out of curiosity and others because traditionally the event was usually a fun activity of which to be a part.

By ten o'clock the church hall was heaving with excited participants. RK, with Poppy in the buggy and Daniel and Kirsty eagerly jumping up and down, was among them. However, as instruction sheets were handed out, teams allocated numbers and departure times recorded, "What, no car!" was a frequent exclamation followed closely by the question, "How can it be a car treasure hunt, then?" Completely nonplussed Jennifer simply smiled and said firmly, "You'll see." Bemused, the contestants went on their way, shaking their heads. They found it to be totally different to the entertaining days, planned in previous years, by Adam and Laura.

Lord Edmund de Vessey usually ferried a car load of elderly residents from The Close around the course. Armed with copies of the day's itinerary their sharp eyes and minds enjoyed peering through the car windows searching for hidden village oddities, then, sitting back in their seats pondering over and solving the clues.

Knowing this, Jennifer Pedwardine planned the route with suitable adaptations to accommodate the less agile. For the majority the treasure hunt was on foot, in and around the village.

"Who hasn't got a TV in Ferry Lane?" was another frequently asked question.

"I thought everyone had a TV!" was the much repeated reply until someone spotted that the letters t and v were missing from the name plate of No 6 Ferry Lane, '*Cres of the wa e*'.

Both Sergeant Tom and P.C. Dan mingled unobtrusively amongst the competitors ensuring their safety and the free flow of visiting traffic to the village. The de Vessey Estate, as usual, provided a field for car parking to prevent potential mishaps along the narrow lanes between pedestrians and drivers unfamiliar with the awkwardness of their twists and turns. After this event work was commencing to turn the field into a proper car park as promised by Lord Edmund. Job applications were already coming in to the PC for the position of car park attendant during the busy summer months. It had already been agreed to issue access passes to villagers with vehicles.

"Charging us £5! Daylight robbery!"

"No, making certain they are not misused or the privilege abused," boomed Lord Edmund. "We simply haven't the room for hundreds of vehicles to traverse our lanes. The only exceptions will be emergency vehicles, the Mini-Hopper and the College bus. We'll make provision for visiting coaches on the car park."

"So we need to prove we live here in order to drive to our homes?"

"No, the pass shows you have an automatic right of access because you are a resident in the village."

"What about delivery vans?"

"No problem. The scheme is intended to prevent the flagrant snarling of our narrow lanes, that we experienced last summer, occurring again."

As the treasure hunters eagerly sought for answers to the clues Dan particularly kept a look out for Robyn Dickinson-Bond wanting to acquaint her with the progress that had been made with regard to her nocturnal intruders.

When he finally caught up with her he explained, "They have been apprehended and charged following the identity parade in which you participated."

"Oh!"

"So you shouldn't have any further problems with unwanted visitors."

"That's a relief."

"Further incidents came to light through undercover investigations by the drug squad in Norwich which also involved the trio."

"What about the silenced shopkeeper?"

"That matter is still under investigation."

"Don't let them give up on that, Dan. There are people in this village who would welcome closure on that incident, and soon," RK turned to leave.

"Come on, children, let's go and solve some more clues. See you later, Dan."

Dan was pleased to see RK back to her carefree self and deliberately withheld the fact that Billy Knights had given his city colleagues the slip. The drug squad were not unduly perturbed about this because they believed they could break down the two suspects already held in custody. When Billy's whereabouts became known and they picked up the threads again the police hoped to haul in even greater 'fish'. Meanwhile, surveillance of activity in and out of the Newton Westerby harbour would continue and a quiet eye would be kept on RK's safety.

As Dan moved on to mingle amongst the clue finding participants he remembered he had forgotten to inform Robyn that police investigations had exonerated Joe and Josh Cook from any involvement in the Kemp's accident at Christmas. This was because further evidence had come to light that pointed the enquiry in a totally different direction. *I'll fill her in on that info at some later date.*

The treasure hunt certainly proved to be a fun day with a difference but one full of laughter and merriment.

To the astonishment of the participants the clues finally led the problem solvers to the garden at Bakers, the former village bakery now the home of Miss Pedwardine. Most of the villagers had seen no further than the hedge and fence that abutted the lane so were eager to view beyond the boundary. Amazement was the reaction of them all as they stepped through the open garden gate, apart from Alex, who on her return to the garden simply revelled in the delight of others as they enjoyed the unexpected hidden beauty all around them.

"What a tremendous success today has been," RK commented warmly to Alex.

"I'm glad you've enjoyed it."

"This is a fantastic setting to meet at the end of what has been a fascinating trail around the village," RK commented as her eyes travelled around the garden vista and she gasped in appreciation at the luscious spectacle before her.

"It is lovely, isn't it? I was mesmerised the first time I walked through the gate."

"I'm sure it takes a lot of hard work to maintain this standard but I'll just be content to sit in this spot and enjoy the beauty of someone else's handiwork."

Alex murmured in agreement then asked, "Is Adam not with you?"

"No, he's gone to spend the day with Laura at the hospital, so the children and I have had great fun unravelling Jennifer's cryptic clues." RK pushed Poppy's buggy next to Bethany's while keeping a close eye on Daniel and Kirsten as they skipped to join Lily, Keir and Pansy in their exploration of the garden. The two toddlers slumbered side by side as the adults clustered together to discuss the achievements of the day.

"Yes, an excellent suggestion of yours Alex," Stephen Cooper quipped, as he assisted in the distribution of hot dogs and burgers from the barbeque, veggie as well as traditional.

"Not at all," replied Alex in her quiet unassuming manner. "All the credit is due to Miss Pedwardine's imaginative expertise."

"Splendid teamwork," congratulated Doctor John diplomatically, beaming at all around him, including Jilly Briggs and her youthful band of helpers as well as the village stalwarts surrounding Miss Pedwardine distributing coffees and teas.

"Well done, Jennifer," complimented Lord Edmund. "We'll have to co-opt you on to the PC, can't hide skills like yours under a bushel."

Embarrassed by the unexpected plaudits Jennifer simply replied, "What would happen to all of this if

I was tied to stuffy meetings?" Her arm swept out to encompass the horticultural mosaic in front of them all.

"My dear, we appreciate your willingness to open up this lovely space for us to enjoy, today, but I'm sure you still have much to offer our community. You may be retired but you haven't opted out of life, have you?"

Jennifer smiled at those around her. "Of course not but, even in retirement, I am kept very busy and I don't always have time to fit in everything I would like to do each day."

Undeterred, Lord Edmund persisted. "I'm sure you can spare the occasional hour once a month to contribute expertise from the vast wealth of knowledge you have acquired so that the current residents of our villages may benefit."

With pursed lips Miss Pedwardine had the final word, "We shall see."

However, the pleasure of the treasure hunt day soon receded into memory as the village prepared for the annual arrival of summer visitors who swarmed like flies to this idyllic unspoiled haven.

CHAPTER SIXTEEN

Despite the onslaught of summer visitors to the village the clearance of Kezia's Wood continued in earnest. Chit Beckingsdale had been instructed to handle the work under the watchful eye of Lord Edmund and Doctor John. With an army of willing volunteers from the village, as well as the team of students from Easton College on work experience, Chit painstakingly cleared the area metre by metre starting from the lane and working back towards the centre of the scrubland. His brief was to clear the rubbish but to make certain nothing of historic or horticultural value was lost. The operation became quite an attraction to locals as well as holidaymakers all keen to know what was going to emerge beyond the undergrowth. Bystanders congregated at some point on most days to give advice or ruminate about the wood's hidden secrets.

However, the throb of holidaymaker's hustle and bustle and the excitement generated by the wood clearing project seemed to pass the Catton family by. Their only involvement was Adam's input at the office into the provenance of the deed of ownership. Their horizons were occupied and coloured by preparations for Laura's homecoming. The upheaval in the house affected them all. Since her stroke nothing could shake Adam's belief that one day Laura would return home. Unsure how she would cope with the present facilities in their home a tremendous amount of dialogue and planning had taken place between Adam and Ben Durrant over many months in anticipation of that day. This was to ensure that not only were all of Laura's needs met, but the alterations catered for the needs of the whole Catton family, as well as retain the character of the 18th century property that had been in Adam's family for generations.

In the initial stage of the discussions Ben had been nominated by Lord Edmund to be spokesman for the Parochial Church Council discretionary fund and approach Adam on their behalf. "You'll do best, my boy," Lord Edmund boomed, clapping a hand firmly on Ben's shoulder, "you are an accomplished architect, have excellent communication skills and foremost, his best friend."

Since that directive, Ben had waited for an opportune time to chat over the proposed plans with Adam. It had come a few days later when, following their evening meal, he glanced through the window and saw RK leave the Catton house at the end of her working day looking after Adam's children.

"RK's on her way home, Rache, so I'm off to Adam's house," Ben called up the stairs.

"Will you be long?" Rachel was at that moment tidying the bathroom after Mark and Rhoda's evening bath. She had listened to their prayers, told them a story, and the children were now tucked up in bed almost asleep.

"About an hour, I expect, Sweetheart, depends how long it takes me to convince him of the PCC's proposal."

"Tread carefully, dear, Adam's a proud man."

So, Ben had left his house, stepped briskly across the lane and appeared on the Catton doorstep, armed with his laptop. Within minutes of Ben's arrival the two young men gravitated into the kitchen where Adam flicked on the kettle and made a pot of tea.

"Good of you to stop by, mate. Is there any news of Dave returning to the village?" He opened a cupboard as he spoke and drew out a couple of mugs from the shelf.

"No, he doesn't seem to have plans in that direction at the moment."

"Not heard anything of Jansy either." He placed a packet of biscuits on the tray. "I thought she might pop in to see Laura more often, with her being based at the hospital, but apart from the very first week of Laura's admittance we've hardly seen anything of her."

Adam carried the tray of tea from the kitchen and the two men relaxed in the sitting area of the family room. Ben felt the best way to approach the topic he'd been assigned was to plunge straight in.

"You have a lovely home, Adam, but how do you envisage using the space when Laura comes home?"

Surprised, Adam raised his eyebrows, "You in to reading thoughts now, Ben?"

Ben smiled and shook his head. "No, just wondered how you plan to cope with the inevitable changes."

"That very thing has been tossing about in my mind for the last few days until I don't know whether we'll be living upstairs and sleeping downstairs or vice versa, putting up walls or taking others down. It's a mighty headache, mate."

Ben placed a hand on his friend's arm. "Before you continue, Adam, as you see, I've brought along my laptop this evening. On it I have a computer program onto which we can put your ideas, juggle around with them and, maybe, come up with a workable solution."

After a thoughtful moment Adam stroked his chin then said dubiously, "Sounds a great idea but what about cost?"

"Let's look at what's required then see what's feasible."

"Right," Adam leaned forward to view the screen.

"Where do we start?"

"With what you've got."

"Measurements and such, you mean?"

"Yes, and facilities, for instance bath, shower and toilet. Then we'll consider obstacles such as steps or stairs, walls, doorway too narrow, opening the wrong way or even in the wrong place. We'll look at where to put a bed and whatever else Laura may need to be comfortable and mobile."

Adam nodded his understanding as Ben switched on his machine.

Ben had a blueprint of plans he believed would be ideal for this lovely old family home but he wanted his friend's input so that Adam would feel he was the one making the vital decisions for the necessary alterations to the house.

"I'll just take a few measurements so we'll have everything accurately to scale."

Thoughtfully, Adam watched as Ben walked around his home, measured walls, windows and doorways. After making notes he sat down and sipped his tea.

"All set?" Adam enquired.

Ben nodded, and prompted his friend to share ideas. He listened attentively to Adam's random observations and then, with the keyboard, built up 3D pictures on the screen with some of his suggestions.

"If we have Laura's bed downstairs, so she's part of family life, it would restrict either the sitting or dining areas or where the children play." Adam shrugged his shoulders and sighed, "It's not easy, is it? We've often spoken of having a conservatory but never got around to it. Now I wish we had."

Ben's nimble fingers danced across the keys. He swivelled the laptop to face Adam. "Something like this, you mean?"

Adam leaned forward. "Mmm, ye...s...s, but would there be room for a bed?"

Ben drew in a bed, to scale, as well as a cabinet. "And there's also sufficient space for a small table and a couple of chairs."

"Mmm! But where could we put in a shower room?"

"Aah, the all important necessity." Ben moved the cursor round again. "What do you think of this?"

Adam gazed intently at the screen. Lines appeared others disappeared as Ben drew the floor plan of the Catton home.

"Oh, you've put it alongside the kitchen wall jutting out on to the patio!"

"Yes."

"Won't it be a bit small?" Adam shuffled to the edge of his seat and looked again.

"You've moved the kitchen window and..."

"So the shower room will be longer."

Adam's finger traced the image as he peered more closely, "...and also the back door is in a different place."

"For easier access."

"I see, the kitchen wall has gone that divides it from the dining area and... there's a new one here, cutting it off from the sitting area."

"Kitchen diner?"

"Uhmm!"

Both men were quiet for a time then Adam got up from the sofa and paced the area where the proposed new wall would be built. He purposefully strode to open the French windows and, although dusk was rapidly enveloping all within its path, he stepped outside and looked intently at the lawn and patio that could become his wife's new living quarters.

Ben followed him out and counted, in steps, the measurements so Adam could get an idea of the eventual size of the room.

Ben quietly put spoken words to the layout of the plan, "Patio doors here into Laura's conservatory room, th..."

"But Laura loves these French windows."

"We could adapt them, but sliding means greater flexibility and consequently, more room."

"Right," Adam hesitantly replied.

"Not convinced?"

"No, I know how much Laura enjoyed pushing open those French doors, "to bring the fragrance and beauty of the garden into our living space," she frequently said."

"I'm sure it's not impossible to reach a compromise so that Laura doesn't lose what is important to her."

"That will be good, Ben." Adam walked thoughtfully towards the outside wall of the house. "The extension you plan is going to be quite a size, isn't it?"

"Yes, with an en suite shower, toilet and wash-basin, or in modern parlance a 'wet room', to the right adjoining the present kitchen wall. The conservatory can be separate allowing quiet and privacy, or having glass doors of some description, open and all-embracing into a family kitchen cum dining room, extending at the far end onto the back of the front door porch as the utility area of the kitchen. Dep..."

"Not sure you could do that."

"Why?"

"Old property, conservation and all that."

"I see. Is it listed?"

"Don't think so but I seem to remember when Dad had the internal alterations and modernization done for my Mother, there were restrictions on changing the external appearance."

"Could someone in your office check the legal situation for us?"

"I'll attend to that in the morning. The deeds are lodged there, too, should we need them to verify the situation."

"Good! Now, depending where you want to place the kitchen units the access door into the kitchen from the hall can be changed."

"I like the idea of a separate lounge but am not sure about the hallway."

"Why?"

"That wall jutting out looks odd."

"There could be a door at the end, like this."

"Mmm," Adam pensively stroked his chin. "I'd like to keep the toilet under the stairs for the children's use."

"If that's the case, we could take 6ft by 3ft off the lounge next to it, just so." Ben indicated the changes on the screen. "It could then be used as a storage area for shoes and school bags or hanging room for coats. The hallway wall could be shortened as long as it isn't a weight bearing wall."

"Aah! I see."

Ben showed the existing house plan in blue then superimposed Adam's suggestions in red over the top, along with some alterations of his own. Then illustrated each room in 3D with the ideas they had spoken of.

"Oh my!" Adam's finger hovered over the screen as Ben drew the modifications.

"There's a good space behind that proposed new wall that encloses the stairs, cloakroom and loo, isn't there?"

"Yes. So, what about developing it as the children's new play area with built in cupboards along the far wall for their toys and there would also be a slot for your computer desk under the window here?" This time Ben took Adam on a virtual tour of the proposed alterations to the house so that he could get a feel for the projected changes.

"Mmm, that's a possibility. Must keep the toilet for the children's use, though."

Adam clapped his arm along Ben's shoulders. "You've done wonders, ole boy, and given me much to think about."

Ben grinned. "I'll print this out when I get home so that you can mull the plans over and share the proposals with Laura."

"Thanks, mate."

"Nothing will be changed that doesn't meet with your approval. Upstairs will remain intact, too."

"That's good."

Ben saved the program, closed down his laptop and rose to go home. "I'll let you have this in the morning." He walked towards the front door. "See you, Adam. Thanks for the tea. Love to Laura."

"But we haven't discussed the cost."

Ben turned and smiled at his friend, then quietly said, "Philippians chapter 4 verse 19, Adam."

"But…"

"No buts!"

Before settling down for the night Adam looked up the Bible reference Ben had quoted as he left, "…my God will meet all your needs according to his glorious riches in Christ Jesus." Tears welled up in the eyes of the intensely resilient man.

Finances had become tight, since Laura's illness, but he hadn't said a word to anyone. He felt the wellbeing of the children was of paramount importance so willingly dipped into his savings to pay RK to care for them, but with Laura in hospital, they also had to manage without her salary. Daily trips to the hospital and parking fees were also proving quite an expense. Alterations to the house, on the scale that Ben proposed, were certainly beyond their means at the moment. With a heavy heart he bowed to rest his aching head into his hands. *Thankyou, Lord! I don't know how you're going to do it, just teach me to trust that you have it all in hand and know the answer.*

Adam's prolonged discussions with Ben had resulted in judicious renovations to the house with the proviso that further adaptations could be made as and when the need arose. When Adam had sought advice from Doctor John he, too, had suggested that hand rails and ramps might be required at some stage to aid Laura's recovery. "Decisions about where to place them might be best left until Laura's in situ."

The explanation Ben had given him of the PCC's community discretionary fund award, to help meet the cost of the house renovations, left Adam flabbergasted.

"I can't take that."

"You're not being asked to take it. It's being offered, with no strings attached, to meet Laura's needs to enable her to cope with living in this community, all you have to do is graciously accept it on her behalf."

"That is incredibly generous of the PCC."

"If, at any time in the future you are in a position to make a donation to the fund I'm sure it would be gladly received to enable this discreet helping hand scheme to continue in the village."

So, the Catton's beautiful home had been thoughtfully adapted by Ben Durrant and his workers at Durrant's Master Builders to accommodate Laura's disability, predominantly paid for by the special fund set up by Lord Edmund with Adam's full agreement.

"Lord Edmund's foresight and feeling for our village is tremendous. Look at the renovation and modernization he's instigated on the old estate cottages."

"Yes, but it's not just about bricks and mortar. He genuinely cares for the well-being of the people in our community. He believes everyone is entitled to, not only a decent home but also a reasonable life-style, and does his utmost to ensure each person has that opportunity."

"I'm so very grateful for his generosity to us. It will make such a difference to Laura and our family."

"He's always taken his responsibility to the villagers seriously…"

"Yes, I feel he still behaves like the feudal Lord of the Manor."

"…but since the tragic death of his son followed by the loss of his wife he's viewed us more like his extended family and passionately wants to show that he cares about us all."

"And I suppose the discretionary fund is one way he can do that."

"Yes, it is. When he sets his heart on a cause he fights for all he's worth until it is accomplished."

"I guess he put forward the cash for the discretionary fund in the first place."

"I'm sure you're right."

CHAPTER SEVENTEEN

It was towards the end of the summer that Laura was finally discharged. She had been in hospital for four and a half months and latterly spent nearly five weeks in the special rehabilitation stroke unit in preparation for her return home. Adam was overjoyed that at long last they could be reunited as a family. As Laura had begun to make progress he had taken Daniel and Kirsten separately over to the hospital to spend time with her. When she transferred to the stroke unit Laura had a private room so Adam took all three children to see her.

Daniel and Kirsten took it all in their stride chatting to Laura about the building work that was going on at home and describing the changes that were taking place. When they realised she couldn't always respond to them they simply gesticulated with their arms and got animated about activities they were involved in at Church and school while Laura nodded in all the right places and spoke words that were becoming easier for her to pronounce. Daniel or Kirsten readily jumped in to finish off words that proved too difficult to enunciate. But for Poppy it was a bewildering experience. The surroundings were unfamiliar and although her brother and sister called the lady in the bed 'Mummy' she didn't look or sound like her Mummy. So she clung to Adam.

"On the day Laura comes home, Adam," Dr John advised, "I think it might be less traumatic if the children were not in the house when the ambulance brings Laura home."

So, RK arranged to take Daniel, Kirsten and Poppy to Jenner's Mill for the afternoon where they could play with Lily, Pansy and Keir, see the animals and help to collect the eggs.

Trixie offered to prepare a meal for the family so that when Laura was settled, and RK and the children returned home, they could share a meal together. "They've watched the workmen making changes and they've known the building works were to enable Mummy to come and live at home, but it hasn't seemed real."

"Good idea, it's been hard for them to picture Laura in this new style home. She's been in hospital for such a long time. This way, they'll see her in place, in her room when they walk into the house."

However, whilst Adam and the children were thrilled to have Laura home it took some while for them to adjust to an inactive and inarticulate mother. Laura, too, at times struggled with the changes to her status within her own home and wavered over the smallest of issues. Adam was worried by the lack of confidence in his wife and endeavoured to encourage her in the slightest achievement in order to boost her self-assurance and regain her poise.

RK appeared to be a permanent fixture in the house and the village looking after the Catton children and supporting Laura in her rehabilitation. Her daily presence in their home helped them all to cope with the changes more smoothly. Although she enjoyed her work, at the end of each day, she looked forward to making her way to the retreat on the beach. She was unreservedly content with life in Ferry Cottage having put the unpleasant experiences behind her.

Most of the children in Newton Westerby found her a fun person to be with and usually gravitated towards the little group when they were out at the play-park, on the beach, taking walks down by the quay or exploring the heath, so that frequently RK had an entourage following her like the Pied Piper of Hamlyn. She took Daniel and Kirsten to all their activities, and to Church, but saw no need for a personal commitment herself. She was amazed at Adam and Laura's firm faith in view of their circumstances and the poor prognosis regarding Laura's ill-health.

"I really don't know how you can continue to believe in God," RK said to Laura on a day that had been particularly trying. With great effort Laura reached out her hand and touched RK's arm and smiled, "Y-you w-will."

RK shook her head, "Never!" In the silence that followed RK recalled her father's words, "Religion's a crutch for people with no back bone. Show your mettle, work hard and you'll succeed." *But Adam and Laura's approach to God and religion is quite different. He's someone real to them and part of their daily life. They don't treat Him like a crutch, more like a dependable friend; speaking as though He was actually sitting in the room with them.* Quite often Laura's words came back to her and RK puzzled over who was right, her father or her new friends.

As time passed a disciplined routine was established. Laura went regularly to physiotherapy at the hospital and Adam worked patiently with her at home when he got back from work each evening. They were both determined she would succeed.

Roger Cooper's return to the village was a joy to Emma but also proved a blessing to many of the Newton Westerby residents and the Catton family in particular. As the junior partner of his father's practice he became Laura's GP and he was a great encouragement to them both. RK found, too, that Doctor Roger, as the villagers began to call him, (apart from his brother Stephen and his cohorts who dubbed him, Rog the Doc) not only had a listening ear but came out to visit when he was needed and was only a phone call away with advice when she required it for Laura or the children.

The older young people and young marrieds also enjoyed RK's quirky sense of humour and most delighted in her company particularly Dan Prettyman, though he continued to guard his heart. He frequently extended invitations to barbeque evenings, youth fellowship activities and house group Bible studies. She didn't readily accept the invites but on the occasions she had gone along RK was amazed at the warmth proffered to her and the pleasant manner in which the evening passed. No one preached at her, condemned her for not attending church or criticized her decision to have nothing to do with Christianity. Instead, she found that with good grace they listened to her views and encouraged her to enter into the lively debates and discussions with animated confidence.

Annette Andaman, the Cooper sisters and Emma Kemp also requested her presence at girlie evenings in their homes and RK was quick to reciprocate their friendship, pleased to entertain them to supper evenings at Ferry Cottage. These occasions were such a joy for RK. With no inhibitions set by her parents she felt free to do as she chose. Through the daily school runs she also built up a firm friendship with Rachel Durrant and was frequently invited to share mealtimes in their home. As time passed she quickly got over the unease that had been caused by the unwelcome night-time intruders and thoroughly enjoyed living in a haven so close to the sea.

The setting of the cottage was a magnet to the young folk although the unkempt garden was getting more of a wilderness as each day passed.

"It's not easy to fit in gardening," RK confided to Emma one day when she was in the village shop, "and if I'm really honest, not really my scene, despite being a farmer's daughter."

Before evening, that news had winged its way around the village. When the lads heard RK's dilemma they said, "Let's have a party!" So Stephen Cooper and Nicky Andaman organized a knife and fork party with a difference. All the guests were instructed to bring not only cutlery knife and fork but "a gardening fork, spade, hoe or trowel and a seat are essential."

Emma donated gardening sacks for weeds and fruit gateaux for sweet, Billy Cooper gave the girls sausages and burgers, while Pauline tucked in a parcel of veggie varieties for the staunch vegetarians, Hilary, Annette and Stephen. Uncle Roy and Aunt Bernice sent along a selection of easily tended perennial plants with Justin and Jilly Briggs baked a large batch of rolls and baps.

On the morning of the party a box appeared on the step outside Ferry Cottage packed to the brim with home grown salad. A large piece of white card was lodged between the lettuce and a bag of tomatoes on which was written, 'ENJOY!'

"I wonder where this has come from."

"At a guess, I'd say Jenny Ped."

"Miss Pedwardine?"

"Yes."

"How can you tell? Do you recognize her produce?"

"No, just the cryptic note is very much her style."

"Really?"

A week before the planned event at Ferry Cottage Tessa Jenner had taken along a pair of her goats to clear as much of the overgrown grass in the garden as possible. She tethered them to curb their natural instincts to jump over the boundary wall and Nathan popped in each day to milk and feed them and re-position the tether stakes.

Then, having thoroughly completed their task the goats were transported back to Jenner's Mill but to the clean-up party Nathan brought a mower so that he and Ryan could tidy up the remaining grass. They painstakingly edged it to make a neat looking lawn while others dug over and weeded the surrounding borders in readiness for the donated plants. Quite a number of young people had gravitated to Ferry Cottage armed with all manner of implements to assist in the tidy-up and each task was accompanied by a great deal of leg-pulling, laughter and hilarity.

Half-way through the proceedings Stephen, self-appointed chef at the barbeque to ensure veggie and meat remained separate, yelled, "Food's ready!"

There was a race to the kitchen sink to wash before eating and grab a chair to position in a semi-circle close to the barbeque.

"Justin, will you give thanks?"

Conversation stopped.

Justin glanced at RK, not wishing to cause her offence, and the other guests held their breath. Slowly RK nodded her assent.

"Father God, thankyou for the bounty of Your hand, the beauty of nature, the richness of friendship and the provision of food. Bless this home and our hostess as together we participate in this special time. In Your name, Amen."

"Thanks, RK, for letting us share this wonderful oasis, bless you," said Annette as she leaned across and placed her hand on RK's shoulder.

"Yes, you've created a delightful space that's great for meeting together." Raucous laughter greeted Miranda's words as the friends gathered round the barbeque to get their food.

The unintentional joke was not lost on RK who chuckled as she reached to take the hot dog Stephen passed to her. "You're the ones who've done the work and I'm so grateful. The garden looks superb."

"You are fortunate, RK, to have such a fantastic spot. It's both restful and refreshing." Murmurs of agreement rippled round the munching group of friends enjoying their food and each other's company.

"What a view! I'll join you any time, RK, breakfast or supper, to feast my eyes on this incredible scene."

"Yeah, it's amazing, thanks to our Creator God."

Following that evening RK gave more thought to what made her new friends tick. *They are lovely people, kind, and thoughtful, generous, fun and yet there is something else about them that I can't put my finger on. Maybe it is something to do with this God thing.*

CHAPTER EIGHTEEN

As the autumn unfurled its kaleidoscope of rich burnt amber colour the village prepared to celebrate the marriage of Roger Cooper and Emma Kemp. Swept along by the euphoria of the occasion RK got involved with a number of festive arrangements. The couple planned a simple Church ceremony with an unpretentious family get-together afterwards but a number of the villagers had different ideas. "Nothing outlandish but something worthy of Emma and her Doc," was the consensus of opinion amongst many villagers.

Jilly Briggs was organising a reception for family and close friends in the church hall following the lunch time ceremony conducted by Rev Hugh in Saint Andrews Church. By arrangement with the College, Jilly co-opted fellow students of Rosie Jenner to practise their skills waiting at tables, dressed in formal attire, as well as the mundane task of clearing tables and washing up. "It will be good work experience for them," she persuaded the College authorities.

"The women in the WI and Women's Guild who are part of the flower arranging team would love to decorate the Church for you, Emma," offered Penny Darnell, "and also make posies for table centres in the church hall."

Lord Edmund offered the family coach which was stored in a disused barn. "Have no need for it now so it requires a thoroughly good clean." Trixie organized a willing team of workers to wash and polish the lovely old carriage and her sister Maisie made new upholstery to replace that which the mice had nibbled through.

"Ryan's a dab hand with mechanical things, as is RK. I'm sure they'll check over the wheels and suspension to ensure all is in safe working order."

"No horses now, I'm afraid, but I'm sure the Beckingsdales at Hall Farm in Newton Lokesby will oblige," Lord Edmund propounded.

In the evening of the wedding day the young folk of the village planned to hold a hog roast in honour of the newlyweds masterminded by Roger's brother, Stephen, but very much aided and abetted by his uncle, Billy Cooper, who was providing the hog and supervising the cooking of it. A number of people in the community owned plastic or canvas gazebos which they were invited to erect on the Village Green and everyone with garden tables and chairs was requested to make them available. All the residents of the village were invited to share this special occasion with Emma and Roger. "Just don't breathe a word to the couple."

Justin and Adam were arranging a musical interlude for the enjoyment of the young couple and all who had the inclination to gather on The Green to wish them well. Aunt Bernice had a foot in both camps, having an ear for Emma's nuptial aspirations when Emma came to call, and she was also au fait with the young folk's plans, via meal time discussions with Justin. She and Roy carefully kept abreast of all the arrangements to ensure there was no clash or compromise of interests.

Amidst the excitement of all this happy preparation a very subdued Jansy returned to the village to attend her brother's wedding as bridesmaid to her long time school friend. Emma did her best to draw her friend out as they chatted about arrangements for the ceremony while Jansy was having a final fitting for her dress at her Aunt's in Newton Lokesby but Jansy slickly eluded any reference to her personal affairs, Dave or the past and adroitly turned the conversation back to Emma's marriage to her brother.

"Which salon are you booked into?"

"I'm not. Rachel's offered to do our hair on the morning of the wedding."

"That will be nice. What time?"

"About 10am."

"In your flat?"

"Oh, no, I'm getting ready at Green Pastures. Aunt Bernice has cleared a room just for our use and is storing my dress and yours, when it's complete, as well as the one Alex will be wearing."

"Not leaving from Alex and Graeme's, then?"

"No, Aunt Bernice and Uncle Roy have been so supportive since Mum and Dad's accident, with the business as well as personal things, that when they offered their home for our special day I felt it would be a way of thanking them by giving Aunt Bernice opportunity to participate in the planning of a wedding. She hasn't got a daughter and she won't be quite so involved should Justin one day get married."

"Jansy, please stand still," admonished the dressmaker as her niece fidgeted around.

"Sorry, Aunt Maisie."

"You will be, my girl, if I catch you with one of these," warned Maisie nimbly juggling a handful of pins as she deftly turned the hem of the bridesmaid's dress.

"When is your brother Drew travelling down from Edinburgh for the wedding?"

"He and Morag have decided not to come to the wedding."

"Why's that?"

"'Drew still carries a lot of angst against Roger for marrying me for what he terms my inheritance."

"That's seems a little churlish, I must say, and a rather childish reason for spoiling your special day," blurted Jansy and she stamped her foot to emphasize her displeasure at Drew's actions.

"Concentrate, girl, turn slowly."

"Yes, Aunt," said Jansy sheepishly and rolled her eyes upward as she grinned impishly at Emma.

"Oh, that's not all he's grieved about. Drew continues to wrangle about the legal aspect of Mum and Dad's will with regard to the Stores and what Drew feels is his right to a third of the weekly income from the Stores but that's all in the hands of the solicitor, thanks to Uncle Roy, who continues to handle that aspect of things for us."

"I didn't realise you were still having aggro about all that nonsense Drew brought up when your parents first died."

"Unfortunately, it's still ongoing but Mr Capps-Walker is dealing with it all so Alex and I don't concern ourselves with it other than pray that Drew will again find peace of heart. I'm just very sad that Drew has become so embittered. It's unpleasant having animosity between us for no apparent reason."

As she watched the dressmaker at work Emma recalled the last conversation she had with her brother Drew over the telephone regarding the sale of the Village Stores. It brought back unpleasant memories of the smooth talking stranger. His visit had obviously been instigated by Drew.

'I've received an excellent offer for the shop, flat, bungalow and cottage, Em. Now that you're getting married, and working at the school, you won't have time to run a shop. I guess you'll be glad to be relieved of the responsibility of the Stores and all that entails. The buyer is coming on Tuesday 17th at 11am to view so make sure you're available to show him round.'

Drew slammed the phone down as Emma gasped in shock, 'We are not for sale.' With shaking knees she staggered out of the office to find Rosalie.

'Can you hold the fort?'

Concerned by Emma's pasty face and distressed demeanour Rosalie came around the counter and whispered away from the ears of the customers who were milling in the aisles, 'Are you OK?'

Emma nodded, 'I must go and see Uncle Roy.'

He, bless his heart, had immediately put the matter into the hands of their solicitor, Mr Jocelyn Capps-Walker, prayed, given Emma a hug and assured her that in time all would be well.

"I can't believe your brother's refused to attend your wedding." Emma's mind had been miles away and was brought back to the present with a start when Jansy spoke. She quickly recovered her poise and replied,

"Well, I assure you it's true. Drew has no wish to be part of my wedding plans. He simply wanted to snatch all my dreams away from me in one fell swoop and didn't even wish me happiness for my wedding day," Emma sighed sorrowfully.

"Jansy! Do you want to get pricked?" She had begun to vigorously shake her head at Emma's words.

"Ooh, no!"

"Then sta…"

"I know, stand still."

"Well, do it, girl!"

Emma laughed. "You never could be still for more than two minutes together even when you were a girl you were always on the move."

"So, who's going to give you away, Graeme?"

"No, we decided to ask Uncle Roy. Since the accident he's been such an encouragement to both Alex and me. Early on he assumed the father figure role and continues to look after our best interests. We shall be forever in his debt. Roger and I felt this was one way in which we could acknowledge all his kindness to us and one that he would not refuse."

"So where will you live? Are you moving away?" Jansy asked.

"Oh no, for the time being we're going to live in the little flat over the Stores."

"I always imagined you'd venture to foreign climes."

"We're quite content to stay at home where we're needed."

"There now, girl, that's it. Walk slowly across the room for me, please, Jansy," Maisie cast a critical eye over her handiwork as Jansy moved in accordance with her instructions.

"That'll do, you can get changed."

"Thankyou."

Within a short space of time the two friends were on their way back to Newton Westerby.

"What about work?"

Emma turned to look at her friend in surprise.

"I shall continue to run the Stores and teach part time at the village school, just as I do now and Roger will be involved in the practice with your Dad."

"So, no plans to explore the great unknown?"

"Hardly, we're both really happy to put down roots here. We have got plans to expand, though."

"Really, what are they?"

"Well, we intend to move into the cottage that was once Alex and Graeme's as soon as the renovation and redecoration is complete. I shall finally have my coveted studio and Roger will have a study." Emma smiled at Jansy with excited contentment.

"Life will be a bed of roses for you, then" commented Jansy wistfully.

"Jans, I believe we shall be blissfully happy because we both feel this is the will of God for us at this moment in time but there's a lot of hard work ahead of us."

"Why's that?"

"We've almost completed the conversion of the main area of my flat into a coffee shop and tea rooms. We think it's an amenity the village has needed for a long time."

"Gosh, that's an ambitious undertaking, however will you cope?"

"Well, we have superb staff covering the Stores led by Rosalie, and Jilly and her team is top notch in the catering department, even Mum would approve. We're also involved in the apprenticeship training scheme being run from Lowestoft College; Rosie Jenner is taking the catering/cooking diploma and young Maxine Cook is due to commence the shop management course. Once they've completed their studies I've promised them a permanent position. There are also other students who will require work experience and practise in these areas in forthcoming terms."

"So the future looks assured?"

"As well as it can be, with the SOS campaign and possible PO closure constantly hanging over our heads. Melvin Andaman has been a tremendous help. He's taken to the office side of postal work far better than I anticipated. I think both he, and Rosalie, are relieved he doesn't have to get up at 3am anymore to go to the sorting office and then prepare and do postal deliveries."

"I'm surprised you've got Maxine Cook working in the Stores, considering what her Dad and Josh got up to. I'm sure her presence in the shop doesn't go down well with some of the community particularly as the Cook's actions have left you in this predicament."

"Predicament?"

"Yes, thrusting on you the responsibility of the Stores, unable to fulfil your dreams, because they tampered with your Dad's car causing your parents' deaths."

"No, that's not so," said Emma quietly. "Surely you heard that though Joe and Josh were charged and convicted of the burglaries and assaults nothing was proved against them with regard to the cause of the accident. Case dismissed was the verdict given with regard to Joe's possible involvement. As far as Josh was concerned, his finger prints were all over the car but so were many others that were unaccounted for, so it was inconclusive."

"But…"

Jansy stopped speaking as Emma shook her head.

"I was in court and witnessed Joe interrupt proceedings. He addressed the bench and said, 'Mr Judge, Oi admit to stealen' from Lord Edmund an' …' he went on to list a whole lot of burglaries, assaults and misdemeanours he'd organized. 'Oi admit to helpen' stitch up Nicky an' clobberen' Mrs Vicar but Oi hen't killed no one. Mr Kemp's a good sort, he's helped me out plenty an' Mrs Kemp's bin good to my Michelle with food an' things so's Oi hen't got no reason to kill them. Oi's a-bin a fewell, an' Oi'm sorry.' "

"That doesn't mean a thing."

"I tend to believe him. Why would he lie? He'd got nothing to lose and, for all he's been a scoundrel since he lost his job at Sizewell, I think his inherent honesty came to the fore at the trial."

"My word, Emma, you've changed. Where's your cynical zip? You've become somewhat trusting and forgiving."

"That's what the Christian life is all about."

"Now you sound just like your Dad."

Emma smiled to herself as Jansy bid her farewell. *What a compliment; to be compared to Dad. Thankyou, Lord, for Your work of grace. And thankyou, too, that I am fulfilling my dreams in a way I could never have imagined. I'm marrying the most wonderful man who loves me unreservedly. I am teaching children at school in my own village and I have the opportunity to indulge my artistic flair when I dress the shop windows just as I please and to cap it all I am carrying on the family tradition of running the Village Stores.*

When her friend had gone Emma reflected that not once had the conversation included any aspect of Jansy's life, it had all centred on her and Roger, their marriage and future together. Even when Aunt Maisie had mentioned that she still had Jansy's wedding dress cluttering up hanging-space and it was about time she made use of it, did Jansy refer to Dave or the past.

In fact, seldom did anyone else in the village refer to Dave Ransome. He was still away from the village, fishing off the coast out of Brixham. Although his trips home had been very scarce over the last few months he faithfully kept in touch with his sister, Rachel and her husband, Ben.

"He's heard nothing at all from Jansy," Rachel confided to Emma, "and it appears on the surface that all ties between them are severed but when I last spoke with Dave he said 'I can't forget her, my heart still beats fast at every remembrance of her.' "

Dear Father God, I pray for my two friends who were once so close to You, and one another.

CHAPTER NINETEEN

The morning of the wedding dawned through an autumnal haze. The chilliness of the air did not deter Emma from putting on her thick fleece and slipping out of the back door into the garden of Green Pastures. Retracing the steps of six months earlier, which she had taken with Roger following her graduation, Emma recalled with clarity the moment when, at the end of her graduation day, he so romantically proposed to her.

On reaching the river she stood in quiet contemplation at the water's edge and savoured, with gratitude, all that had taken place in her life since the start of the year. She recalled the tragedy that had taken the lives of both her parents and turned her own life up-side-down. *How Mum would have revelled in the preparations for this day and Dad would have spruced himself up to look important as the proud Father of the bride. 'I'll even close the Stores for you m'girl' she could almost hear him tease.* Tears spilled unbidden down her cheeks. She looked out across the water but saw nothing but the dearly loved faces of those precious people in the picture of her mind. Time seemed to hang suspended till other images nudged her memory and flickered into the frame.

The struggle of balancing study with the day to day running of the Village Stores; the supportive staff, Rosalie and Jilly who willingly went the extra mile; the decisions and new initiatives that overnight became her responsibility; the compassion and loyalty of friends and family, Alex and Graeme, Aunt Bernice and Uncle Roy and so, so, many more; the aggro with Drew and Morag; the anxiety created by obnoxious strangers and a possible takeover; the clearance of Kezia's Wood and the astonishing finds that were being unearthed, all tumbled into view, vying for her attention.

Then she remembered Roger; remembered how he had stood in this spot and held her hand and vowed, '*I love you now, my dearest Emma, and I will love you for always.*' He had then lovingly embraced her and sealed his declaration with a tender kiss. Never would she forget his next words. '*You are very desirable, my luscious Carrots, but that loveliness is not mine to share until our wedding day.*'

Now, today was The Day. Her heart sang. Briskly she returned along the pathway, in order to commence her preparations for celebrating the day, to be greeted on the doorstep by Aunt Bernice with arms opened wide.

"Dearest Aunt Bernice what would I do without you?" Emma said as she accepted the warm, motherly embrace offered to her.

Bernice kissed her niece's head as she held her close. "My dear girl, God gives us each other for times such as these."

Emma sniffled as tears threatened to tumble down her cheeks as emotions rose to the surface.

"I can't tell you how glad I am that He gave me you and Uncle Roy, you've been my rock during the last few months," she whispered hoarsely.

Bernice hugged her tightly. "That's what family is for."

However, for Jansy, the day of the wedding was a strain. She had made no contact with Dave during their estrangement but seeing the radiant happiness of her brother and her friend, as they pledged vows to one another to last a life-time, confirmed in her heart what she had blatantly thrown away. Keeping up the pretence, that all was well, proved very difficult.

Unknowingly, over the last few months, Jansy had become unwittingly entangled with an unscrupulous young House Doctor, who along with a colleague, abused Jansy's trust and undermined her professional integrity. However, it was quite some time before Jansy became aware of any misconduct.

She had reached the pinnacle to which she aspired and attained her Sister's post on the paediatric ward. Always meticulous in her paperwork she picked up on discrepancies in the drug records that she couldn't account for so, reported her findings to the management. The furore that followed was messy. When Jansy learned that the culprits were Doctors Stead and Hollis she was mortified. She was annoyed that someone she trusted had so treacherously planned to dupe and deceive her.

Although she was not directly implicated the incident still tainted Jansy and her position. *I've been such a fool. Whatever will Dad say about my stupidity?* She was so ashamed and hoped that her parents would not hear of her predicament, at least, until it was all sorted out. She certainly didn't want anything to leak out at the wedding.

Seated at the top table enabled her to remain aloof from inquisitive friends and relatives. However, the interval between the Wedding Breakfast and the informal celebration on The Green in the evening was proving a problem till Stephen came up to her and said, "Jans, would you like to see the progress we've made in Kezia's Wood?"

"I'd love to see what you've been up to. Let me just pick up my stole I think it may be a little chilly outside."

"You look good, Sis. That colour suits you."

"Thanks, Bro, you don't look so bad yourself in a suit and that tuxedo is simply fab," she complimented, knowing the difficult task Emma and Roger had had to persuade Stephen to wear such formal attire.

As they walked arm in arm away from the church hall Jansy quietly commented, "I understand, amongst other things, you've taken up prison visiting, Bro."

Stephen shrugged his shoulders nonchalantly. "Not really, just helping out a mate."

"I've heard there's more to it than that. It seems Josh has turned over a new leaf since you started to visit him regularly," Jansy persisted.

Stephen shunned the plaudits directed at him over the change in Josh's behaviour so didn't willingly respond to his sister's inquisitiveness about his involvement with Josh's rehabilitation so muttered, "I simply suggested he channel his skills in more positive ways and get involved in the learning programme on offer at the institute and he took me up on the challenge."

"That's great, Bro'," she congratulated.

"Oh, shush, Jans, it's nothing."

"OK, OK, so you don't want to talk about Josh but what can you tell me about your other venture?"

The change in Stephen was palpable. As they continued walking down the lane to the site he chatted animatedly about the project their father had instigated. "For a depth of about twenty metres, the right hand side of the site has been cleared, along Main Street down to what appears to be a cobbled lane. All intact, lovely old, original cobblestones, probably straight off the beach. It's taking longer than was first planned because it's unknown territory and both Dad and Lord Edmund are anxious that nothing gets destroyed needlessly. The College boys had to stop coming because of exams but there's been stacks of support from the village.

"They've discovered important trees and shrubs and also a rare orchid. I think that's why Dad insisted on Chit supervising, because he's knowledgeable about arboretal things, rather than have builders simply bulldozing their way through.

"Two weeks ago we found a wall. Turned out to be an outhouse and then to his horror Ryan stumbled into an earth closet as he was pulling at some brambles. He was even less enamoured when an irate mother rat scurried out underneath his twisted legs. The door had fallen off its hinges and bracken and brambles had shrouded it for years but it's good solid wood so I hope eventually to do something with it."

"It all sounds really good," said Jansy when she could get a word in.

They sauntered passed the shrubs and trees on their left hand side. "It's amazing how big the area is," said Stephen gesticulating with his arms the width and breadth of the site.

"Well, here we are," he indicated a clearing between the woods and a thatched property to the right.

"A cobbled lane here, too?" Jansy nodded towards a pebbled pathway emerging from the undergrowth to the right of the cleared area.

"Yes, isn't it exciting? We're not sure if this is on our land or…"

"Our land? Whatever do you mean?"

"Well, Dad had this idea to buy the land for my 21st Birthday with a view to me developing whatever was found into a woodwork studio and a storage place for all my books but Adam discovered that the land actually belongs to the descendents of Annie Kemp, which, in effect, is most of the village so Dad couldn't purchase it. However, the property at the end of the row seems to have been deeded to Alex and Emma's Great, Great Grandmother, so pro tem I have a temporary lease until the legal boffins sort out all the official jargon."

"What an exciting project!"

"It is and new things are emerging every day. As I said earlier we're unsure whether the cobbled lane is on this property or belongs to the cottage next door or may even be a public roadway because it's been hidden for years. But can't you imagine a cart and horse plodding down here?"

"You're right, it seems very atmospheric, almost as though we've been transported back a 100 years or more in time."

"I'm glad you can sense that, too. I sometimes feel I'm the only one who feels the history of this place so many just want to see the area cleared. Adam has also unearthed an ancient map of the village which suggests a row of properties on this site. We think, maybe, built from east to west."

"That is exciting. I've love to see that."

"It's being treated like gold dust at the moment. He found it in Mr Capps-Walker's grandfather's old files that had gathered dust in the attic in his office building in Norwich."

"What an astonishing find."

"I won't suggest you walk on the soil in case you spoil your wedding shoes but if you can manage the cobbles I'd like to show you our latest find." Excitedly Stephen tucked his sister's arm through his and supported her on the uneven surface. Slowly they made their way along the bumpy pathway till they reached a spot where a large cobbled area stretched out to the left like a courtyard before a single story building. It didn't appear to have doors or windows, had many bricks missing from the walls but presented as a wide, open space that stretched a long way back to another wall under roofless rafters.

Jansy raised her eyebrows. "I see you're opting for healthy outdoor living," she teased.

Stephen grinned. "No, I'm still kipping down at the UEA midweek and lodging with Mum and Dad at weekends."

Eagerly he pulled his sister forward then, knelt down on one knee spread out his arms before the derelict building and said dramatically, "Behold, my carpentry showroom!" He turned back to look at Jansy and said sheepishly, "Well, at least my woodwork shop in embryonic form."

"You are such a joker, Stephen, but dream on."

"You've got no imagination, Jans."

"No need, you've got enough for both of us."

Stephen got up and enthusiastically pulled her nearer to the building. "Look closer, what can you see?"

Jansy stepped forward but Stephen grabbed her arm protectively, "Not too close, we've had to erect an electric fence to protect the property from looters."

"Looters?" she exclaimed.

"Yes, looters! What do you think this is?"

Jansy shook her head, "I've absolutely no idea."

"A blacksmiths."

"Really?"

"Yes, look there's the chimney and place for the fire and anvil. This courtyard is where they brought the horses to be shoed by the farrier. We found all the implements and tools that would have been used in a smithy. I got Jilly Briggs brother-in-law, Rob Hawksworth, to come and photograph everything in situ as soon as articles were found, thankfully, because the following night we found a couple of fellows with a van trying to take everything away, hence the reason for the electric fence. As soon as Lord Edmund heard about it he offered us a disused stable in which to store all the finds. Someone from the Museum service came to identify, date and value them. They wanted to take them away but the PC objected most vociferously. So, they're under lock and key up at the Manor until the project is complete and it is decided how best to display them."

"Display them?"

"Yes, they're a valuable part of the history of our village. There's still a lot of practical work to be done as you can see but also an awful lot of research about this parcel of land we are rediscovering. The more I think about it the more I would like to display the history of our village in a living museum."

"Stephen, that's quite an undertaking."

"I know and I can't do anything about it until we have unearthed all the secrets this tangled jungle holds."

CHAPTER TWENTY

By the following spring Laura Catton had made tremendous progress in her walking and talking but her right side was still proving difficult to respond. Daily, Adam patiently, yet persistently, took her through her exercises to increase her arm and leg movement and improve her coordination.

"Come on, Sweetheart, one more time. That's good," he lovingly encouraged.

Laura grimaced. At times she became exasperated with his doggedness but when they assessed how far she had come in the last year they shared tears of joy and thankfulness. Her speech too, was improving and Laura felt relief because she was able to make herself understood after months of frustration.

Together, they gave thanks to God for the encouraging signs of recovery. Laura looked up at Adam affectionately and put out her left hand to touch his face. "I-l-lo-love you. Th-th-thankyou for b- be-being so d-de-t-termined and m-ma-making me p-p-persevere. I-th-think on my own I w-w-would have g-gi-given up l-l-long ago."

"Not you," Adam held her flaccid right hand between his hands and gently massaged it, then tenderly lifted it to his lips. "I w-w-would, you know!" She grinned lopsidedly.

One day Ben called in to discuss further alterations that were needed to enable Laura to get around the house more freely. He quickly drafted the areas where more ramps and handrails were required on to his laptop, and then asked Adam, "What's that lean-to on the left hand side of house?"

"Oh, that's Dad's old office. My mother had it sealed up after he died. I've never given it any thought."

"Is the door still there?" Ben began to run an expert hand across the wall of the lounge tapping and listening as he did so.

"Might be, I'll send her an email. After being a widow for almost ten years she remarried six years ago, as you know, and is now living in Canada as the wife of James MacDonald Todd. She gave the house over to Laura and me on her marriage. I guess she never thought of a time when we might require that space." Adam refrained from adding that Mr Todd had insisted he pay his Mother the market price for the property even though it was his inheritance by right as the only son of his Father. Had he been acting on behalf of clients Adam would have fought tooth and nail to uphold their entitlement but his Mother seemed so happy with the new man in her life he acquiesced because he didn't want to create unnecessary friction between them. The loan he had taken out to meet this commitment was the reason for his current depleted funds.

"Mmm! I think it could be just here." Ben's fingers tapped a section of the wall to the left of the chimney breast which made a different sound.

"You could be right."

"I'll leave you to make contact about gaining access then, Adam, but I think that's valuable space you could bring into family use. For instance, your computer desk could be moved into there, book shelves built to line the walls to accommodate all your books, files and the like, and as the children get older provide a quieter place to do homework, and so open up the lounge area more for sitting and relaxing."

"You're always forward looking, Ben."

"I suppose in my job aiming to utilize all available space becomes a habit. Talking of which, have you any plans for the outhouses next to the kitchen, what looks like the old coal shed and washhouse?"

"Not given them any thought, to be honest."

"Shall we go and have a look at them? I have one or two ideas that you might like to consider."

"C-ca-can I c-come, too?"

"Yes, please do Laura. Perhaps you can keep us from making any too outlandish suggestions."

Laura smiled and hooked her good arm through Adam's extended one and accompanied the men through the open glass sliding doors that led from the dining area to the conservatory. Ben turned to the right, undid the French window, and stepped out on to the patio.

"Do you like where we repositioned your French windows, Laura?"

"Y-y-yes, I'm s-so g-g-glad you k-kept th-them."

Ben stood to one side as Laura leaned heavily on Adam and gingerly lifted her leg over the threshold. *Uhm! I can see the ramp needs to be shallow just here to enable Laura to manoeuvre across from the conservatory to the patio, and rails to the left.*

Ben scribbled a reminder in his notebook before striding across to the outhouses. He pulled at the first door which was incredibly stiff to open. "Need some oil here."

"I doubt it's been opened for years. As a child I remember old Sims, from Newton Marsh, carrying sacks full of coal on his shoulders and the crunching noise it made as he tipped them over to fill up the bunker. We boys enjoyed climbing in there and hiding behind the boards but after a delivery it took a few weeks for the pile to go down before we could play in there again."

"Oh, I remember those days, I used to come here to play and never wanted the day to end. What games we played!"

"When I was about eleven it was my task to refill the coal scuttle. I always overfilled it in order to encourage the pile to go down but I invariably struggled to carry it across the sitting room and always managed to spill some chunks on to the carpet. Did I get a roasting from Dad!"

"I recall the day, too, when we all got thrashed for messing up our clothes because we were larking around in the coalhouse when we'd been warned not to."

"Oh, yes, and Alex Kemp got sent to bed without her tea because she'd ripped her best coat on a nail in there as she climbed over the boards so she was well hidden from the catchers."

"Those were the days! What fun we had!"

"Dad, also, went each autumn on the log run. Did your Dad go? I know Mr Kemp and Roy Durrant were part of the crew. I forget who else, but they took wagons and saws and went to the woods on the western side of the Manor estate and helped with the coppicing, as well as the pruning of fruit trees in the orchard. The men were rewarded with logs for their day's labour. I had to assist in stacking them this side of the boards in the coalhouse. They helped to eke out the coal supply throughout the winter when the house was heated only by open fires. I loved the smell of apple tree burning the best."

"That aroma always signalled the approach of Christmas to me."

Laura fidgeted uncomfortably.

"Sorry, Sweetheart, you weren't here in those days. Please forgive us for reminiscing."

"N-not at all. I en-j-j-joy l-list'nen'."

"Just getting tired and uncomfortable?" Adam put his arm protectively around Laura's shoulders.

"Mmm."

"Back to the business in hand, Ben?"

"Right. These are fantastic spaces that can be made to work for your family needs." Ben raised his tape measure rule along the walls and wrote down measurements in his notebook. "I know you have to retain the original exterior but I suggest we upgrade the interior and make the coal and washhouses into a playroom. We could also erect a roof over the present patio area, possibly corrugated plastic, and enclose that far side from roof to floor in shatter-proof glass. It would provide somewhere dry, light and airy for the children to play where Laura can see them."

Laura nodded her approval with enthusiasm.

"I c-cou-could b-b-be-c-c-come in-v-v-volved in th-their d-day to d-day life, again."

"Yes, my Sweetheart that would be good."

"If the children are playing in this part of the house is there any reason why they cannot use Laura's ensuite facilities? I would recommend that you do away with the W.C. under the stairs. You could then make that space into a storage area for coat and shoes. It might be nice to open up the stairs into the lounge, making the long hallway unnecessary as you have a porch by the front door."

"That's an interesting suggestion, don't you think, Laura?"

"Y-yes."

"If I cast my mind back I seem to remember when my grandparents lived in the house that area was a large hall. I recall, too, as a very small boy coming in through the front door straight off the lane. It was actually in front of the stairs, and on the left-hand side there was always a fantastic, blazing fire. Let's go in, I'll show you."

Without more ado Adam bounded into the house leaving Ben to help Laura negotiate her way back to the sitting room. He repositioned a chair for her so she could continue to be part of the conversation. Excitedly Adam paced the area as he recalled the earlier structure of the house as it had been in his grandparents' day.

"The stairs were more open and, of course, there was a dividing wall in what is now the sitting room. The front door was situated where the window by my computer now is."

"I don't remember that," said Ben "I always came in through the door with the porch when I came round to play."

"Oh, I think that door was the original way into the kitchen."

"What a lot of changes! You ought to write up a history of the house whilst it is still so fresh in your memory and keep it with the deeds before all these changes are forgotten. Ask your Mum, too, what she remembers."

"I c-cou-could do th-that," Laura became quite animated.

"Yes, Sweetheart, that would be brill," Adam put his arm around his wife, "Now that you're more mobile we could fix up your laptop so you could work at it with ease." *Must speak to Roger, though, about how much I can let Laura do.*

While each season had its own particular delights Laura loved spring the best, with the freshness and fragrance of emerging foliage and flowers, new life and new beginnings.

Oh, Lord, I pray for a new beginning to wholeness, a fresh start. I long for a return to normality in my dealings with the children. In her mind she never stumbled over words but, because she was still faltering over some words, conversation was, at times, frustrating especially with Poppy. Laura breathed in deeply as she looked out of the window of the conservatory, her place of confinement for such a long time. Her eyes gazed across the garden and revelled in the signs of new life evident there.

A rooster crowed and blue tits and sparrows competed for space on the bird feeder Adam had fixed to the cherry tree that graced the lawn. Laura smiled as they chirruped happily. As they mingled, whilst busying themselves about their normal early morning activities, she identified with the necessary routines of life. *I do hope the clearance work doesn't destroy their habitat.*

Beyond the boundary wall at the bottom of the garden she caught glimpses each day of the work taking place in Kezia's Wood and marvelled, along with many other villagers, at the discoveries that were being made; lovely old properties, architecturally intriguing, but desperately in need of restoration. It was hard to believe they had been hidden undetected for so long. Soon the name Kezia's Wood would be quite inappropriate although Chit Beckingsdale was ensuring the land wasn't wholly denuded of trees and shrubs, selecting some fine established specimens to enhance the gardens of the rediscovered buildings. *I'm glad he has the good sense to leave something for our feathered friends.*

Following Ben's last visit, to discuss additional house alterations, Laura had pushed the boundaries out further so that she could be involved in small household tasks and activities with the children. Today, she was going to be allowed to help sort out the old office.

Within the week Mrs Todd had willingly given her permission to reopen Adam's father's former study. However, when they finally gained access it was evident that the room needed not only a great deal of sorting but also a thoroughly good clean. Spiders and other creepy crawlies were having a field day with the myriad sheets of loose and boxed papers scattered about the room.

"L-l-le-let m-me help do th-this."

Adam raised his eyebrows quizzically. A quick phone call to Doctor Roger, while he was in the kitchen making morning coffee, to ask about the advisability of allowing Laura to do this, resulted in Trixie organizing a cleaning team to help with the physical work, enabling Laura to sit and read through the many documents and papers that had accumulated so many years ago. *Don't molly-coddle her, Adam. If Laura wants to do it then encourage her to exercise her mind and her body,* was Doctor Roger's advice.

So, painstakingly Laura worked through paperwork on the shelves, her floppy right hand nestled in her lap. In the drawers and box files she found many receipts and invoices that were no longer required but one crumpled piece of paper caused a great deal of interest and excitement.

"L-l-look, Adam, a p-pr-pre-premium b-bond in your name."

Adam leaped across the room, took the yellowed, musty paper and scrutinized it closely. His eyes lit up and he grinned at Laura before wrapping his arms around her in an enthusiastic bear hug.

"Oh, Laura, what a find!"

Excitement pervaded their every thought and move for the rest of the day because stapled to the bond was a faded letter which intimated that ERNIE had picked out the bond number in the monthly draw.

"I have no idea if Mum and Dad ever claimed on this prize." Adam pored over the documents intently.

"If the b-b-bond is st-still v-valid w-would th-there be enough to p-pay for the p-pr-proposed new b-building w-work?"

Adam flung his arms around Laura and hugged her again. "More than enough, Sweetheart, and there might even be a significant sum left over to donate to the Lord Edmund's PCC discretionary fund that helped to fund the first phase of the renovations to our home."

A quick call to his mother to check his eligibility to the bond followed by another to the claims office to verify the validity of the bond resulted in a very sizeable cheque being delivered to the Catton house in due course.

Adam uttered a silent prayer of relief and gratitude that their financial worries were taken care of, as he recalled Ben's words of so many months ago from Philippians, '...God will supply all your needs...'

Throughout Laura's slow recovery, RK's presence in their home was invaluable. She'd willingly adapted her tasks to accommodate Laura's needs, as well as, ensured that the children were well cared for. While Adam had initially taken extra days off from work, when Laura first returned home, it was RK who had assumed the burden of extra work that care for Laura required. The children loved her and had taken to her firm but gentle, humorous manner when she first began to look after them at the onset of Laura's stroke.

To Adam and Laura's delight RK had, just lately, begun to accept invitations to attend house groups and fellowship meetings at church in addition to the social events and activities of village life. She was thinking deeply about what she was hearing, asking many questions about the teaching in the Bible as it relates to daily living, and as a consequence changing her opinion about the Christian life that she had imbibed from her staunchly atheist parents since childhood.

P.C. Dan was a more frequent visitor than most to the Catton home. The friendship he shared with RK was very special and he was thrilled to see her heart changing before him. The vulnerable side of her drew him but he knew he still needed to be cautious. Despite her recent profession of belief in God he was pretty certain the belief did not include a personal relationship with Jesus Christ. Until that happened, she was off-limits to him. He hoped his heart could remember that.

However, a recent fall from her motorbike on a trip, a long overdue holiday to her parent's farm in the Lincolnshire fens, had incapacitated her and Adam was unsure when she would be well enough to return to work. He did not know the extent of RK's injuries, having received only one brief phone call from Mrs Dickinson-Bond, which informed him that RK would not be able to return on the planned date because of an accident.

The Catton family were bereft without her and many others in the village missed her sunny, though oft times quirky, nature. Quite a number, the children amongst them, sent notes and cards but not one person received any further news in return. Even Dan heard nothing from his friend.

CHAPTER TWENTY ONE

As the spring days began to lengthen and the easterly winds lose their penetrating chill, Jansy Cooper decided to return to Newton Westerby, on an infrequent visit, to stay with her parents. It was good to be home and she looked forward to leisurely days ahead, devoid of responsibilities, concentrating on her own areas of need rather than those of her patients.

"I'm off, Mum," Jansy called as she fastened the lead to Benji's collar. "I'll not be long, just down the lane and along the beach. Let the North Sea breezes blow away some of the city cobwebs."

"Any in particular?"

"Oh, yes, but nothing for you to worry about." Time enough to share, not wanting to burden her mother, yet. The memory of allegations at work and the tangled web of lies and deceit Doctors Stead and Hollis had woven around her still churned her stomach over even though the hospital board had exonerated her. She didn't feel ready to discuss it with her family.

"Well, my dear, I'm sure you'll find fresh east coast air will clear the head and the heart," replied her mother with more cheerfulness than she really felt. Trixie was concerned by the pallor of her daughter's face. On her return home for a short break from her position as Sister-in-charge on the paediatric ward at the Jenny Lind specialist children's hospital in Norwich Jansy seemed overly fatigued. Her eyes lacked lustre and her brow was constantly furrowed. Trixie was unsure of the cause and did not want to probe too deeply. Her daughter would speak when the time was right. Trixie was just glad to have her home after so long away and looked forward to cosseting her. *I do wish she and Dave could sort out their differences, though I'm sure it's more than the estrangement that is causing the drawn, haggard look and tenseness Jansy tries to conceal.*

"I'll pop in and see the progress Stephen's made at Kezia's Wood."

"Yes, do, he'll be so thrilled to show you all that has been accomplished."

"I guess I'll meet one or two people I know on the way but I promise not to accept more than one invitation to coffee." Being brought up in the seaside village where her father was GP meant Jansy was well known to most people, apart from the summer holiday makers and the ever increasing day trippers.

Forcing a smile Trixie came into the kitchen and said, "Will that be possible?"

"Well, I'll do my best without upsetting too many of the villagers," Jansy grimaced.

"Lunch is at one. That fits in best with your father's schedule, today. Enjoy your walk."

"We will. Come on Benji." Jansy wasn't going to allow the disquiet she felt spoil such a glorious morning. It was a little fresh but the sun was shining and the coastal gardens were ablaze with colour, the mauve of crocus had given way to yellow trumpeted daffodils which in turn were being superseded by the pink frothy, blossom of cherry trees on one side of the lane echoed by clematis Montana 'Elizabeth', scrambling over walls on the other.

As the pair made their way through the village they encountered a number of locals who were both surprised but glad to see them. Jansy stopped to chat or simply waved. Gradually, the ambience created by the uncomplicated beauty of the gardens and the genuine friendliness of the villagers at seeing Jansy after such a long time, lifted her spirits.

As she passed the vicarage Adam Catton was cleaning windows. He waved when he spied Jansy.

"'Morning, Adam."

"Hi, Jansy. I'm real pleased to see you."

"How's Laura? I trust she's making progress? Please give her my regards."

"Thanks, Jansy, she's doing nicely. Call in if you're passing. She'd be delighted to chat with you," said Adam niftily climbing down the ladder.

"I will," she called. Jansy had great admiration for Adam Catton who had resigned his position at a prestigious city solicitor's office to care for his wife and family following RK's accident but Jocelyn Capps-Walker refused to accept Adam's resignation. Adam was a valued and skilled member of his team and he didn't want to lose his expertise. "Work from home. Make it temporary. Just part time," he cajoled. Adam had eventually acquiesced.

Jansy recalled it was well over a year since Laura had suffered a stroke at the young age of thirty-eight. Adam accepted His boss's conditions, with a few provisos, but had still become the village window cleaner, when RK's expected return had not happened. "It will give me greater flexibility and allow me to choose the hours I work to fit in with caring for the children and attending to Laura's needs," he reasoned.

Some said he was a fool and should have insisted on help from Social Services but Jansy could identify with his decision to be near at hand, a street away was less distance to travel than the many miles from the city if he was needed urgently.

"How are the children?"

"Adapting remarkably well but they miss RK dreadfully. She was superb with them and was a real God-send to our family immediately following Laura's stroke. I can't believe she'd let us down so badly."

"You have no idea when she'll be returning?"

"None at all. No one in the village seems to have heard from her. All correspondence remains unanswered so we wonder if we have the correct postal address of her parents' farm. I've tried calling her mobile number but without any success and foolishly I didn't make a note of the number her mother called from."

"How about you? How's life panning out for you after all the changes?"

"Different!" Adam grinned as he pulled down his ladder. He actually found he preferred the freedom of outdoor life which was poles apart from the restrictions of the office.

Jansy made to move on her way.

"Tell your Mum I appreciate her offer to collect the children for swimming on Friday while I take Laura for her check-up. I accept gratefully." Jansy could see the relief in his eyes. "The kindness of folks is overwhelming, at times."

"They love to do it."

"I know, but I couldn't have managed, in recent times, without people like your Mum."

"It makes her feel less redundant now that Roger, Stephen and I have left home," Jansy explained.

"How long are you home for this time?"

"Oh, just a few days."

"You look as though you could do with some fresh sea air to put colour back into your cheeks. Let's hope the break will achieve that!"

Jansy laughter peeled out. "That's enough of your sauce, Adam Catton," Jansy chided but she knew him well enough, their friendship went back a long way.

"Anyway, Benji and I are on our way to do just that" she said.

"Well, take care and do call in to the house, anytime, Laura will be so pleased to see you."

"I'll do that," she called and waved in farewell as she continued along the path by the side of The Green till it reached the top of the steps. Jansy stood still for a moment and looked across to Kezia's Wood. She was amazed at the transformation that had taken place on the site. "Wow! They have been busy." Benji pulled impatiently on his lead. "OK, OK, I'm coming." Together they bounded down the flight of steps to the lower lane.

Jansy was drawn towards the clearance site intrigued by the spaciousness that seemed to be emerging.

However, before she could take another step to satisfy her curiosity her arm was grabbed and held from behind. Gingerly she turned to face her assailant.

"Oh, Mrs Jenner, you did make me jump."

The old lady stood directly in front of Jansy in order to impede her progress and ensure she listened to what she had to say.

"So, it is yew Jansy Cooper! Thought I recognized yew. Now, yew just tell that father o' yourn..." *Oh dear, give me patience*, pleaded Jansy silently, as Mrs Jenner proceeded on her catalogue of complaints. "...that hoity, toity Miss he has answeren' the phone said I muss..." Jansy, all at once, felt sorry for her long-suffering father, "...might be dead. Then what would I dew? My legs be that bad I can't..."

"Hi, Jansy! Coffee's on."

A voice from across the lane interrupted the flow of Mrs Jenner's tirade. Jansy looked up to see the smiling face of her old school friend, Emma Kemp, now married to her eldest brother, Roger.

"Oh, Em!" she sighed with relief. Jansy carefully disengaged herself from Mrs Jenner, spoke to her kindly and wished her well, before crossing to join Emma, standing by her front door.

"It's good to have you home," Emma greeted her warmly.

"Thanks for rescuing me, that woman does go on so. I'd love a coffee." Emma looked at her friend quizzically. It was out of character for Jansy to be impatient with anyone, yet, she did seem jaded and lacking her natural vivacity.

The friends spent some while in general chit-chat, catching up on inconsequential news, till Jansy glanced at the clock and exclaimed, "We really mustn't keep you any longer, Em, especially on your day off. Benji's itching to have a run along the beach. Perhaps we could have an evening together before I go back."

"Lovely," replied Emma, "just give me a ring. I'm sure Roger would love to spend some time with you." She hadn't sussed out Jansy's problem and guessed her friend needed more time to gather herself together before sharing what was bothering her. She hadn't even shown any interest in the renovations that had been done in the cottage since Emma and Roger had taken it over. In the past, Jansy's natural curiosity would have demanded a conducted tour.

Jansy waved goodbye and as she stepped through the gateway looked again across the lane towards Kezia's Wood. What a difference since she had strolled down here with Stephen in the late afternoon on Emma and Roger's wedding day last October.

At first glance the lane seemed much wider, the trees and bushes that had abutted the lane were mostly all gone and in their place stood a row of derelict but interesting old buildings. Intrigued she crossed over to the other side. Edging the lane now and stretching the entire length, in front of the properties, was an uneven cobbled pathway. *Stephen will be so thrilled at this find. There seems to be a row of five or more distinct dwellings along this stretch not just one as Dad thought at first.* She couldn't satisfy her curiosity any further because barriers prevented pedestrians getting too close to the unstable structures so she hurried along to the property at the far end of the row which had so obviously been lovingly and sympathetically restored and was a great advertisement for the potential restoration of the remainder. *What a contrast to the dereliction and neglect of the other properties.*

Jansy was truly amazed at the transformation of the site. Stephen had worked wonders in the preceding months. She could see that adjacent to the roofless smithy her brother had shown to her with such enthusiasm last autumn an extensive property had been unearthed which stretched alongside the cobbled lane right up to Main Street.

She smiled at the hand-painted sign above the bowed window to the left of the front door, 'KEZIA'S BOOK SHOP proprietor – S.D. Cooper.' She opened the door and walked in, her entrance announced by the jangling bell above the door. The smell of wood and linseed and musty old books assailed her nostrils but the old wooden shelves and cubbyholes reaching from floor to ceiling stacked with books bearing spines the colours of the rainbow enveloped her with an intriguing sense of warmth and cosiness. The central portion of the shop floor was taken up with an ancient shop counter on which were displayed some of Stephen's more priceless volumes in domed glass presentation cases.

"Hi, Sis, like what you see?" Stephen came through a doorway opposite the front door having heard the bell in his workshop.

"It is amazing, Bro. Who'd have thought all this was hiding in the wood."

"Quite a brainwave of Dad's, wasn't it?"

"I bet even he didn't realise the extent of what was concealed by the undergrowth."

"He was absolutely gobsmacked. We've called a halt to the clearance at the back of the other properties firstly, in view of the fact that no one has time to tend long gardens anymore and secondly, because we think some woodland ought to be retained for the benefit of wildlife and the environment and finally, there simply isn't the cash to continue and the PC feels priority should now be given to restoring the buildings that the clearance has exposed."

"A lot of work still ahead, then?"

"Yes, but a tremendous amount of interest has been shown by the villagers and loads of people have offered to help. I think many have this feeling of self-discovery. This is their history. Some of their ancestors lived or worked in these cottages. They have a sense of pride and achievement in helping to return them, not necessarily to their former glory because some of the amenities were pretty archaic, but to a usable state.

"Ben and his team carried out the surveys on the properties to ascertain whether they were structurally safe and sound. Some seem to be more so than others. Temporarily, he had his workmen shore up the existing walls. He then assessed what was required to restore and upgrade the buildings. Durrant's were asked to carry out initial work but as so many residents have offered their services Ben has organized teams of volunteers to carry out certain projects. That's helping to keep down the cost. I am anxious and thankfully, so too, are the PC and housing committee to retain the character and history of the row."

"What a lot I've missed by being away from the village. You must be so excited to have uncovered such an interesting remnant of village history."

"This isn't all we've found."

"Oh?"

"From ledgers we discovered in cupboards in the room at the back of this property it would seem that this building was in fact the home of Granny Bemment and the site of the original village stores which she started.

"Wow, what a find."

"We think her granddaughter, Kezia, took over the running of the shop and when she married John Durrant, she and her husband subsequently bought the property which is the current Post Office. Then, at some later date they acquired the corner property which became the current Village Stores. I think there are bundles of receipts and exercise books itemising the shopping transactions of many village families going back over a hundred years which need sorting out and transcribing."

"What an unbelievable record of village history! Kezia must have been a meticulous book keeper."

"Yes, it has been so exciting but also a little bit unnerving to discover facts about our ancestor's day to day lives and to actually handle documents and ledgers that they handled in the past is rather awesome."

"I can imagine."

"From documents that Adam has already deciphered it seems as if Granny Bemment had a finger in many pies. She was village midwife and layer-out-of-bodies, seamstress and laundress and she brought up her three granddaughters when her daughter died giving birth to her last child, Kezia.

"It appears Kezia was the one who established the shop into a thriving business. She must have done very well because we think although she inherited this cottage she possibly bought others in the row as well as those opposite. Adam is still sifting through the paperwork we found but as you can imagine some pages are faded, a number badly watermarked and yet others torn."

"How thrilling..."

"Come through the back. Let me show you all I've done."

"I really ought to be going. Mum expects me back for lunch at one o'clock and Benji is pulling on his leash anxious to be off."

"Oh!" Stephen's face looked so crestfallen Jansy promptly said, "I'll come for coffee in the morning and you can give me a tour, OK?"

"I'll be in Church in the morning and I'm at Mum and Dad's for Sunday lunch…"

"Let's come after lunch, then, before I return to the hospital."

"That's a date. See you Sis, enjoy your walk."

Benji, delighted to be off again, dashed to the bottom of the lane and on to the beach. The tide was out and Jansy was amazed at the amount of shingle that had built up on the usually sandy beach, and then remembered her mother had said there had been a number of stormy, high tides during the winter. Benji enjoyed his freedom, tearing down to the water's edge and back, as Jansy threw pieces of driftwood for him to fetch that the waves had discharged on to the beach.

Jansy looked out at the rolling sea. It never ceased to fascinate her. She watched as squawking gulls hovered round a longshore boat making its way to harbour. *He must have a catch of some sort* Jansy thought. As it moved closer she recognized the boat as Dave Ransome's 'Sunburst' and hoped it was true. She knew how hard hit local fishermen were by government quotas.

Once, she and Dave had been close but, her need to prove her independence, and his to prove he could make fishing pay, had driven a wedge between them. As she thought of Dave's perseverance she remembered the many who had left the industry, or diversified, in order to keep soul and body together. Families, whose livelihood had been fishing for generations, were suffering greatly. Some she had grown up with had had to uproot and move to alien environments where they had difficulty adjusting to a new way of life. Honest people doing an honest day's work, not like Hollis and Stead, dishonest scoundrels to the core that they were.

Jansy had learnt to her cost that the anonymity of city life was vastly different to that of a close knit fishing village community. She wondered how much longer she could stick it out. She loved her work and had laboured so hard to achieve her specialist nursing skills but she also missed the gentle rhythm of the familiarity of village life.

How she valued these infrequent refreshing breaks at home with her parents. What could she do if she lived here? She certainly didn't relish travelling into the city each day. How she had fought with Dave over that very issue. Back to back late or early shifts would leave her exhausted, getting to bed after midnight and up again at 5.30am wouldn't be good for her or her patients. Her mind lingered for a moment on the occasion when her father had offered her the position of practice nurse but at the time she was at loggerheads with Dave, so, stubbornly refused to even consider the option of work near to home, wanting to be as far from the village as possible. *What a missed opportunity! If only Dave and I...*She sighed and shook her head whimsically.

An exceptionally loud splash followed by an anguished bark alerted Jansy from her daydreaming. She frantically looked around for the dog.

"Benji! Benji!"

She set off across the beach but the more she hurried, the more the shingle hindered her progress.

"Benji! Benji!" she shouted.

There was no sign of him. A sense of urgency pushed her on till she put her left leg out, but there was nowhere

264

to put it down; no beach, no shingle. Her eyes stopped searching around her. She looked down, her whole body rapidly following. Then she saw him. Benji was in the water of the harbour thrashing about and frightened. Jansy let out a strangled cry as within seconds, her arms flaying around windmill fashion, she joined him. The shingle ridge had completely obliterated the harbour edge.

As she surfaced Jansy caught her breath. The water was bitterly cold and the current swift. She rapidly scanned the surface of the water. When she spotted Benji she tried to swim towards him but her clothing dragged her down. When he heard her voice the frenzied splashing ceased and, even though her strokes became more laborious, she gently coaxed him to swim with her nearer to the harbour wall. It took all of Jansy's concentration to achieve any sustainable movement.

She reached out a hand to the wall but there was nothing to hold on to. She searched frantically for something to grab, a life-belt, a foot hold, anything. There was only a solid twenty foot wall, covered in green slime, towering above her. Her heart sank. She felt sick.

"I mustn't panic. I must stay calm. I must keep moving. Good boy, Benji, come with me," languidly she uttered the last words out loud.

Slowly, Jansy followed the line of the wall anticipating that at some point she would find a way out of the water, a mooring rope or a ladder. However, cold and fatigue were beginning to take their toll. *Surely, there must be a buoy! Where are the boats? Where's Dave's boat? I can't even ask you to help me God because I've ignored you and left you out of my life too long. Another consequence of my stubbornness!* She was finding it difficult to stay afloat and drifted towards the centre of the river.

"Help! Help!" she yelled as loudly as she could. With great effort she thrashed her arms on the surface of the water to create as much disturbance as possible. Benji caught on and valiantly barked and splashed. Jansy stopped, kept her head above water, and then, commenced the procedure over again hoping to gain someone's attention. She lost count of the number of times she repeated this routine. She was getting drowsy and comatose, unable to concentrate and think coherently. *Oh, God, I do need you!*

Vaguely aware of noise and voices she could fight the oblivion that engulfed her no longer and sank into the dark abyss.

With horror Dave witnessed the incident as he steered the 'Sunburst' through the harbour mouth, so he called the coastguard for assistance, and then gently eased his boat along the channel searching for dog and girl. By the time the lifeboat arrived he had located the pair. His heart lurched when he recognized them as Jansy Cooper and Benji!

With expertise born of experience the lifeboat crew rescued them both. Benji was taken to the Animal Rescue Centre where vets were on hand to monitor his condition. Jansy was airlifted to the Norfolk and Norwich Hospital where her condition caused considerable concern as she was barely conscious and suffering from hypothermia and the possible threat of pneumonia.

Her journey from the unconscious state to the conscious was bewildering and frustrating. She became aware of someone calling her name, holding her hand, a familiar smell. Work! Jansy shivered. She was cold, so cold. She tried to talk, to open her eyes, to ask for something to keep her warm but the words wouldn't come. Unbidden, scenes with Jeremy Stead and Steve Hollis flickered through the pictures of her mind, interspersed with the gentle voice of her father. Little Mrs Jenner floated in and out, still chattering about her ailments. Then she smelt fish and heard Dave's deep voice, followed by that of her mother, gently stroking her brow and talking softly of everyday things. She saw a vague silhouette of Laura Catton, then dear Emma with a paintbrush in her hand, by the side of the harbour.

Jansy tried to pull herself away from the muddled darkness that seemed to be holding on to her. It was such an effort dragging herself towards the light, the warmth, the familiar. The more she attempted to reach out, the more she was held back. Her eyes wouldn't open. Words would not come to be spoken.

"Sister Janice, Sister Janice," a firm voice called out.

"No..o, no..o," Jansy mumbled. "Janss..s, J..ansy."

"Dear Jansy," said a voice sitting beside her and a hand gently squeezed hers. "She's coming back to us."

Gradually she opened her eyes and focussed on the familiar face looking down at her with love and tenderness.

"The Lord be praised!"

"Oh, Dad," she whispered.

It was many days later that Jansy was allowed home, weak but alive. Her mother fussed round her like a broody hen, her father guarded her protectively and Dave became a frequent visitor. He was as devoted as ever. It was as though the rift between them had never happened. At times Jansy found their cosseting rather claustrophobic.

She had explained numerous times about Benji disappearing into the water, the build up of shingle and the unprotected sea wall that contributed to her falling in after him.

"Something needs to be done about that," said Trixie in her determined voice that signalled action. "It can't be left so open. It's so hazardous and dangerous. Next time might be fatal for someone."

"Oh, Mum, don't say that," said Jansy.

"She's right, my dear," said Doctor Cooper thoughtfully. "I'll bring it up at the next Parish Council meeting. See what we can do."

"Thanks, Dad."

Whilst Trixie campaigned for warning signs and more accessible life belts and all the trappings of safety she felt necessary, Jansy renewed her strength strolling through the village in the late spring sunshine, accompanied by Benji, keeping well clear of the harbour edge.

The episode, too, had given her pause for thought with regard to her spiritual well being. Where was God when she needed Him? A question she had asked so many times was answered quite distinctly through this near tragedy; He was there all the time. She'd looked for Him in the wrong place and at times not looked for Him at all.

CHAPTER TWENTY TWO

A number of months afterwards, as the balmy days of summer embraced the village with their warmth, Jansy sat on a rustic bench in the tranquil setting of the garden at Bakers absorbing the stillness and serenity of that place. She had taken time off sick following her escapade in the harbour then, after further deliberation and discussion with her parents, decided to hand in her notice at the hospital.

"When you feel well enough the position of practice nurse is still vacant if you care to give it some consideration," her father suggested.

A small sigh escaped her lips as her eyes gazed at the loveliness surrounding her. She wasn't a gardener but she did appreciate the palette of colour that had been achieved with skilful planting combinations by someone far more knowledgeable. *If only I could piece together the various facets of my life into such tidy compartments I wouldn't be so tangled up with all the loose ends I now have to deal with.*

Jennifer Pedwardine had agreed to open her beautiful garden to the villagers, on certain occasions for quiet contemplation, following the success of the treasure hunt the previous year. Jansy had missed out on that event but Emma introduced her to this hidden oasis soon after her return home from the ordeal in the harbour.

Together, the two friends shared precious moments here. In the peaceful ambience of the garden Jansy unburdened her heart.

"I've been so very foolish and selfish, Em," she cried, the tears coursing down her cheeks unchecked.

"Jansy, the Lord knows all about your actions, your thoughts and feelings. He still loves you," Emma said confidently.

"But, my life was a sham," Jansy spluttered, "I pretended to be a Christian. Em, you have no idea how shallow I was. I knew all the religious jargon and when we were teenagers it was easy to fool everybody. I blatantly went through the motions of church ritual. I deceived you and Dave, Mum and Dad, and a host of other people. I'm so ashamed of how badly I treated those who loved me."

"Oh, Jans!" Emma put her arm affectionately across Jansy's shoulders and said thoughtfully, "being self-centred seems the easy option but, in reality, it's the more difficult. I know, I went that way myself for a long time, much to Mum and Dad's dismay."

Jansy nodded in agreement. "It seemed easy to touch up my outward appearance to make it appear as though I had it all together. My attempts to look good did fool most people except Mrs Darnell. She saw right through me. She's an incredibly perceptive lady."

"So, that's why you had to get away?"

Jansy slowly nodded her head. "She pointed out that I was not only trying to deceive others but also myself. I wouldn't listen. I was determined to succeed but I deliberately left God out of my plans."

"He didn't leave you, though."

"No, when I really needed Him, He was there. When I was struggling in the cold, dark, water and called to Him to help me, I believe He saved me from drowning."

"I'm glad about that. I would have missed having you as my sister-in-law," Emma teased through glistening eyes.

In response Jansy gave her a warm, teary smile and said, "I also believe, truly believe, that He allowed me to be rescued in order to save my soul. Did you know Mrs Darnell came to see me in hospital? She told me in no uncertain terms that the Bible says to be saved, it is necessary to repent of your sins, accept forgiveness and believe in Jesus as Saviour.

"She quoted a verse from the book of Romans, 'If you confess with your mouth, 'Jesus is Lord,' and believe in your heart that God raised him from the dead, you will be saved.' We talked about that for a while then she graciously listened, as she always does, to my rabbitting on about doubts and fears.

"Quietly, she explained God's plan of redemption, and suddenly, it was as if blinkers were taken from my eyes. I could see clearly, for the first time, what salvation really meant."

"Dear Jansy, I'm just so happy for you," Emma sniffed and wiped the back of her hand across her eyes.

"Do you know, Em, for years I thought working hard at my job, helping other people, achieving my full potential and trying to be the best I could be was enough to get me to heaven?"

"Mmm, we all think we know better than God how to run our lives and prepare for eternity."

"I think He used my ducking in the harbour to bring me to my senses."

Emma nodded and replied softly, "As He used Mum and Dad's accident to bring me to mine."

"Anyway, since I came home from hospital I've been up to the vicarage fairly frequently and shared some lovely sessions with the Vicar and Mrs Darnell looking at verses from the Bible. Do you know, Em, as the Rev Hugh explained them, the words just came alive for me!"

"Isn't it amazing when the truth of the Bible becomes real and meaningful for your life?"

In a brisk movement Jansy got up, looked up toward the heavens, raised her hands above her head, then turned towards Emma and declared excitedly, "I'm forgiven, Em, forgiven! It's a wonderful feeling." She came before Emma and clasped both of her hands, "I'm sorry for treating you so shockingly over this past year, but thankyou for remaining my friend. It means so much to me."

The friends prayed together, shed tears and hugged as they celebrated the wonder of God's restoring power.

"Dear Emma, thankyou for your love and unconditional support. I truly thank God for the example of your life." Jansy swallowed and her eyes teared up as she remembered her inconsiderate treatment of Emma. She took a moment to gain control of her emotions, and then looked around the garden, "I praise Him, too, for the balm of this place."

"It is special, isn't it? Miss Pedwardine has worked wonders in the garden."

"When we first came in I kept expecting her to come round the corner and tell us off for being here," laughed

Jansy when the feared appearance of Miss Pedwardine had not materialized.

"My feelings exactly," agreed Emma, "but Dad said we would see a change in her when she retired and he was right."

"She's more approachable now than she was as headmistress, isn't she?"

"Yes, she treats us as equals, not as adolescent schoolgirls, and that dear lady has also learned when to put in an appearance for visitors and when to remain unseen."

Since forgiveness had washed over Jansy, her spirit had been renewed and hope restored. The knowledge of the redeeming grace of God for her, because she had confessed her sins, brought tremendous peace to her heart. The garden had become a precious sanctuary to Jansy and she returned time and time again. *Father God, thankyou for loving me. I know I must deal with my wrongful attitude and actions of the past before I can move on to the future. I hurt so many people by my wilfulness. Please help me to be strong and trust in You as I ask for their forgiveness.*

Today, Jansy had arranged to meet Dave here, in the place she thought of as sanctuary, to talk about the past and discuss their future. They both recognised that reconciliation required heart searching frankness before the healing process could begin.

"I'm a bit apprehensive," she had confided to Emma.

"Be open and honest but, above all else, be yourself," counselled Emma. "I'll be praying for you both."

So, surrounded by a plethora of scents, Jansy soaked up the warmth from the sunshine, amidst the rich tapestry of colour woven by the many plants, and waited. She wasn't as calm as she appeared. The sensations in her stomach echoed the turbulence in her mind as thoughts somersaulted at the prospect ahead. A meeting with Dave was inevitable. Although he'd had a hand in her rescue, and visited her often in hospital and at home, someone else had always been in attendance, so that they had not had opportunity to address personal issues.

Today, she had arrived early in order to think and compose herself. Time passed and the sun having reached its zenith moved on. Jansy continued to sit under the canopy of trees in Jennifer Pedwardine's luscious garden till the shade kissed her with its coolness.

Will Dave come? Jansy thought anxiously. *I treated him so very badly.* She bit her lip and looked nervously in the direction of the gate when she heard the latch open. *Lord, please guide me to do your will.*

Dave cautiously approached Jansy, his heart thumping as apprehensively as hers. When she looked up at him, he smiled and reached out his hands to her.

"My dearest girl!" That special endearment. It still made her heart flutter.

"I'm so glad you came," Dave gently squeezed the extended hand Jansy had lifted to meet his.

Jansy returned his smile and said, "I couldn't keep away. I had to come to ask for your forgiveness."

Dave shook his head, "No recriminations, Jans."

"I didn't mean that. Just that, maybe, we need to share our thoughts and feelings."

"Openness and frankness, you mean?"

"Yes, I can't bear anymore misunderstandings."

"We've both been through a lot during the last year."

"Mmm! It hasn't been easy."

"Life's experiences seldom are."

"Yet God's presence has been in them all."

"Yes, not always apparent at the time but…"

"…all the same His love was gently chiselling the stubborn places of our hearts."

"You're right."

Their stilted conversation stopped abruptly and they sat together in the stillness for some time. The silence was only broken by a creaking tree branch and the occasional chirruping of birds.

Oh, Lord, please give me the right words to share with Jansy what is in my heart, Dave prayed.

Seated inches away from him Jansy sat quietly. Her heart, too, was petitioning her Heavenly Father.

Then, Dave turned and, looking directly at her, opened his mouth and his heart. Jansy returned his gaze and listened as Dave described the wrench of leaving her, over a year ago, and the monotony of the endless, spacious days spent at sea.

"The pain of separation from you was like a knife through my heart, Jansy."

"Oh Dave, I am so very sorry," Jansy murmured as her eyes puddled up.

"It did force me to look deep within myself and recognize how utterly worthless I was on my own."

Dave went on to explain about his hours of solitude, his interaction with the Brixham fishermen, the helplessness he felt after the beating Billy Knights and his companions put him through, as well as the care of the Mission canteen staff and the superintendant's invitation to the cafe-church which led to him attending the Bible study.

"Let me tell you about that. It was based upon the book of Jude. As the Mission man led the study the Lord spoke quite distinctly to my heart through His Word." Dave looked very distant at that instant as though he were reliving those special moments.

"I never realized before, but that little letter of Jude issues a challenge to us to grow in faith, pray in the spirit and remain in God's love but also teaches how that is possible. I had difficulty focussing at the time so I asked the chap sitting next to me to underline the words in my Bible, 'to Him who is able,' able to help me faithfully do those things, and I looked back at them over and over again.

"Never had the days been so lonely, Jans. How I missed you! I looked out at the sea that stretched all around me for as far as the eye could see. I looked to the north, turned round to the south, gazed east and then west and couldn't see where it ended. I looked down and couldn't calculate its depth. My little fishing vessel seemed small and insignificant as it bobbed around on the immense ocean. I'd placed so many hopes in that little boat then stupidly allowed it to come between you and me.

"I learned in that moment the vastness of God's love. It stretches even further than the sea. It covers all, including me and my failings, you, too, Jans, even though at the time you were so far away, with a mantle of peace and forgiveness. How I thanked God for the reminder that He is far greater than the universe He has created yet He loved me enough to send His Son to die for me and prepare a place for me to live with Him in eternity.

"I was devastated when you brushed me aside, Jansy, in favour of your career. I thought I was everything to you and that somehow I had failed you, that I hadn't shown you how much I loved you. How conceited is that! Then, His still, small voice nudged me. 'To Him who is able,' able to keep me, able to guide me. How I prayed for that guidance, Jans."

"I'm so ashamed that my stubborn selfishness caused heartache to so many people, but especially to you," Jansy murmured with regret.

"Then one morning something deep within me urged me to come home."

"The prompting of the Lord, I expect," Jansy whispered.

Dave nodded and got up from the bench.

Jansy followed his movement with her eyes and said quietly, "How glad I am that you obeyed, otherwise we might not be having this conversation."

"I learned an important lesson in those moments of solitude, that when we're in His plan, He guides us, and we hear His directions clearly."

Dave moved back to sit nearer to Jansy. He looked at her steadily and reached out to take up one of her hands.

"Dear Jans, I don't want to rush things but I would like us both to take time to listen for the guidelines the Lord has for our lives."

Jansy nodded her head in response. "Mrs Darnell advised me to pray and stay in the Word if I truly wanted to live in the Lord's will. Ever since that day I've been trying to do just that."

"I am so very glad. Thankyou for listening to me, Jans." He released her hand only to look earnestly into her eyes. "I know it's probably painful but are you able to share what has happened to you during the past year?"

At first, Jansy twiddled nervously with her fingers. Then, taking courage from Dave's honest outpourings she took a deep breath and began to explain her actions and the feelings that drove them.

"I was desperate to prove I was capable of getting to the top of my profession, that I could achieve success by my own ability and not because I was the Doctor's daughter. When Mrs Darnell suggested I address the issues that were bothering me about my future career and our life together I ran away. I couldn't face them or you nor Mum and Dad. I pushed my love for you to the very back of my mind and left God out of the equation altogether.

"I'm ashamed of the way I treated you and sorry I didn't take time to discuss my concerns with you.

"Stead and Hollis, were junior doctors at the hospital. Working with them day after day I got quite close to them, Stead in particular. I trusted them. When I was busy with a patient and they needed to administer medication to other patients I allowed them to use my drugs cupboard keys to gain access to what they required. But they had been siphoning drugs from the paediatric ward to feed other's habits and line their own pockets. I had absolutely no idea what they were doing. Apparently, it had been going on long before my advent on the ward.

"I was so ambitious I used people to achieve my goal. Stead was a challenge because I was unable to manipulate him. I was so naive I didn't realise he was the one manipulating me. I virtually threw myself at him hoping it would influence my appointment as ward sister. I realise now I was dabbling in dangerous issues in order to get my own way. I wouldn't be surprised if you hated me, Dave, because of the way I behaved. I know now I treated you abominably. You probably see me as being as bad as Stead and Hollis.

"Their activities implicated me because I was Sister on the ward and, however innocently, I became entangled in their duplicity. I'd been going out with Jeremy Stead on a number of occasions over a few months, which didn't look good for me when his involvement came to light, but it was all a sham. He didn't have any feelings for me. It was just part of his plan to use me to gain access to drugs in order to make money dishonestly.

"I was devastated that I had been compromised both emotionally and professionally. I found it hard to understand how Doctors committed to healing lives should deliberately engage in activity that would destroy lives.

"I've learned recently that Billy Knights, the deckhand on Laura Catton's cousin Mark's boat, was the go-between. Stead and Hollis gave Billy what they had acquired from the hospital and he supplied them with drugs he smuggled aboard while out fishing. They then sold them onto a dealer in Norwich. I believe Mark was as duped as I was.

"Apparently, their Norwich venue became too hot, the police net was closing in so Billy suggested future exchanges take place in the unlit delivery area at the back of the Village Stores in Newton Westerby till Uncle Mick saw them one night. Billy kept a high profile in the village over that Christmas period to ascertain if anything leaked out about his clandestine meetings at the Stores. The villagers seemed to be unaware of his activities but he couldn't be sure that Uncle Mick hadn't already contacted the authorities so he had to be silenced before he could speak out about what he had seen.

"Billy then switched his meeting place with the Doctors to the garden of Ferry Cottage where RK spotted them. Stead and Hollis were angry with Billy for allowing them to be seen with him, not once but twice. They really thought they were invincible and, because the drugs were mostly smuggled in and out through the tiny ports, drug pushing in the city would never be traced back to them. They were careful to ensure that drugs stolen from the hospital went to the continent via Billy's cohorts and the drugs sold in the city were those acquired from Billy Knights or his associates when they made the return trip. Mark, who is as honest as the day is long, still finds it incomprehensible that Billy was involved in such furtive operations and actually conducted them in his boat right under his nose.

"RK reported the incident that took place in her garden and was given police protection until the men were apprehended. This was because police intelligence, having ruled out Joe and Josh Cook as the perpetrators of the Kemp murders, found that growing evidence pointed to the possible involvement of drug and trafficking smugglers in the car 'accident'. Witnesses to their illegal activities proved to be a threat and had to be eliminated.

"I've only recently been able to piece together some parts of the jigsaw because for quite a time I had all but severed my links with the village so was unaware of the connection between furtive goings-on in Newton Westerby and missing drugs on the paediatric ward in the hospital. Nor was I aware that you had been attacked because you'd seen Billy with his dealers. It's a shock to learn we've both been caught up in his net of deceit."

"My dearest girl, I'm sorry you've had to cope with such humiliation on your own."

Tears flowed uncontrollably down Jansy's cheeks.

"Oh Dave, don't be nice to me. I treated you horribly and all you did was show how much you cared."

Dave moved closer to Jansy and touched her cheek. "I could never hate you, Jans. There's a great deal of difference between you, Billy and Doctors Hollis and Stead." Tenderly he lifted her tear stained face to look into his.

"There is?"

"Certainly; Billy, Stead and Hollis seem to be totally unrepentant of their actions and how they have impacted upon other people," Dave said solemnly. "Whereas, with you, I see nothing but regret over the way you acted. I also see genuine sorrow for your behaviour towards your friends and family, and even me. In fact, I see a transformation in you and a real desire to be different."

"You do?" Jansy whispered.

"Absolutely!"

"How can you be so sure?"

"I can see it in your eyes. There is a new radiance about you and you seem to be at peace with yourself and those about you. When you speak you say what you mean rather than take your time to weigh up what you think people want to hear before speaking."

"How right you are! I always knew the correct jargon and developed a mask for churchified situations. I wanted people to think well of me."

"Not until the challenge of conflict came into your life did that mask drop."

"You're so right. It was hard to continue pretending when what I wanted was not in accord with what God directed. Mrs Darnell saw through me and realized how false I was because she told me in no uncertain terms that in pretending Christianity I was deceiving you, God and myself."

"Is that why you shut me out and ran away?"

"Yes, I couldn't face being found out and the last thing I wanted was for you to know I was a fraud."

"Was loving me all pretence?"

"Oh, no Dave, I genuinely loved you but my selfish ambition wouldn't let me put God first in my life or consider your hopes and happiness above my own."

"My dear Jans!"

"I deeply regret hurting you, Dave. I know God has forgiven me and my salvation is real. I've been amazed at how differently I now view things."

"For the better?"

"Yes, I realise there can be no place for pretence in my relationship with God, with you or anyone else, for that matter."

Dave's face gave nothing away as his hands came gently to her shoulders. He bent forward and tenderly kissed her cheek. "I love you, Jansy."

Jansy looked across the garden through glistening, unseeing eyes. She then turned back to Dave, brushed a hand across her face, in an attempt to stem the flow.

"I wanted to be free to do what I wanted to do but in all I achieved I was still restless and, so often, quite out of my depth. Now through God's grace I've learned what true freedom is." The words were uttered in a great rush.

Dave reached to take her hand, "My dearest girl, I am so very happy for you."

Eagerly he reached to take both her hands into his, "Shall we start again?"

Jansy moved with a start, "Oh, no, Dave."

"Jans? Please explain," implored Dave, his face furrowed with consternation.

"We can't go back to the beginning, that would be a backwood step, but we can move forward and build on the lessons we have learned, together," Jansy's eyes shone.

"You mean get married?"

"Yes, please."

"Let's go and talk with Rev. Hugh and then I have somewhere special I want to show you, where we'll engage in a lifetime's project that we'll work at together, an anchor, that will ensure neither of us gets out of our depth again."

This time it was Jansy's turn to frown but he didn't enlighten her, just held out his hand to her. Eagerly she grasped it.

"Let's have an autumn evening wedding ceremony," she suggested, "followed by a village barbeque on the beach."

"And a honeymoon on the boat," Dave teased.

"Dave!" Jansy tilted her head and shaped her rosebud mouth into a playful grimace.

"Are you leaving so soon? I've just put the kettle on for tea." Jennifer Pedwardine called to them as Dave opened the back gate. He looked first at the former headmistress and then at Jansy whose blue eyes danced with love as she fought to suppress the giggles that were threatening to emerge.

"Miss Pedwardine, whilst a cup of tea would be most welcome, we find we have some urgent unfinished business to attend to. Perhaps we could come on another occasion and take tea with you?"

"Tomorrow, 3.30pm!"

"Yes, Miss!" Dave and Jansy replied in unison.

EPILOGUE

The ever shrinking days of summer were packed with arrangements for the planned autumn nuptials.

"We'll never be ready in time," Jansy fretted.

"Don't get so het up, Jansy, so many hands have been offered to lighten the load I'm sure everything will be accomplished just as you desire in readiness for your big day," Trixie calmly assured her.

Any spare moment, as far as work commitments permitted, was devoted to decorating and preparing the cottage that Dave had purchased more than a year ago as their home. Jansy was amazed that Dave had gone ahead and bought it. Yet she was pleased he had. She had to admit the cottage was proving to be every bit the asset Dave and RK had tried to convince her it was. Even the garden that had until recently been so resplendent in its summer garb now glowed peacefully, its vivid colour replaced by the gilded sheen of autumn, blending so splendidly with the colour scheme chosen for her special day; burnt amber and sherbet lemon!

As she walked from her parent's home on the arm of Doctor John along the pathway towards the open door of the church Jansy seemed to quiver in the dusky light of evening as the gossamer threads in her billowing sleeves glistened with the iridescence of dragonfly's wings. The busyness of the last few weeks was forgotten as she anticipated the joy of future days. The autumn gold of the trees provided the perfect backdrop for the gentle processional father and daughter were taking together backlit by the setting sun, its rays causing the fruits woven into the coronet anchored on her blond curls to sparkle with the richness of jewels. Branches moved playfully this way and that with every bit of breeze an accompaniment to the swishing movement of her ivory bridal gown.

A smile appeared on her rosebud mouth as she pictured the delight on Dave's beloved rugged face as she walked up the aisle to join him at the altar. The year so recently passed had been a steep learning curve for them both, bitter experiences overturned into an arena of happiness. To their cost they knew that doubts and uncertainties cause confusion and mistrust leading to a complete breakdown in relationships. Fortunately, they had discovered the way of gladness and reconciliation when the oil of joy and forgiveness poured into their hearts and love was rekindled. Tenderly Dave courted his 'dearest girl' and the dormant spark within each of their hearts blossomed like the opening of a budded rose, fulsome and fragrant.

The organ played, the choir processed, the congregation fidgeted, Emma came forward to greet her friend as she approached the church porch, her simply styled prim-rose coloured dress high-lighting her rich auburn hair. She wore it down, at Jansy's request, and Rachel Durrant had woven lemon rosebuds into it. Both girls carried bouquets of burnt amber roses entwined with wisps of seasonal foliage and sherbet lemon nasturtiums.

"Am I OK, Em?" Jansy rushed up and asked nervously.

"You look lovely, Jans, doesn't she Doc?" Emma smiled as she bent to straighten Jansy's train and then reached out to titivate her shoulder length veil. *Don't cover your face, Jans, I want to see you clearly as you come up the aisle* Dave had asked.

With that request in mind Emma carefully ensured the intricate floral circlet was firmly secured and the delicate lace veil would not slip. "These hips and haws glow like precious gems amongst the flower buds and perfectly match your amber tear-drop pendant."

"Thanks, Em. Is Dave OK?" Jansy jiggled around trying to peer round the porch along the aisle towards the front pew.

"Stand still, Jans," mumbled Emma with hair- grips clamped between her teeth, "while I secure this side of your coronet."

Jansy let out a quiet sigh.

"There now, all done. Dave's fine and he'll think you look wonderful." Her poise and self-assurance instilling calmness into her anxious friend.

John stood to one side beaming at his impatient daughter. He put up his arm. "All ready now?"

"Yes, Dad," she whispered, "I'm ready." She squeezed his arm and raised shining eyes which spoke volumes.

"Let's go and join this man of yours."

The notes of the organ crescendoed and the con-gregation rose as one to greet the bride who, had not Doctor John been sedately holding on to her firmly as he walked on the solid flagstones, would have flown to meet her groom.

Jansy was oblivious to the smiling faces that greeted her arrival, her feet barely touching the ground, as she winged her way along the nave towards the one waiting for her.

Her eyes fixed on his manly stature, the broad shoulders and dark wavy hair. Her stomach flipped and her heart beat faster. *How I love that dear, dear man!* Her brother Roger, resplendent as best man, leaned over and whispered in Dave's ear. He turned. His eyes locked with hers. The love emanating from them drew her like a magnet. He mouthed, "I love you" and when she reached his side he squeezed her hand and for her ears alone he said, "You look so lovely, my dearest girl." His special endearment for her. Her heart skipped with joy.

Side by side they sang the hymns of worship chosen for the occasion and when Rev Hugh invited them to stand before him and face one another to make their vows Jansy knew without a shadow of a doubt that this was the right thing to be doing. *The past is gone and forgiven; together we stand on the threshold of a new and sacred relationship.*

After the legal requirements were dealt with and the vows of intent had been given, the congregation were surprised by an additional unscripted declaration by the groom to his bride followed by a response from Jansy to Dave.

"Jansy, I will always cherish and care for you. I recognise you are a person in your own right and have different needs to my own but I will endeavour to listen to you and learn alongside you the many things we, as yet, do not know."

"Dave, I truly love you. I will support you in your role as the head of our family. I will learn to share my thoughts and feelings with you to minimize any future misunderstandings."

Without taking his eyes from her face Dave reached out towards Jansy and took both of her dainty hands into his rough work-worn ones and as one they declared, "We love the Lord with all our hearts and thank Him for redeeming love and new beginnings. We promise to read His Word and pray together and by His help grow in Christian love."

The organ began to play, 'The Lord bless thee and keep thee,' as hand in hand the young couple mounted the steps to kneel at the altar as man and wife.

The choir's joyous anthem of praise filled the Church with a jubilation which was equally matched by the tumultuous applause that almost raised the rafters as the newlyweds processed down the aisle following the signing of the marriage register. Eyes brimming with happiness looked to the left and then the right along the rows of pews at the familiar faces beaming in delight. Jansy and Dave acknowledged the good wishes with nods and smiles punctuated by her infectious giggle.

Just as they reached the archway by the porch Ben Durrant called out to them, "Stop for a moment." He focussed the lens on his camera then clicked the button to capture the radiance on their faces. "Nothing stiff and formal," Dave and Jansy had instructed. "Just pictures of people as they are, enjoying our special day with us." So, no set poses were planned but Ben, whilst intent on adhering to their wishes, wanted to ensure they had a worthy record of this day to look back upon. He had also entrusted his camcorder to Ryan Saunders who was a whiz with machines of any description and appointed Nicky Andaman as his able assistant to keep a look-out for quirky and interesting shots.

The joy of the occasion spilled over onto the Village Green then down to the beach as everyone followed the young couple to partake of the barbeque wedding supper masterminded by Uncle Billy Cooper and Jilly Briggs. Glowing coals on a brick built stove highlighted the venue and burning candles secured in jars wedged into the sand marked clearly the pathway to follow. Hand in hand they tripped across the sand towards the location that had been prepared for their celebration.

"It's magical to be by the sea-shore as the sun bids goodnight and the moon begins to show it's glistening light on the waves," Jansy said playfully swinging Dave's arm.

"It's even more special, Mrs Ransome, to have you in my arms and melt into your shining eyes as I kiss you as my wife," and Dave tenderly drew her to himself.

"Hey, you love-birds, break it up. It's time to eat. We're starving even if you're not," laughter followed Stephen's declaration. Their brief romantic interlude was shattered as they were soon joined by friends and family, and the youngsters boisterously playing around them. Dave smiled at Jansy then caught up her hand as together they moved forwards to greet their guests as they arrived on the beach.

"What a marvellous idea, you two, to meet on the beach in the evening," called Nicky as Ryan continued to film the newlyweds as they welcomed friends and family to the Wedding BBQ Supper.

"This is so lovely to be by the sea as dusk turns to night on so balmy an evening," said Emma as she strolled arm in arm with Roger to the meeting place and her thoughts were echoed by many as they meandered from the church including Laura who valiantly tackled the sandy pathway, escorted by Adam, so that together they could offer their good wishes to the happy couple.

"Such a shame RK isn't able to enjoy this special occasion," Annette called over her shoulder."

"Yes, she so loves the beach and the rolling sea."

"Who'd have thought the warm weather would have lasted this late into autumn?" commented Trixie as she came forward to kiss her daughter and new son-in-law.

"Isn't it good that we have a bright moon in a clear sky, tonight?" Jansy gazed across the shimmering glaze on the rippling waves.

"We're fortunate, too, that we have very little light pollution spilling over from the village that would spoil the effect," agreed her father.

"Yup, we be blessed with no street lights," Dave's father added as he joined them.

"The palette of the night sky is amazing." Doctor John's remark had everyone near to them instantly raise their heads to see the spectacle for themselves.

Jansy looked up in awe at a night sky becoming spangled with stars and constellations set out so plainly they could almost have been drawn there.

"Incredible!" she exclaimed.

"Yet, every so often when bright smudges appear in their midst you are reminded they are but the tip of the iceberg," added John.

"It makes one feel so small and insignificant." Jansy snuggled closer to Dave. He placed his arm protectively around her shoulders.

As they focussed on the vista above them the scent of the honeysuckle tumbling over RK's garden wall was overpowering causing a number present to ponder on the absence of their friend. From Kezia's Wood, sounding ever closer, were the cries of tawny owls twit-twooing in the dark. Along with the ever rippling tide each added to the perpetual reminder of the many components of God's created world.

Dave nodded. "Dearest girl, you and I are a small, yet precious, part of the Almighty's plan but as we learn to live in the centre of His love we will endeavour never to be out of our depth again."

Lightning Source UK Ltd.
Milton Keynes UK
UKOW06f1920190917
309503UK00007B/773/P